HOUSE OF
HERNANDEZ

ALSO BY MIMA

The Fire Series
Fire
A Spark Before the Fire

The Vampire Series
The Rock Star of Vampires
Her Name is Mariah

Different Shades of the Same Color

The Hernandez Series
We're All Animals
Always be a Wolf
The Devil is Smooth Like Honey
A Devil Named Hernandez
And the Devil Will Laugh
The Devil Will Lie
The Devil and His Legacy
She Was His Angel
We're All Criminals
Psychopaths Rule the World
Loyalty Above All (there are no exceptions)

Learn more at **www.mimaonfire.com**
Also find Mima on Twitter, Facebook and Instagram @mimaonfire

HOUSE OF HERNANDEZ

MIMA

HOUSE OF HERNANDEZ

iUniverse books may be ordered through booksellers or by contacting:

iUniverse
1663 Liberty Drive
Bloomington, IN 47403
www.iuniverse.com
844-349-9409

Because of the dynamic nature of the Internet, any web addresses or links contained in this book may have changed since publication and may no longer be valid. The views expressed in this work are solely those of the author and do not necessarily reflect the views of the publisher, and the publisher hereby disclaims any responsibility for them.

Any people depicted in stock imagery provided by Getty Images are models, and such images are being used for illustrative purposes only.
Certain stock imagery © Getty Images.

ISBN: 978-1-6632-4381-2 (sc)
ISBN: 978-1-6632-4390-4 (e)

Library of Congress Control Number: 2022915032

Print information available on the last page.

iUniverse rev. date: 08/16/2022

CHAPTER 1

Honor. It's not a word we hear much anymore, probably because it doesn't mean much anymore. We live in a society that's quite comfortable letting it all hang out, with little concern with reputation and the legacy left after they die. Who are you, and how will you someday be remembered? Will those who speak of you do so fondly, lovingly, and respectfully, or will you be spoken ill of, or even worse, completely forgotten?

To be honored is to be respected. And respect is something money can't buy, but it can be manipulated.

Jorge Hernandez knew all about honor. Despite his ruthless style of retaliation or his cartel background, he went out of his way to create an illusion of brilliance. It didn't matter if it was one of his many businesses or the volunteer work connected to his brand. Jorge knew it was all about perception. People needed to view him as a powerful man who had moved to Canada and taken over the business world, where he was ruthless and always found his way to the top. Then there was his family, and that was what made him shine.

"Maria, I have told you already," Jorge pointed toward the door in his home office. "Not everything is for you yet."

"I didn't say it was," His 15-year-old daughter whined on the other side of the desk. Her big brown eyes widened, causing him to look away. There was such an innocence about her, such an intense longing to be as powerful as her father. She wanted to learn everything, but it wasn't the time. "But this isn't a bad meeting. Is it? Isn't this about your book?"

"There are no *bad* meetings," Jorge corrected her while shaking his head. "I do not want to overwhelm you with everything at once. You are only 15. You do not have to learn everything about the family business today. Enjoy life, be a teenager. It only happens once."

"Thank God for that," She muttered and looked down. "*Papá,* I want…"

"Maria, please, I do not like it when you whine," Jorge cut her off. "Enough! *Si,* I do appreciate your enthusiasm for learning everything. I really do. However, you must calm down. You had many lessons during the summer. Today, we are only talking about my memoir. That is all."

She hesitated and made eye contact with him, studying his reaction before relenting.

"But if there's anything important," She said as she stood up and turned her body slightly as if preparing to leave.

"Maria, this here is about *House of Hernandez* coming out," Jorge reminded her. "That is all."

His phone beeped, and Jorge glanced at it. He looked back up at his daughter, who was almost at the door.

"*Te amo,* Maria," Jorge couldn't help but smile at his daughter as she reached the office door. She quickly swung around, and her face lit up.

"I love you too, *Papá,*" She giggled and reached for the doorknob, then she was gone.

The door was barely closed when Jorge's secure line rang. He cringed, took a deep breath, and answered.

"What can I do for you, Athas," Jorge spoke bluntly to the Canadian prime minister, "have a body you need me to get rid of, or what?"

The exasperated sigh on the other end caused Jorge to be annoyed.

"Can we *not* start every conversation this way," Alec Athas muttered. "I thought you said that we would…"

"This here is a joke," Jorge cut him off as he glanced toward his bulletproof window. "We can still joke, can we not?"

"In your world, it might be considered funny," Athas started. "But in mine…"

"In *my* world?" Jorge cut him off and leaned closer to the phone. "Let me remind you that the line in the sand between our two worlds, well it disappeared this summer. Do not talk like we are so different, Athas, because we are not. I'm just better at all this than you."

There was a silence, followed by Athas attempting to backtrack.

"Look, I'll never be able to thank you enough for what you did," Athas sounded stronger when he spoke. "If it wasn't for you, I could be in prison right now."

To this, Jorge's head fell back in laughter.

"*Amigo,* for being in politics this long, you have not realized yet that a man in your position, he does not ever pay for his crimes," Jorge reminded him. "What is it they say? Rules for *thee* but not for *me*? If you were found with that body, the story would be so fucking spun, you would've been spun right out of the room, and it wouldn't even be your house anymore. Do not pretend that you are on the same level as a normal Canadian or that you aren't above the law because you *are,* so it would not matter if I had not helped you that day. However, you're heading toward another election, so we had to keep things clean."

"Still, I do appreciate what you have done."

"This here is fine," Jorge shrugged and leaned back in his chair. "The beauty of owning a crematorium is that bodies, they just go missing."

"The police keep saying it's a dead-end," Athas reminded him. "That Marshalton just disappeared."

"Hey, you know, Marco, he made it look like the man leave the country with a lot of money," Jorge reminded him. "My IT specialist, he can do anything. As far as everyone knows, he's off to a tropical island, laughing at all of us."

"I don't think he's doing any laughing these days," Athas muttered, causing Jorge's head to fall back in laughter.

"Anyway," Athas let out another one of his long, exasperating sighs. "I think I'm going to call the election next week."

"Is this so?"

"I'm thinking Sunday? Monday?" Athas continued. "I have to meet with the Governor General; it's a whole procedure."

"Isn't everything?"

"It's politics, after all."

"That is the same time my book comes out," Jorge thought for a moment and grinned. "You know, it is usually the politician putting out a book just in time for the election, not the man people *wish* was running."

"Sometimes I wish it *was* you running," Athas reminded him. "Since you're my advisor, why bother with the middle man?"

"Because, Athas, I do not want to deal with the daily horseshit you must deal with," Jorge insisted. "I *own* you, but this does not mean I want to *be* you."

"As you keep reminding me."

"I may not be in the running," Jorge continued. "But it does not mean that the people don't want me. Who knows? Maybe one day, I will run for prime minister and win, of course."

"Of course," Athas spoke with sarcasm in his voice. "I'm not sure how you can be so confident. The media, they'll look for dirt, trust me…"

"I *own* the media."

"You own a *portion* of the media," Athas reminded him. "But the biggest slice of the pie…"

"*You* own," Jorge reminded him. "The *traditional* news media in Canada, it is owned by *you*. So start acting like an owner. Only give them the money when they say what you want. Don't be stupid, Athas."

"It's not exactly moral…"

"Neither is murdering someone in your home," Jorge cut him off. "But you do not have such an issue with that, now do you?"

Silence followed, and Jorge grinned.

"May I remind you that this here is easy," Jorge started again. "You say what the people want, and you *know* what the people want because you check polls. They want jobs, money, health care, the usual. It is that easy. Smile, be charming, flirt with the women, that kind of thing. This here, it is not hard. Your government funds the news. Make sure those fuckers say what you want them to say or cut their funds. Do all that, and this election is yours."

"But you need good policies," Athas replied. "Promises that incite hope."

"That is what I am saying," Jorge shrugged. "This here, it is not hard, Athas. Politicians are now celebrities. *Act* like a celebrity. Don't act like a pussy though, because people need to feel like their prime minister can stand their own against more powerful countries."

"So, in other words, act like you?" Athas dryly asked, causing Jorge to laugh.

"Well, this here sounds like a good plan," Jorge clapped his hands together. "After all, the people, they love me."

"That's what you keep telling me."

"That's what I *know*," Jorge reminded him. "Remember that news show asked what Canadian they would like to see run in the next election…"

"Yes, and your name was at the top of the list," Athas replied. "I think you've mentioned it a few times."

"Well, Athas, it is good that you remember."

A glance at the clock reminded him that it was almost time for his next meeting.

"But Athas, I must go," Jorge said as he pulled his chair ahead. "But remember, the most important thing is to show your strength, your power, but remain down-to-earth and likable. But most importantly, know that this here is your reputation, your honor. That is what people will remember. That is your legacy."

Even after their conversation ended, Jorge sat with his thoughts. So few considered their legacy. They only focused on the here and now. But it was honor that made some people stand out. Jorge had gone to great lengths to maintain his honor, and nothing was going to stop him.

CHAPTER 2

"No, this here will not be happening," Jorge shook his head, glanced past the others, and looked at his wife, Paige. Even from across his desk, they shared a powerful look. "I have a family that needs my attention and businesses to oversee. I do not have the luxury of running around the country to do this here book tour."

"Was that in your contract?" Paige calmly asked, raising her eyebrows as her blue eyes grew in size. "Were you supposed to?"

"It wasn't," Tom Makerson spoke up. "I have to do some touring since I wrote the memoir, but there's nothing in the contract that obligates Jorge to do the same."

"Me, I could care less about this whole book thing," Jorge reminded them. "This here was only to discourage others from writing fake biographies about me since this one is authorized. The less people know about me and my life, the better."

"You mean your *fictional* biography," Diego Silva abruptly spoke up, his body jittering around in the chair as he laughed at his joke. "None of that is true! People would fucking die if they knew your actual past."

"Literally," Chase Jacobs added, giving Diego a frustrated side look. "This ain't something Jorge wants people to know about."

"Ok, there is some truth to the story," Jorge attempted to calm things down, glancing first at his longtime Colombian friend, then back at Chase, the youngest member of the group. "Now, this here, is a more....digestible version of the truth. But it is true. There is nothing in there to dispute."

"It *is* all true," Makerson jumped in as he glanced toward Diego. "We didn't get into...you know, everything, for obvious reasons. But we talked about Jorge growing up in Mexico, how he got involved in his father's coffee business..."

Diego let out an abrupt laugh and dramatically rolled his eyes before crossing his legs, glancing toward Paige, then Marco Rodel Cruz, who sat at the far end of the desk with a tablet in hand.

"As I was saying," Makerson continued, his voice tense. "Everything *is* true, we just focus more on his current businesses, why he started them, that kind of thing."

"Well, *kind of* why I started them," Jorge muttered.

"Yeah, he started the crematorium because he cares so much about preserving the dead," Diego said before abruptly laughing, this time alarming everyone in the room. Jorge could sense the discomfort within the group.

"Diego, please, can we..."

"And he took over the pot industry because he has a *sincere* interest in natural healing," Diego continued in an exaggerated tone that grew louder. "And he started the bar *just* to name it after his daughter!"

"Ok, Diego, this here is enough," Jorge cut off his friend, noting the concerned expressions around the desk. "I think we all understand that the book, it is not completely real. That was never the point. It is no different from the fictional accounts of celebrity lives that they write. Can we move on, *por favor?*"

Paige shared a concerned look with her husband, while Chase glared toward Diego, who appeared unaware of the general vibe in the room.

"As I was saying," Makerson took a deep breath. "I will step away from my duties at HPC news for a few weeks to tour around, talk about *House of Hernandez* in some interviews, that kind of thing. I will sporadically come back to the office to check in, but I think Tony and Andrew have a handle on things while I'm gone. Of course, we have a great staff, so everything should be fine."

Jorge nodded.

"And honestly, I think I will still pop in on the show whenever I have time to discuss the news of the day," Makerson continued. "It's online, so it's not like I have to be in the studio. Of course, we're still trying to figure things out, but I think that should work."

"This here, I like," Jorge nodded in approval. "And we can have the book launch, maybe at the bar?"

"Yup," Chase replied as he sat up straighter in his chair. The half-indigenous man had once been the quietest member but now was taking a more prominent role. "Maria wants to help plan it."

Paige let out a giggle.

"*Mi amor,*" Jorge turned his attention toward his wife. "Maybe you could help with this?"

"I will," She nodded. Her mannerisms were much more relaxed than those of Diego, who sat beside her. Jorge noted that his mood had suddenly changed. "Maria has some elaborate ideas, but some are good too."

"I will take whatever help I can get," Chase continued. "I don't know *shit* about planning a party."

"*I* can plan a party," Diego loudly jumped in again. "You guys are amateurs. Are you forgetting, that I'm…"

"Diego, please, let us calm down," Jorge attempted to bring things down a notch.

"No one forgets you're gay, Diego," Chase was more abrupt this time.

"I wasn't going to say because I'm *gay,*" Diego turned toward Chase. "I was going to say because I used to plan parties. Back when we had the…"

"That was more Jolene," Chase referred to Diego's sister. "She did all that. I *know* because I worked for her and…"

"Ok, can we please get back on track," Jorge abruptly cut them off. "This here, let us not go down memory lane. I do not care who plans this stupid party. I promised the publisher that we would have a book launch and the bar, it seems ideal. That is the most I will be involved with *House of Hernandez.*"

"It's already topping on Amazon for pre-sales," Makerson noted. "I mean, that's pretty impressive."

"People want to learn all about me," Jorge boasted. "This is not a surprise."

"Sir, I must say something," Marco finally spoke up as he looked away from his iPad. Shaking his head, the Filipino had concern on his face. "There is a lot of excitement online, but others wish to dig more into your past. When I hacked some major publishers, I see where they think a lot is not being told, but fear you would sue them if they couldn't prove it."

"That would be the least of their worries," Jorge muttered as he gave Marco an appreciative nod. "Anything else?"

"There is just talk, sir," Marco continued. "But it is concerning."

"We knew that this could happen," Makerson reminded him. "We just have to emphasize that the book is the *only* authorized biography that you'll be doing. Maybe it would be best to address the rumors and try to diminish them right away."

"Maybe suggest that you have a common name in Mexico," Chase started. "So if they suggest rumors, you can remind them that it may be another Jorge Hernandez?"

"This is a possibility," Jorge nodded.

"We don't want to overdo that or any narrative," Makerson suggested. "It might cause too much attention. That's something we might casually toss out but not focus on. Once you make something the narrative, people catch on and start to pick away at it."

"Be like the government," Diego loudly spoke up. "Say it's a conspiracy theory. That's what they keep doing about Marshalton....."

"Ok, again, this here, let us not get into it," Jorge attempted to smooth things over and shut Diego up. His erratic behavior was irritating him. "The bottom line is to discourage anyone from looking too deep into my past."

"Maybe we should put out fires as they come up," Paige suggested. "Let's not get ahead of ourselves. This might not even be an issue."

"Plus, Athas is about to announce an election," Jorge continued. "So, I must put my attention on that as well. I cannot waste time on problems that do not exist yet...and may not."

"There have been rumors about the election swirling for some time," Makerson nodded. "I'm glad it's about to become official. That will divert a lot of attention away from *House of Hernandez* and, in turn, you. That might save us."

"I definitely could use some saving," Jorge grinned. "I need a break from all this insanity. Putting out the fires Athas starts is enough to keep me busy."

"There are a lot of questions around why Marshalton went missing," Paige quietly reminded him.

"This comes up a lot, sir," Marco affirmed. "People, they do not all believe the story he just left."

"My informant from the Toronto Police assured me it's tucked away," Jorge nodded. "And the RCMP is barely lifting a finger since they found information that he left the country. It's a waste of resources to look into something that seems pretty clear."

"I think any fires Athas starts," Makerson suggested. "Will be from his own stupidity. They usually are."

Jorge's head fell back in laughter, causing a nervous Diego to jump.

"Jesus Christ, Jorge," He shook his head and rubbed his face. "Too early for loud noises."

Jorge said nothing but exchanged looks with his wife.

"You know," Jorge finally said. "I think that is all for today. We have covered all the bases necessary at this time. We will talk, maybe later in the week."

"I will keep you posted on things," Makerson said as he started to stand.

"Thank you," Jorge replied as the others followed, his attention turning toward Diego. "You, we need to talk before you leave."

Diego sat back down as the others made their way toward the door, leaving the two men alone in the room.

"Diego, I do not know what is going on with you," Jorge bluntly spoke. "But you are acting strangely this morning."

"Nothing," Diego shook his head. "I have been busy running *your* company."

"Oh, well, if this here is too much for you," Jorge shrugged. "I can find someone else to do it."

Taken aback, Diego's mouth fell open.

"Something is going on with you," Jorge repeated as he moved ahead in his chair. "And you are going to tell me what it is *now*."

"I'm just stressed," Diego grew defensive.

"I know we have had some incidents in the past with you day drinking…"

"No, I'm not drinking," Diego confirmed. "I have this prescription. It's just making me feel a little…off."

"What is it?" Jorge pushed.

"Just this…."

"Diego, I am tired," Jorge shook his head and studied Diego. "I do not have time for this nonsense. What is *really* going on?"

"Nothing…"

"Diego, I sold cocaine for many years of my life" Jorge cut him off while watching him. "And right now, you remind me of someone who is using it."

Diego didn't answer. Instead, he burst into tears.

CHAPTER 3

"And so what he is telling me," Jorge gestured dramatically, almost hitting the shot of tequila that sat before him. "Is that he has been doing this all along? Do you think this is true?"

Chase glanced down and folded his arms over his chest. He finally looked up and around the empty bar while shaking his head. Opening his mouth to speak, Jorge jumped in before he could.

"I mean, I give him everything," Jorge continued to rant as he glanced down at his shot. A sense of disappointment rang through his voice. "He has been my *hermano* for all these years. How could I not know about the drinking? The cocaine?"

"Maybe he hasn't been doing it *all* along…" Chase began, but Jorge was already shaking his head.

"This here, it has been going on a long time," Jorge finally spoke with a sadness in his voice, his eyes meeting with Chase's again. "I do not understand. Years ago, we talked about this, you know? That we would leave the drugs behind. We could focus so that we would not have any weaknesses. And I find out, that Diego has been doing it regularly for years. As CEO of my company and my associate. I did not know."

"But he's gonna hide it," Chase reminded him as if attempting to reassure Jorge. "He knows how you feel about this kind of thing. He wants you to think that he's clean, you know…he worries about what you think of him. Even yesterday, when he told you everything. You said he was upset?"

"He cried," Jorge said and took a deep breath, reaching for his shot. He hesitated before knocking it back. It burned all the way down his throat. Jorge finally regained his composure. "He tell me that it has been years. That he needed it for the energy, to keep going. He is just using it more and more."

"I never saw that side of him," Chase said. "I don't think, anyway. But when I first met Diego and stayed at his place, he did seem to have a very secretive side, you know? I was also pretty wet behind the ears, being just a kid. I had no idea how someone doing coke would act. And I mean, Diego has always been a bit crazy, always been jittery and hyper, so I didn't think anything of it. He drinks such a crazy amount of coffee."

"But I should have seen it," Jorge spoke with regret. "After all, I have known this man for over twenty years. When did things change?"

"Maybe they never have because he's always been into something, you know?" Chase reminded him with a shrug. "Didn't you say when you first met Diego that he partied a lot? He was probably never really clean, and if he was, it wasn't for long."

"He say he's tried to stop different times," Jorge started to struggle with his English as he grew more upset. "When I think back, there were times he was very depressed and maybe he was trying, but he did not want to say."

"He didn't want you to think he was weak," Chase reminded Jorge. "He cares what you think, Jorge. Diego always has. He probably tried to do it alone and realized he couldn't stop. So, he started again. I feel bad that he didn't feel he could tell anyone."

"Everything always reaches a breaking point," Jorge reminded Chase. "We can only sit on our secrets so long before they explode and our whole lives get blown to fuck. And here we are."

"He seemed to come undone at the meeting yesterday," Chase's eyes softened as he uncrossed his arms and reached behind him to brace himself against the bar. "I was seriously getting annoyed."

"I could see that," Jorge replied with a grin. "We all were, but you know, I think, he was just being Diego. But something was very different, and I could not deny it anymore."

"So," Chase started but stopped to yawn and stretch. His body was massive, emphasizing what incredible shape he was in, reminding Jorge that he was getting a little soft lately. "What now? What can we do?"

"I do not know," Jorge admitted. "Paige, she is looking into it. She says Diego has a lot of trauma or something from his childhood. He has a lot of unresolved feelings he must address, or he will never truly be able to recover from this problem. Me, I do not know about this kind of thing."

"That makes sense," Chase nodded. "But, you know, don't we all? We all have shit from our past."

"Yes," Jorge nodded and silently remembered how Chase had tragically lost a child years earlier. His remaining sons were slowly moving out of his life, focusing more on their step-father. "Chase, tell me, how do you live with your demons? I am curious."

At first, he didn't answer. Shaking his head, Chase shrugged as if he didn't know what to say.

"I mean, how do you…"

"It's not easy," Chase finally admitted, briefly looking down at his feet. "I guess boxing or working out has saved me. It's my way of not losing my mind. It always has been just what I did."

"This here makes sense," Jorge nodded. "It is much more productive than what Diego has chosen."

"We do what we know," Chase reminded him. "But what about you? You had a lot of shit in your past."

"Me," Jorge shook his head. "I keep living my life. Paige, she says I have a lot of anger from when my brother died. It has also made me very protective of my family."

"You *are* very protective," Chase added.

"No one threatens my family and lives to talk about it," Jorge reminded Chase and took another deep breath. "And Diego, he is my family, in many ways. He always has been, and now, I must help him."

"So, he's taking time off work?"

"That is the plan," Jorge shrugged. "But I do not know. This here, I will leave to Paige. She is my angel. She will figure this out."

"Can you imagine?" Chase hesitated. "I mean, what kind of person Diego is without the drugs? He can't be the same guy, you know? It might be kinda weird."

"Could it get much weirder?" Jorge countered, causing Chase to laugh just as there was a knock at the door. "That must be Marco."

Chase went around to answer it. He greeted the Filipino, who pushed his bicycle beside him. Leaning it against the wall and removing his sunglasses, Marco walked across the floor. He wore a fedora and had a laptop bag swung over his shoulder.

"Good morning," He respectfully spoke as he approached the bar and sat beside Jorge. "How are things today, sir?"

"We got a problem, but nothing we can't handle," Jorge admitted. "I had a conversation with Diego yesterday. Long story short, he may have a drug problem."

"Oh sir, this is true?" Marco's eyes widened as he looked between Jorge and Chase. "Is this why he acted so strangely yesterday?"

"In fairness, don't he always?" Jorge found himself making light of the situation, immediately regretting it. "I should not say such things. It is a serious concern."

"I hope he is ok, sir," Marco said as he placed his laptop bag on the bar.

"Want anything to drink?" Chase asked the IT expert, pointing at the bottles behind him. "Or coffee? Water?"

"Yes, coffee please," Marco nodded. "Thank you."

"So, what you got for me today, Marco?" Jorge asked with some reluctance, fearing that more problems were about to be introduced. "Wait, Chase, has Clara been in?"

"Yes," Chase nodded when asked about the older lady who checked for listening devices and other potential issues. "She checked this morning."

"Sir, things seem quiet," Marco admitted as Chase sat a cup of coffee in front of him, followed by cream and sugar packets. "I do see chatter about Athas soon announcing an election and how they plan to bring him down."

"But why?" Chase shook his head. "He's done something worthwhile. He's helping indigenous communities get clean water. He's tightened laws, so the police aren't as corrupt, like…what do people want?"

"Money," Jorge answered his question. "An election is coming, they want you to piss money on them and give them nice things, or they do not vote."

"Sir, our voter turnout is quite low," Marco shook his head. "They do not vote anyway."

"We gotta get people to the polls," Chase said as he poured a coffee for himself.

"We only gotta get them to the polls if they vote for Athas," Jorge reminded him. "The trick is to get that to happen."

"Youth is the key," Marco said and pointed toward his laptop. "They do not always vote, but when they do it appears to be for moralistic ideals. Make the world a better place."

"See this here, it is all boring," Jorge shook his head. "What we gotta do is shake things up. We gotta make Athas a rock star. We gotta make him seem cool. This is how we get people excited about voting."

"Give old people more money," Chase suggested. "They always say seniors barely get anything to live on."

"Families too," Marco jumped in. "Sir, everything is so expensive now. That is how normal people feel. They feel like the government doesn't even care."

"These here are good points," Jorge nodded.

"But it doesn't matter if the media turns against them," Chase reminded them. "We got some of it, but the mainstream can be brutal. They hate Athas."

"He funds some of them," Jorge pointed out. "You would think they'd be a little more favorable."

"There's that girl over at the news channel," Marco began to laugh. "Sir, they say she has a crush on Athas. What if we were to have *her* interview him? I would say she would make him look *very good*."

"Oh, I know the one. It's Holly Anne Ryerson," Chase nodded. "He just gotta flirt with her….you know, give her a little attention."

"Nah, he's not gonna flirt with her," Jorge shook his head and thought for a moment. "He's going to fuck her goddam brains out."

CHAPTER 4

"You're a politician," Jorge shot back at Alec Athas, who sat across from him with a nauseated expression on his face. "Your whole life is about being whored out, so why should this be any different?"

"My whole life," Athas attempted to correct him with strength in his voice that quickly waned. "Is to help the people. Not to sink to that level."

"Really, Athas?" Jorge sat back in his chair and glared across the desk. "Do you think you are in the position to take the moral high ground? I clean up a dead body in your home not so long ago, but you are here telling me that you are too virtuous to fuck a journalist? Is that where we are now?"

"I…" Athas quickly deflated in front of him. "That, it wasn't.."

"This here, I do not care," Jorge quickly cut him off. "I do not care if you kill this man because he tried to fuck you over or because he insulted your haircut. I do *not* care. The point is that you have already sunk low to keep your position. Why would this here be so bad?"

"How do you even propose I do this," Athas shook his head. "Or that Holly Anne Ryerson will go along with it or not cry rape or something. I mean, I have to be careful."

"Marco has hacked her phone, and this here is her fantasy, *amigo,*" Jorge reminded him as he tilted his head, showing a sinister grin. "Athas, you must learn that you always find someone's weak point. And her weak point is her pussy. And for some reason, she wants you in it. I do not understand why, but it would be like taking candy from a baby."

"Oh God," Athas shook his head. "I can't believe what you're proposing."

"You have your people suggest having an *intimate* interview with her," Jorge started and stopped for a moment. "As a way for people to get to know the Greek God outside politics. Like, you know, what do you watch on television? What is your favorite book? Do you prefer chocolate or vanilla?"

His last comment came across salaciously. Jorge enjoyed torturing Athas, who was squirming, his face full of tension.

"I would recommend vanilla," Jorge spoke salaciously. "You know since she is a white girl."

Athas gave him a dirty look.

"And hey, this Holly Anne lady is plain looking," Jorge shrugged. "But she got big tits, and from what Marco found out when he hacked her account, she hasn't been fucked lately, so you got her where you want her."

"I just don't think…"

"Athas, I do not want to hear it," Jorge shook his head. "I tell you, she is interested in you. She has told her close friends. She is giddy like a teenage girl. Knows everything about you."

"And she's going to keep her mouth shut?" Athas asked suspiciously. "This isn't a trick to fuck me over."

"Athas, if I wanted to fuck you over," Jorge reminded him. "I would have when I found a man with a bullet through his head in your office. No, this here will help get mainstream news on your side."

"Wouldn't it be easier to give them money," Athas shook his head. "And not hurt someone in the process."

"You are not hurting anyone," Jorge insisted. "She gets to live her fantasy."

Athas continued to look upset.

"Give them money," Jorge thought for a moment. "The economy is bad. You would like to help them out. They compete with all these American streaming sites. That's your excuse. They will give you great coverage. Then fuck her brains out and make sure she gives you one hell of a review."

Athas looked disgusted, but this didn't bother Jorge.

"Trust me," Jorge insisted. "I know what I'm talking about. People are weak. You have to find their weakness. And we found it with her. And it's you."

Athas didn't agree or disagree but appeared physically ill when he left the office. After he was gone, Jorge started to laugh out loud as he glanced at the bulletproof window, almost as if it were a person, but he quickly composed himself when his door slowly crept open. A toddler entered the room and bashfully looked around.

"Miguel, *ven aqui,*" Jorge managed to catch the little boy's eye as a big smile appeared on his face. "Come see your *Papi!*"

The child giggled before running across the floor and behind the desk, where Jorge swooped him up in his arms.

"Miguel! Are you my next meeting?" Jorge teased as he brought the child down onto his lap. "I certainly like you a lot better than my last meeting."

"I don't know what you said," Paige's voice came from the doorway. "But Alec was in an unpleasant mood when he left."

"Yes, well, you know Athas," Jorge shrugged as his wife made her way across the floor and sat across from him. "He does not like the truth. I tell him that he has to give these news assholes more money to keep them happy before an election, and he acts like this does not always happen. He must learn to play the game."

"Alec isn't much for games," She gently commented.

"Athas isn't much for politics either," Jorge reminded her, "but that's his fucking job."

"Jorge!" Paige's eyes widened as she glanced toward their child, who was watching his father with interest. "He's picking up on everything. Remember the time he started using that other word…"

To this, Jorge laughed. The previous year, Miguel heard the word 'kill' in the house, which resulted in him sporadically yelling it out whenever he took the notion. This made him unpopular at daycare.

"Miguel, he has much bigger things on his plate," Jorge teased as he looked down at his son. "What are you up to today?"

"Well, we decided he would stay home from pre-school because he wasn't feeling well," Paige said as she looked at her son. "So he played with some blocks, then had breakfast with his stuffed cow."

"Did the cow," Jorge looked down at his son. "Did he eat all your food?"

"No," Miguel shook his head. "He try. *Papi,* I say no."

"Oh, I am sorry," Tala stood in the doorway. The family's nanny held her cell phone up and shook her head. "I was on the phone, and I turn…"

"Tala, it's fine," Paige cut her off, turning around. "You had a call. I was there. He was eating breakfast."

"But Tala, maybe you should take him," Jorge suggested as he kissed his son on the top of his head. "Paige and I, we must discuss some business."

"Oh, yes, sir," The Filipina lady rushed over. With a big smile, she reached to collect their son. "I take him for a walk. It is a beautiful day!"

"Thanks, Tala," Paige said as the nanny walked out of the room.

After she was gone, Jorge and Paige exchanged looks.

"You saw Diego? Do I even want to ask?"

"He insists he's fine," Paige shook her head. "That he doesn't need help. That he needs to spend time with Sonny and…."

"Oh, that child," Jorge shook his head, referring to Diego's boyfriend. "At least he does not have him moved in."

"Well, there was talk of that too," Paige muttered, "and Sonny's a man in his twenties. He's not *exactly* a child."

"To me, he is," Jorge corrected her. "And if Diego wants to be a sugar daddy, this here is fine. But first, he has to get his shit together."

"I keep trying to talk to him about treatment and getting help, but…"

"He will not listen?" Jorge pointedly asked.

"No," Paige shook her head.

"Well, he's going to listen to me," Jorge stood up. "I cannot have weakness in my organization, and this here, it is a weakness."

"Just don't be too harsh," Paige gently asked as she rose from her chair. "I know you're worried about him, but try to show some compassion. Don't be a bully."

"Paige, when have I ever been a bully?" Jorge asked as he stood up. "What Diego needs is a reality check. He is not a weak man. I cannot have that in my family. He needs help because Paige, I cannot have a cokehead on my team."

"I hate to break it to you," Paige said with compassion in her eyes. "But I think you have, but if it makes you feel better, I didn't know either."

"Yes, well, this here stops now," Jorge shook his head. "I am going to talk to him."

"Just please," She asked as they made their way to the door. "Pick your words carefully."

"Oh, Paige, believe me," Jorge stopped to reach for the doorknob. "I assure you I will be picking them *very* carefully."

She didn't look convinced.

Making his way out of the house, Jorge walked next door and knocked on the door. A few minutes passed before Diego answered. He wore a robe and appeared tired, deflated, like an exhausted version of himself. It was hard to see.

"Diego, we must talk," Jorge insisted as he pushed his way into the house. A tiny dog looked up from a massive stuffed bed in the next room, then sunk back in. In the kitchen sat Sonny at the table. He was also wearing a robe.

"It is almost 10 in the fucking morning," Jorge looked toward the kitchen, glancing back at Diego. "Do people not get dressed now?"

"Oh, I was making some calls," Sonny started to answer, jumping up from the table, almost losing his robe. "And…"

"Do you not work today?" Jorge cut him off. "Do you not still work for me at the production house?"

"I just thought," Sonny stumbled on his words. "I would…"

"Go to work," Jorge instructed. "I will take care of Diego."

Looking back at his longtime friend, he didn't feel pity for him. He felt shame. It was time to get him back on track.

CHAPTER 5

"Now," Jorge gestured for Diego to sit on the couch. "That he is *finally* getting ready for work, we can talk."

"Look, I…" Diego started to explain but got a look from Jorge, and immediately stopped. His head lowered in shame.

"Diego, we are not doing this bullshit," Jorge insisted as he sat beside him. "I need you to be powerful. I need you to be strong. I need you to run my goddam company. What is it that Paige suggested you decided was not good advice?"

"It's not that it's bad advice," Diego attempted to explain with a bit more vigor. "I just don't think it will work for me."

"Ok, so tell me, what is it?"

"She thinks that it's trauma from my childhood that is messing me up," Diego shrugged. "That I seek your approval and work too hard to go over and above to impress you, but I swear that she's wrong. It's…"

"She's right," Jorge cut him off, causing Diego's shoulders to slump as he shrunk in size. "But Diego, this here, it is not always a bad thing."

"I don't understand."

"Diego, I need you to get better," Jorge reminded him as he pointed toward the wall, indicating his house. "My family, they need you too. If something were to happen to me, you have two kids that are your godchildren. They need you. Paige will need your support. You must help my Maria learn to lead the family. So you see, you are valuable, and yes, in a way, it does matter what I think. I do not expect you to kill yourself at work every day, but I wish you to do your best. If you need to hire people to help, then do so, but at the end of the day, I count on you to oversee everything. You are one of my key people, Diego. You are also my friend, my *hermano,* and I need you to better. We all do."

"I know, I do, I know," Diego spoke with sadness. "But I don't got my *own* family. It's not the same."

"Diego, you are a very wealthy man," Jorge reminded him. "If you want a family, you can have a family. If you want children, you can have children. There is adoption, those…you know, surrogate mothers. You can get married. And it is not just about that. You must be strong for all the employees at *Our House of Pot.* They need a leader that assures them of jobs, of their livelihoods. That is your family as well, and you are their *Papá.* You must know this here. Your life matters and you have responsibilities. This isn't just about you."

A spark of hope filled his eyes as he sat up straighter. He looked like he wanted to say something but remained silent.

"We need you to get better."

"Ok," Diego finally managed, appearing to be on the verge of tears. "I can do that."

"So, I will send Paige over here," Jorge said as he stood up. "And you will listen to whatever she says you should do. She is your angel. You know, she would never lead you in the wrong direction."

"I know," Diego spoke with vulnerability in his voice and cleared his throat. "I know."

"Then please, I ask you," Jorge hesitated for a moment. "*Beg* you to take her advice. Listen to her. She will help you."

"I will," Diego assured him.

"Ok, I thank you," Jorge nodded. Awkwardly shuffling around, he glanced at the door. "I must go now. I have a meeting, but please, listen to her."

Jorge turned and headed toward the door, leaving Diego with his thoughts.

Getting in his SUV, Jorge flew out of the driveway and down the road. Hitting the button on his steering wheel, he listened to the phone ring.

"Hello," Paige answered. "Are you still at Diego's?"

"No, I just left there," Jorge replied as he watched the traffic ahead. "But he will do whatever you say."

There was a pause.

"You didn't threaten him, did you?" Paige muttered into the phone.

"No, Paige," Jorge began to laugh. "*Mi amor*, I explain to him that he is important to us. We need him. Not just to run *Our House of Pot*, although I did explain why this is important because employees rely on him to keep the company going each day, so they have jobs. I also tell him that our family needs him and that he is a part of it. Paige, I tell him many beautiful things that inspired him, and I also made him promise that he listen to whatever advice you have for him. When you go to his house, you will see a different attitude. And if you do not, please let me know so I can talk to him again."

"I will," Paige sounded enthused. "This is great. I hope he listens."

"Paige, whatever you need him to do."

"I have a private counselor to work with him," Paige replied. "He'll help him work through past trauma and the physical withdrawals. After they meet, he can decide the best way to deal with this, but I've talked to him and checked all the credentials."

"Whatever must be done, Paige," Jorge insisted as he sat in traffic. "Please do it."

"I will, I definitely will," She agreed.

"I am heading to my meeting at the production house," Jorge said as he glanced around. "So, I will have my phone off while there. But you know where to find me if you must."

"Will do."

He ended the call. Taking a deep breath, he thought for a moment then called Chase.

"Morning," He answered right away.

"*Buenos dias*," Jorge replied as traffic slowly started to move again. "I am on my way to the production house. I want to tell you that I reasoned with Diego this morning, and he has agreed to get whatever help he needs."

"That's a relief," Chase replied. "It didn't sound like he was going to listen."

"I gave a compelling argument," Jorge insisted. "He has a lot of people counting on him. He just had to be reminded of that fact."

"I think we all need that from time to time," Chase agreed as the sound of a truck backing up could be heard in the background.

"You got an order there?" Jorge asked as he eased closer to the production house.

"Yeah, the truck just got here," Chase replied. "Let me know if you need any help with Diego…or anything…"

"*Gracias.*"

Jorge ended the call just as he left the stream of traffic to head to the Hernandez Production Company. He could see the familiar vehicles that indicated everyone was already in the building. When he spotted Marco's bike leaning against the wall when he walked in, he knew the whole gang was waiting for him.

"Sorry I am late," Jorge announced upon walking into the boardroom. Marco looked up from his laptop while Tom Makerson, Tony Allman, and Andrew Collin looked in his direction. "I had to talk to Diego before coming here."

"Is he…ok?" Makerson asked as his face twisted up. "He was acting strangely at the meeting the other day."

"He might have some issues with drugs," Jorge said as he closed the door. "But in the news, you will say he has not had a vacation in years and decided to take some time off to rejuvenate."

"Maybe we shouldn't mention it at all," Tony suggested as Jorge took his usual spot at the table. "Unless it's brought up."

"Might be better to be proactive," Makerson suggested. "So it won't look like we're hiding anything."

"Sir," Marco jumped in. "I can look to see if anyone is questioning his time off."

"Perhaps that would be best, and then we will see," Jorge agreed. "Maybe people, they will just think it is normal vacation time."

"That's fair," Andrew spoke up as he leaned back in his chair. Unlike the others, he dressed unprofessionally, wearing a ripped jean jacket and a Tupak t-shirt. "You know, you gotta throw the dogs some fresh meat if they're hungry, not if they're sleeping. What kind of drugs are we talking about here?"

"Cocaine," Jorge replied flatly, hoping to change the subject. "And this here does not leave this room."

"Fuck, you gotta be paying him *well*," Andrew commented. "That shit is not cheap."

"He *is* the CEO of *Our House of Pot*," Makerson reminded him. "Can we move on?"

Andrew shrugged like he didn't care.

"So, we're about to start the campaign promoting the *House of Hernandez* documentary that coincides with the book coming out," Tony jumped right in. "We want to leave it a few weeks from the actual book release. Strike while the iron is hot, but we don't want people to skip the book either."

"Good idea," Jorge nodded. "I like this."

"You watched it and thought it was good?"

"Like I tell you before," Jorge shrugged. "This here, it is perfect."

"It goes nicely with the book," Makerson added. "Hopefully, it doesn't take from Athas' fire too much when he announces the election. It's happening close together."

"That there does not bother me," Jorge assured him. "Speaking of which, we must make Athas a rock star once he finally announces this election. I thought he would by now, but it is good that he has not yet. He plans to throw money at the traditional media to keep them thinking pleasant thoughts about him. That and we…..we got another plan."

"Other than building him up in our reports?" Makerson asked suspiciously.

"We got this here reporter that has a thing for Athas over at…"

Marco grinned. Andrew immediately noticed his reaction, and his eyes widened.

"Oh fuck off! That one? Oh man, she don't exactly hide this shit either," Andrew laughed. "Remember Tony? We watched that clip where they're making fun of her interviewing Athas before. There was practically a puddle under her chair. It was so obvious."

"I must not have seen this here interview," Jorge replied. "But it seems to be common knowledge."

"Do I even want to know?" Tony cringed, and Marco giggled at the end of the table but immediately attempted to hide it.

"Oh no, you aren't going to…." Makerson turned to Jorge. "I mean, you aren't seriously thinking…"

"He needs good press," Jorge attempted to justify his decision. "And well, she needs…."

"Yeah, we know what she needs," Andrew laughed and clapped his hands together. "Wow, talk about politicians getting down and dirty! And she's just got that kind of look. The smart, plain-looking ones always are buck wild and…"

"Ok, can we not do this," Tony put his hand in the air, while Jorge grinned and raised an eyebrow. "This is…are you sure this is a good idea? We don't need Athas to be a 'me too' case when he dumps her later on."

"She won't have proof of anything," Jorge insisted. "And we will cross that bridge when, and if, we come to it."

Everyone knew what that meant. No one said a word.

CHAPTER 6

Alec Athas hated journalists. As a social worker, he hated how they glossed over actual social and economic divisions only to exploit the vulnerable. They never talked to homeless people to ask how they got there but instead took b roll shots of them slumped over on the ground, with urine stains on their pants and a needle rolling around nearby. However, since becoming a politician, his hatred grew into intense loathing.

And now, he sat with Holly Anne Ryerson, a woman who rose through the ranks because she came from a well-connected family, not because she had talent. She was incredibly awkward. Had he not spoken with her before, Alec would feel sorry for the middle-aged woman. However, having had light, ridiculous interviews with her previously, Alec had long lost respect for the journalist.

"So, tell me, what is the last book you read?" She asked as the two sat close together on his couch, after her insistence that it would make the shot look 'tighter'. Her knee was touching his, something the camera wouldn't capture. He wondered how often this happened, the viewer unaware.

"I haven't had much time to read lately," Alec attempted to sound calm, and friendly, even though he thought the question was frivolous and a waste of time. "I have a stack of books by my bed that I hope to get to…one of these days."

She laughed and seemed to move closer to him. Alec shared a fake smile with her and wanted this to be over. As much as he despised this woman, glancing over her body, he did think he could manage to follow Jorge Hernandez's obnoxious instructions to 'fuck her brains out'. Something was intriguing about her curves; that had to be his focus. Holly Anne was known to speak highly of those in the public eye, with the ability to heighten their profile, but she was also known to rip people apart and leave them to die. At first glance, you would never guess it, but Holly Anne Ryerson was the journalistic equivalent of Jorge Hernandez.

"I guess leading a country does take a lot of your time," She joked, and he laughed, even though he was growing annoyed. "Tell me about your favorite television shows."

Alec named off a couple of shows from her network. As if he ever watch either. But this was the kind of fake bullshit expected when you were a politician. You had to play the game. Unfortunately, the stakes kept getting higher.

The questions continued, with Alec jumping through all the hoops. He felt a wave of simmering anger continue to burn inside him, a fury that had only increased the longer he was in politics. His hatred for everything it stood for despite the little positive he was able to accomplish. A part of him didn't want to announce an election the following morning, but they had already planned his press conference. And here he was, having a meaningless interview with Holly Anne to make him appear more approachable and down-to-earth. Since when did people want their politicians to be like them?

"If you weren't the prime minister of Canada," She continued to speak. "What would you be doing now?"

This sounds like a question you ask a pop star, not a prime minister.

"Well," Alec managed to fake another smile. "If I wasn't the prime minister, I would still be in social work. I got involved in politics because I hoped to impact policies. I saw so many gaps being ignored and hoped that a role in government would allow me to address them in a way I simply couldn't while working in social work."

This was an opportunity for Holly Anne to dive into a topic close to Alec's heart, but the look in her eyes made it immediately apparent that it wasn't happening.

"So, do you have any sisters and brothers?"

The nauseating interview continued. The ridiculous questions were better suited for a first date than a pre-election announcement. Alec remained calm, even though the anger inside him continued to build. This wasn't a side of him that he either liked or recognized. It was dark, cold, and a world apart from who he used to be. Was this what politics did to people? Is that why so many politicians stopped caring? It was a game. It was political theater. Nothing was real. How did people think it ever was?

The interview finally ended, and Alec couldn't wait to stand up and break his awkward positioning on the couch. Holly Anne thanked him as she made her way across the room to turn off the camera. Alec removed his mic and hauled out his phone to see if he had any messages while she put her equipment away. Alec felt free now that this farce of an interview was over, relaxed and like himself again. He wanted Holly Anne to leave so that he could try to shake off the experience and move on. He did a lot of that lately.

However, the first message on his phone was from Jorge Hernandez. *Remember what I told you.*

Glancing at Holly Anne, Alec felt the heaviness return to his body. What did she want? What did she *really* want? Why was she a journalist? In a moment of impulse, he asked her that very question. She stopped what she was doing, stunned by what he asked, and attempted to explain.

"Well, I mean, I went to journalism school and…"

"No, that's not what I'm asking you," Alec abruptly cut her off. "I asked *why* you're a journalist. Why do you want to do this kind of work? What would *you* do if you weren't a journalist? I'm curious."

His questions seemed to give her a jolt. With an amused expression, it was clear she was reading too much into why he asked. At this point, Alec didn't care.

"Well, I thought it would be fun," She whimsically shrugged. "You know, you get to meet a lot of people and stuff. I like being on television. I like having conversations. I don't know."

Alec forced a smile and nodded. Sarcastic remarks bounced through his head, but he managed to bite his tongue before they touched his lips.

"You know, it just seemed like the perfect fit," She said as she finished packing up and glanced around. "It must get pretty lonely in this house."

Alec could almost hear Jorge Hernandez laughing. He got such a perverse joy in watching other people show their weaknesses. Whether Holly Anne knew it or not, she was starting to lay her hand on the table.

"It can be," Alec played along. "But I, unfortunately, don't get to spend a lot of time here."

"I suppose," She turned toward him. "You know, I would love a tour. I would like to see what the rest of this place looks like."

"Sure," Alec nodded and agreed, feeling as if he was an actor in a bad porn flick. "I can show you."

"Thanks," Holly Anne nodded as she walked toward him. "I would love to see that stack of books by your bed. I can imagine it's quite impressive."

They exchanged looks. Alec said nothing but started to walk, and she followed.

Passing the office where he murdered someone earlier that year, he suddenly felt the same rage flowing through his body as they made their way to his bedroom. It was almost overwhelming as his heart started to race, his body grew warm, and he clenched his jaw. Everyone wanted something from him. Everyone wanted to manipulate or control him. She was just another one of those people. She was just another vulture.

Walking into his room, he stopped and gestured for her to join him. She appeared pleased as their eyes met. She boldly moved in to kiss him. Things happened quickly, but Alec felt semi-conscious, barely aware of what he was doing. He wouldn't remember leading her to his bed or removing his clothes. He wouldn't remember all the ridiculous foreplay she attempted, tips she probably read on a porn star's top ten lists. He wouldn't even remember the powerful orgasm that ended it all as she straddled him, her large breasts bouncing in the air. But he would remember feeling hatred for her, something she probably misread as passion.

It was after she left that the powerful surge of anger disappeared. He was left feeling drained, exhausted, and depressed. Fixing himself a drink, he reluctantly called Jorge Hernandez.

"*Hola,*"

"It happened."

"Oh, you mean, this here interview?" Jorge lowered his voice. "Should we not be talking on the secure line right now?"

"There's no need," Alec insisted. "You already know what was on my agenda for today, and you already know what happened because you insisted on it."

The bitterness in his voice was surprising to Alec. He hadn't realized it was there until he said the words out loud.

"Is that so?" Jorge asked with humor in his voice, causing Alec to grow angrier.

"It is done," Alec bluntly replied. "And I expect a good review."

"Well, Athas, I am glad you had it in you," Jorge mocked him. "Because this here, it might be what you need to do. Remember, some people have more influence than others."

"I'm aware of that," Alec replied. "I'm *well* aware."

"Just remember," Jorge grew serious. "When she calls or texts you about what happened, don't respond. You want no proof. She can also use this against you."

"I won't."

He ended the call and knocked back the rest of his drink.

Jorge Hernandez had no soul. And now, neither did he.

CHAPTER 7

"And *just like that*," Jorge pointed toward the now closed laptop on his desk. "Alec Athas is a star in Canadian media."

Across from him, the prime minister appeared irritated as he bit his lower lip.

"This here is what you wanted," Jorge reminded him as he leaned back in his chair and watched Athas with interest. "You want good media coverage. And now, you got it."

"After I paid them off," Athas calmly replied, even though his eyes were glaring at Jorge. "*Now* they're talking about endorsing me."

"Ah yes!" Jorge pulled his chair forward and leaned on the desk. "You have barely announced the election. They have to pretend to wait. They must see what you are planning for the Canadian people before they throw an endorsement your way. It would look suspicious otherwise."

"Some independent media have reported that I gave them money…"

"Who cares?" Jorge shrugged, and the room fell silent until he spoke again. "You explained why. It is because of the strain streaming services are taking on traditional media. You had to help them compete. After all, they are an old train that keeps clunking along. At least until after the election. That's when you cut their money and cut their throats at the same time."

Alec raised an eyebrow.

"What?" Jorge shook his head. "Did you think you needed them after that point?"

"I assume Holly Anne Ryerson is the same?" Athas asked as he tapped his finger on the armrest of his chair. "Do I cut her throat too?"

"Well, *amigo,* if you wish," Jorge spoke flippantly. "But in my experience, there are easier and cleaner ways to break up with a girl."

"We aren't *together* to break up."

"And if she says otherwise," Jorge raised an eyebrow. "That is when slitting her throat might be an option. But remember, Athas, you have her in a vulnerable position. You have the power here."

"I don't feel very powerful."

"That's the problem," Jorge bluntly replied and noted that Athas seemed to sink a little in his chair. "The problem is that you forget you are the motherfucking prime minister. The problem is that you are so focused on my power over you that you forget that you also have all the power you want. You can fuck Holly Anne or any woman you want, and we will make sure it is covered up. You can lie all you want, and we will cover it up. You can blow someone's head off in your home office, and we will get rid of the body."

Athas opened his mouth as if to respond but instead sighed.

"I can see this information is new to you," Jorge shrugged. "But I thought it was quite clear. You are *not* powerless, Athas, but we all must answer to someone, and in your case, that someone is me."

"I thought it was the public who voted me in."

"The public voted in their member of parliament," Jorge reminded him. "Not you. You're what they are left with when all the dust settles."

"That's very….encouraging," Athas sarcastically replied.

"Well, it is what it is," Jorge laughed. "Athas, you need to get the stick out of your ass and see where you are, what you have. Go fuck that Holly Anne chick again and take your mind off of things."

"I am not sure…"

"Is she at least a good fuck?" Jorge cut him off.

"I hate the woman."

"I didn't ask you if you like her," Jorge shook his head. "That's a discussion you can have with Paige or one of your girlfriends if you wish, but not me."

An awkward silence followed. Jorge glared at Athas, who eventually looked away.

"Considering you once dated Paige," Jorge reminded him. "Your taste in women, it has drastically dropped."

"Again, I'm going to remind you that was over twenty years ago," Athas spoke in almost a whisper. "And *again,* I'm going to remind you that Holly Anne is hardly my taste in women."

"Yes, but does it matter when she's sucking your dick?" Jorge shot back, watching Athas cringed. "Oh, she has not done that yet? Well, there is something else to look forward to when you see her again. When is that exactly?"

"She wants to meet later today," Athas regained his composure. "But I'm not sure if that's such a good idea. She's a little too....involved in this situation."

"This here is what you want."

"Not exactly," Athas replied. "As I already said, it could blow up in my face later. If I dump her after the election, she'll write a hit piece on me or 'me too' me or something."

"She has two choices after the election," Jorge reminded him. "Go away quietly." He stopped and used his fingers to indicate a gun. "Or not go away at all."

"We can't kill her just because she can't keep her mouth shut," Athas stated.

"Really? Is this here a fact?" Jorge asked. "It seems to me that you may be wrong about this, Athas."

"Come on…"

"Hey, maybe you have some feelings for her after all," Jorge teased.

"Just because I don't want someone dead doesn't mean I have feelings for them," Athas countered as he sat ahead in his chair. "Even though that seems to be the case in your perverse world."

To this, Jorge laughed.

"*Amigo,*" Jorge shook his head. "You worry too much. This here, it will not be an issue. All you do is keep her on as a fuck buddy. She will always secretly wish for more but will not tell you. Eventually, she will get tired and move on. I know this because I lived a million lives before I met Paige."

"Do tell."

"Well, if I must," Jorge thought for a moment. "I once had a girl that was a casual fling. She sold drugs for me back when I was a young man working in California. The more we hooked up, the more she sold. She made more money for me. She made more money for herself. It all worked out fine. It was a good arrangement."

Athas was already cringing.

"Then, one day, she decides it was ok to spend a bunch of money that she owed me," Jorge continued. "She wanted a down payment for an expensive car that was not only conspicuous for someone who was supposed to work a dead-end job, but it was also *not* part of our deal. She owed me money."

"I can see where this is going," Athas muttered.

"So we meet up at her apartment," Jorge continued. "And she tries to manipulate me with sex then attempts to say that this here, it is no big deal. She will pay me later. I did not want to alarm her, so I say 'do not worry about this, these things happen', I walk behind her as she was getting dressed and put a bullet in her head."

Athas appeared alarmed even though he probably already knew how the story ended.

"Why didn't you….give her a chance to at least pay you?" He finally asked.

"Because Athas, the power shift was apparent," Jorge replied. "She forget that I was still *her* boss. And I remind *you* that what I was doing, it was illegal. Nothing was stopping her from going to the police. So I stopped her. I did not get to where I am by being careless."

Athas didn't reply but nodded.

Jorge observed his reaction.

It was sinking in.

"You cannot let people get too comfortable," Jorge reminded him. "That is when you have a problem."

Athas attempted to hide his nervousness, but it was apparent to Jorge. He could smell it.

"And you cannot let *her* get too comfortable," Jorge reminded him. "Or *you* have a problem. She must remember that you are the powerful one in this situation, not her. Of course, with this campaign, you will not have much time for her. So there is always that excuse."

Athas nodded as he took in this information.

"So, do we understand each other?"

"I think so."

"Then, you must get on the campaign trail," Jorge said as he pointed toward the bulletproof window. "What is on the agenda today?"

"We're traveling throughout the province," Athas replied. "My itinerary is full for the week. I wanted to touch base before I left."

"Very good," Jorge said as he stood up and turned his phone on, while Athas did the same. Both their phones started chiming, reminding them of missed messages."

"Speak of the devil," Athas shook his head. "I have messages from Holly Anne…"

"Ah, she is not the devil yet," Jorge insisted as he walked around his desk to show Athas out. "But if she can't keep her mouth shut, she might be."

"That's what I gathered," Athas replied as they reached for the door. "We will be in touch."

The two men were barely out of the office when Paige caught up with them, holding her phone.

"Jorge, we have to go to the school," She appeared flustered. "Maria got herself into some kind of a mess."

Athas exchanged looks with the couple.

"Looks like I'm not the only one with my hands full," He gestured toward the door. "I will show myself out."

"What has Maria done this time?" Jorge grew angry. "We made it almost a month with no issues. What did she do?"

"I guess we will find out," Paige quietly replied.

CHAPTER 8

"You are different from the one before," Jorge observed as he and Paige took a seat across from the principal. The middle-aged man nodded as if not sure what to say. "There was a lady here before, wasn't there, Paige?"

"Yes, I believe so," She quietly replied as she smiled at the principal. "What did you say your name was again?"

"Mr. Anthony," He replied in an official tone, sitting up straighter in his chair.

"Mr. Anthony," Jorge mocked him as he glanced at the principal's shiny bald head and raised an eyebrow. "You are definitely new."

"Yes, I am not privy to any information regarding the former principal," He continued to attempt superiority, which humored Jorge. "But sometimes people just move on."

"Sometimes they do," Jorge muttered as he continued to grin, not taking his eyes off the white man sitting across from him. "So tell me, *Mr.* Anthony, what can we do for you today?"

"Is there something wrong?" Paige automatically jumped in, her voice calm but her concern apparent. "Was there some kind of issue with Maria?"

"Well, I wouldn't say an issue," Mr. Anthony replied. "It is more of an extracurricular activity that Maria started that concerns us."

"Is this so?" Jorge grew irritated. "So, this here has *nothing* to do with school?"

"It does since she is introducing it *at* school," Mr. Anthony continued to speak condescendingly. "She has started a club. She claims it is a spiritual club, focusing on improving the world or something of this manner, and a few parents are concerned that it's a cult."

Jorge's head fell back in a loud, abrupt laugh, causing the principal to jump in surprise.

"This here," Jorge continued to laugh, with tears in his eyes. "This is what you call us here for today? My daughter, she is trying to do something good, and it *alarms* people? I thought you principals only call if kids are in trouble for doing something bad, but this does not sound so serious to me."

"We aren't suggesting that she is doing anything wrong," Mr. Anthony quickly insisted. "There are just concerns."

"So, what exactly did you call us for here today?" Jorge asked. "I do not understand. Do you want us to tell Maria to stop her group? To not do good? Maybe you would like us to ask her to create a gang instead?"

"No, of course not," Mr. Anthony appeared uncomfortable but forced a smile. "We aren't suggesting any such thing. We want to learn more about what is going on, maybe even suggest she keep it outside the school."

"It would have to be outside school anyway," Paige commented. "They're in classes here, so they wouldn't have time to participate in such activities."

"Yes, this is true," Mr. Anthony nodded, appearing relieved to speak to Paige. "But she is recruiting during school hours, and my understanding is that they were meeting during lunch breaks."

"I still do not see the concern here," Jorge shook his head. "This all seems quite innocent to me."

"The parents…"

"The parents are worried about *this?*" Jorge asked, growing frustrated. "Most parents here are rich and give their kids everything they want, spoil them, not make them learn how to work or be independent, but worry about my daughter's little group she has started? Are you kidding me right now!"

"We can't speak on how people parent," Mr. Anthony seemed to drop some of his original attitude. "So, I can't speak to that…"

"I can," Jorge cut him off. "Parents, they bring their kids up to be entitled little assholes, and my daughter, who is trying to do something good, something positive, on her own time, is being condemned? This here, it must be a joke."

"I might be the reason behind this," Paige added. "I used to do a lot of online spiritual work with people, and Maria became very interested during the summer, so we started to talk about it a lot. She was reading different books and followed people online with some *positive* messages. So I would think that she just wanted to share it with others. Being a teenager now isn't easy."

"Oh, please, Paige," Jorge shook his head. "Kids today, they have it much easier than we ever did. I did not have a computer growing up. I did not have everything handed to me. I did not sit in front of a device all day then whine about when I had to walk to the mailbox. I mean, kids, they are spoiled today. Especially in this here school. My Maria, she would be the same if I didn't make her get a job, clean up after herself, all these things. I am sorry, but kids today, they do *not* have it hard."

"But stress wise," Paige suggested, and to this, Jorge rolled his eyes.

"At any rate," Mr. Anthony cut in. "I wanted to meet with you today to talk about Maria keeping this outside of school. The parents are concerned."

Jorge rolled his eyes again.

"Did you speak to Maria about this?" Paige asked. "I think that would be the logical step here."

"I did," Mr. Anthony nodded. "And she was argumentative."

Jorge nodded in approval.

"Well, it is understandable," Paige replied. "I don't even understand this myself."

"In all honesty," Mr. Anthony seemed much more relaxed when talking to Paige. "I don't really either, but I have to respect the wishes of parents. And to your point, Mr. Hernandez. I *do* agree that this isn't something I see as bad. Again, we have to listen to the parents and try to accommodate."

"Ok," Jorge decided that he wanted to end this conversation. "We will talk to Maria."

"Great, she's in the other room."

"You took her out of class for this?" Jorge grew annoyed. "I pay this school how much money again? And you take her out of class for *this?*"

"We had to have her talk to the school psychologist to make sure…"

"Oh for fuck sakes," Jorge stood up and glared at the principal. "I pay a lot of money for my daughter to study at this here school, and I want her studying. Can you possibly accommodate *me?*"

"Jorge," Paige jumped up and grabbed his arm. "It's fine. Let's calm down. Maybe we should bring her home, have a conversation with her, and everything will get back to normal tomorrow."

"Yes, that would be ideal," Mr. Anthony appeared nervous as he stood up and gestured toward the door. "Please, I *do* understand your concerns too."

"He's just doing his job," Paige reminded Jorge. "I can imagine some of the parents that come in here must be…difficult."

It wasn't until they were in the car that they approached the subject again.

"I can't believe they sent me home for this," Maria complained as she crossed her legs and threw her laptop bag beside her on the seat. "It wasn't like I was making a bomb, for God's sake."

"Maria," Paige shook her head. "No one here is arguing with you."

"No, but these parents…" Jorge started.

"They thought I was starting a cult!" Maria complained. "Like I even know how to do something like that. I was trying to help other kids."

"That was noble of you," Paige observed.

"Well, yes and no," Maria confessed. "It wasn't just to help kids. It was because I'm trying to create an image. I thought with my moving up in the family, I should create…an impression of someone with only the best intentions. Kind of like how you used to do, Paige, to hide what you were *really* doing."

With much reluctance, Paige finally confessed to her step-daughter that she once had been a trained assassin who used self-help, a spiritual site, to launder her money. It was a way to satisfy the government while explaining her wealth. This was as much about creating fake profiles and payments as it was spreading positivity to her online community.

"This here, it was a good idea," Jorge commented to Paige. "So I can understand why Maria decided to do something similar. After all, who would expect a spiritually awakened young woman to do anything sinister? Is that right, Maria?"

"That's what I was thinking," Maria agreed from the backseat.

"But why didn't you mention any of this to us?" Paige countered.

"I didn't plan it," Maria shrugged. "I got the idea in school one day and created a Facebook group and a couple of videos, and things just took off from there. I didn't think anyone cared about these things at my school, but they aren't just shallow, rich assholes like you always say, *Papá.*"

"Well, Maria, I am not so sure that still isn't true," Jorge corrected her. "They want to jump on this latest thing. I would not count on them to continue."

"Tell me more about this page," Paige asked with interest.

"It's nothing bad," Maria shook her head. "I mostly just posted spiritual quotes and did a little video about how our generation could make the world a better place. I said we should take advantage of this time in history to do better. You know, that kind of thing. It was like a motivational speech. A few of us met to talk about it on lunch the other day, and then the Nazis found out.

"The what?" Jorge started to laugh. "The Nazi? Who is *the Nazi?*"

"Mr. Anthony," Maria replied. "We call him the Nazi because we think he's one. Also like, he tries to make everything joyless. He might be a racist."

"Well, not everyone is racist," Paige corrected her. "Despite what the media tells you."

"I know," Maria nodded. "We think he likes the white kids better because he always has brown kids in his office."

Jorge let out an exasperated sigh.

"Let it go," Paige muttered.

"Yeah, I think it's an exaggeration," Maria insisted. "I think he would be an asshole to me even if I were white."

"So, Maria," Jorge picked up where they were before. "This here group, it is new? I am not sure I feel comfortable with you doing videos online. This here, it concerns me, but for your safety."

"It's a closed group," Maria insisted. "It's private."

"We will look at this page when we get home," Jorge insisted.

"Trust me," Maria insisted. "I know what I am doing. I'm going to talk about making the world a better place, all flowers and sunshine. That's it. I'm not a cult. I'm just trying to do what Paige once did. I'm going to make it look like I'm a spiritual leader to hide who I am."

Jorge gave her a look in the rearview mirror.

"I'm Maria Hernandez," She said, her eyes glued to his. "I'm about to take over the most powerful family in the country."

CHAPTER 9

"If we aren't here to make the world a better place then why are we here at all?" Maria spoke with sincerity on the social media platform. *With wide eyes and a youthful naivety, it was difficult not believing that her heart was in the right place.* *"My goal is to encourage people my age to do better, and hopefully, it only evolves from there."*

"See what I mean?" Jorge pointed toward the laptop on the bar, glancing up to see Chase nodding his head. "Who the fuck would ever believe that this here little girl wants to rule the world?"

"I think they believe it," Chase agreed. "Just not in the way we know she *wants* to rule the world.

"You know, Chase," Jorge said as he closed the laptop. "I worry a lot about Maria. I have for some time. She has been through a lot for her age. Sometimes, I wonder if running this family, if it is a good idea. But when I see this here, I see she is thinking ahead. That she is stronger than I thought."

"Well, she *is only* 15," Chase reminded him. "We have to take that into consideration too."

"Yes, well, according to my Maria," Jorge laughed. "She's only months away from 16! Imagine that, Chase? Even though we *just* celebrate her birthday."

"She's so young-looking, though," Chase commented. "She still seems like the kid I met years ago."

"Oh yes!" Jorge laughed. "Back when you had to babysit her for me."

"I gotta admit," Chase grinned as he leaned against the counter. "When you told me that day that you needed me to *take care* of a girl, I did *not* think you meant babysit."

Jorge threw his head back in laughter.

"I thought for sure you wanted me to kill someone," Chase continued. "I didn't know you even had a kid, let alone that you would trust me to look after her."

"Well, Chase, I saw something in you that I knew I could trust," Jorge shrugged. "I trust my instincts, and I knew you would be perfect to look after her, and really, I must admit, Chase, that was one of your first tasks to see how you did. Of course, you did a little too well because my Maria, she has had a crush on you ever since."

"Yeah, I gotta give her credit," Chase laughed. "She's been pretty consistent with that."

"Ah, this here is fine," Jorge swung his hand in the air. "It is a harmless crush. My Maria, she is a bit of a late bloomer. But someday, when she finds herself a boyfriend, she will move on from her crush on you. That is if I do not kill the little bastard who tries to do anything with my daughter."

"I would not want to be Maria's boyfriend," Chase laughed. "You will scare the hell out of whoever that ends up being."

"Well, this here is a good thing," Jorge insisted. "Then he will keep his hands to himself, *si?*"

"You have to be proud, though," Chase commented. "All things considered."

"You have no idea how proud I am," Jorge confirmed. "But you know, if I am not worried about one family member, there is always another."

"Diego?" Chase guessed as his expression grew serious. "How is that going?"

"I have him at the safe house," Jorge referred to a secret home in rural Ontario where the family could go if they needed to get away from the city. "We decided that it would be best that way. It's just him and his counselor. Someone Paige found. I think this here, it is for the best."

"Any reports back yet?"

"So far, so good," Jorge nodded. "But he has a long way to go."

"So, the party?" Chase changed the subject. "The book launch is this weekend? Anything else I need to know before then?"

"Everything, it is already done," Jorge confirmed. "You need to show up and open the doors for the people preparing it. There will be media here, that kind of thing. As long as our customers know there's a private party that night, I think that is all."

"It's all set," Chase confirmed. "I'll have doormen watching who gets in."

"Well, I hope it goes well, and it goes fast," Jorge shook his head. "I am not looking forward to this at all."

"I thought you'd enjoy the attention?"

"Not when people start asking about my past," Jorge shook his head. "You know I never wanted to do this book in the first place, but was forced."

"With the election going on," Chase reminded him. "Most people's attention is averted."

"Which is what I want," Jorge confirmed. "People need to forget all the rumors, once and for all."

After a short discussion regarding party plans for that weekend, Jorge left *the Princesa Maria* and headed for Hernandez productions to meet with Makerson, Andrew, and Tony. The three were already in a lively discussion when he entered the room.

"You gotta keep the seat toasty for your enemy," Andrew was commenting as he put his arm on the back of the chair beside him as if someone were there. "That's what I always say."

"What does that *mean* exactly?" Makerson raised an eyebrow as he glanced toward Jorge walking in the door.

"Come on, you're the writer," Andrew shot back. "You don't understand words now?"

"I don't understand words that don't make sense," Makerson countered.

"It means," Jorge said as he closed the door behind him. "You must make things as *comfortable* as possible for your enemy so they do not realize they *are* your enemy."

"Yeah," Andrew nodded his head toward Jorge, who took his usual seat, "What he said."

Makerson didn't reply but nodded his head.

"What are we talking about here?" Jorge asked as he glanced around the table to see Tony shrug, "Who is our enemy today?"

"We're just talking about Athas," Andrew replied. "And that guy who double-crossed him then *disappeared* this summer."

"Yes, well, people like that," Jorge shook his head. "They tend to disappear."

Andrew raised an eyebrow but didn't reply. Makerson gave him a dirty look while Tony nodded in understanding.

"So, let us get right to why I am here," Jorge cut off their conversation. "I was just at the bar, and everything is set for the party this weekend."

"Oh, good," Makerson nodded, his demeanor slightly tense. "And then I start the tour from there."

"Just a short tour," Jorge reminded him. "And you keep with what was in the book. If anyone asks you anything else, say that your research did not show anything else."

"Rumors," Tony piped up. "Speculations, maybe even say conspiracy theories."

"Racist rumors since you're a Mexican," Andrew added. "You know, shitheads making things up to get attention."

"That is all," Jorge replied. "Pretend you are a politician. Answer the question you want rather than the one asked of you."

Everyone at the table laughed.

"Speaking of politicians," Jorge glanced around the room. "Why were you talking about Athas when I come in the room? How is our favorite politician doing?"

"We were checking the polls and saying how his numbers have gone up since the summer," Makerson commented, gesturing toward his closed laptop on the table. "The media has been very kind to him."

"Yeah, especially Holly Anne Ryerson," Tony added as he ran a hand over his bald head. "She *sure* gave him a positive review on that news segment."

"Oh yes, up close and *personal* with Athas," Jorge grinned. "I heard about that, but I couldn't stomach watching."

"If you couldn't stomach watching it," Andrew piped up. "Can you imagine how Athas must've felt about…"

"Ok, let's not today," Makerson cut off Andrew and shook his head. "We heard enough of that yesterday."

"Is it true, though," Andrew directed his question at Jorge. "I mean, really? He's whoring himself out to win an election."

"Is this here really that unusual for a politician?" Jorge raised an eyebrow.

"Yeah, but not usually, *literally* whoring themselves out," Andrew said. "I mean, I think…"

"She just seems so…." Tony started and stopped.

"Can you imagine the fucked up sex they must have?" Andrew laughed. "I mean, he must be drowning in…"

"Ok, let's not," Makerson cut him off again. "I don't want to hear you analyze this again today. Yesterday was bad enough."

"I just call it how I see it."

"Can you see it *alone*?" Makerson countered, then turned to Jorge. "If this ever gets out…"

"We say it is a lie and humiliate her," Jorge insisted. "Or maybe we could have this work to our advantage, "If Athas has a little girlfriend…"

"Little?" Andrew shot back.

"Can we just get back on track here?" Makerson said. "So Athas is doing great in the polls. He's already predicted to win the election, provided he keeps a good impression of himself. What else?"

"The new cartel show is starting next week," Tony reminded him.

"The one that *isn't* based on Jorge's life?" Andrew piped up with heavy sarcasm in his voice.

"Yes, this is right," Jorge nodded. "The show that is *not* based on my life."

"I don't know that it was a good idea to have it come out when the book was released," Tony gently suggested. "I mean, there are rumors…"

"But this here will increase interest in the show," Jorge reminded him. "If people comment, we merely give the impression that we did this on purpose to increase ratings. That will make the rumor look fake and us, at worse, having no shame."

"That's not a bad idea," Makerson nodded. "Ricardo is set to do some interviews with entertainment shows. We had someone coach him on how to handle questions."

"This here is good."

"We're doing the first interview, though," Andrew insisted. "Of course."

"Of course," Jorge repeated.

"Everything is falling into place," Makerson suggested. "We just got to keep it on track."

Jorge didn't reply but nodded.

He would keep things on track. And God help anyone who got in his way.

CHAPTER 10

"It looks more like a cocktail party than a book launch," Paige observed as she glanced around *Princesa Maria* and then back at Jorge. "Am I even dressed right?"

"*Mi amor,*" Jorge's eyes swept over the smooth, crimson dress that flattered her curves. "I assure you that you are dressed perfectly for *anything.*"

"Jorge, you know what I mean," She spoke in a begging tone that caused his desires to increase as he moved closer and ran his hand over her back. "I thought this would be more…"

"You know, *mi amor,* we could probably slip into that office over there, and no one would even notice we were gone," Jorge continued to stay on track with his thoughts as his hand slid over her ass. "Maybe we have a family emergency we must attend to or…"

"Chase may not appreciate us *borrowing* his office," Paige whispered back.

"Oh, but we have before," Jorge reminded her as he moved closer, his desires increasing as he visualized their last encounter in the bar's office. "No one will ever know. We are not necessarily the center of attention here anyway. Makerson is."

Glancing across the room, Jorge could see where the author of *House of Hernandez* had various media personalities surrounding him. Jorge slipped his hand into his pocket and pulled out a phone. Turning around, it took him a minute to find Chase, who appeared preoccupied with something Maria was telling him at that very moment. Although Jorge was curious, he was hornier than anything.

"Hey Chase," Jorge grabbed his attention and held up his phone. "There is something we must attend to. Can we use your office?"

"Sure," Chase replied. "Go ahead."

"What's wrong now?" Maria rushed over. "Should I know anything?"

"Maria, we must check in with Diego," Jorge lied. "It is just…"

"We are usually in contact with them daily," Paige rushed to reply. "We realized neither of us has heard…"

"You should go," Maria pointed at Paige, turning her attention toward Jorge. "*Papá,* you need to be over there helping Makerson. The book *is* about *you.*"

"Maria, this is true, but…"

"Maria," Paige calmly replied. "Nothing has officially started yet. Andrew will be live streaming soon. This is just an informal event so far."

"Paige, please, just go ahead," Jorge turned and gave her a look, and she nodded in understanding. "I will check to see if Andrew is close and what is going on with that…"

"Sure," Paige nodded with a smooth grin on her face. "You do what you have to do."

There was something about *how* she said it, that caused his libido to go into full swing. He suddenly didn't care about the party or etiquette, about anything else, as he watched her turn around and walk away as the dress hugged her hips. His thoughts crawled under the skirt as his hormones went into overdrive.

"Maria, I will be back shortly," Jorge dismissively spoke as he looked at his phone, noting that she was shrugging and rolling her eyes. She swung around to walk toward Makerson.

Glancing around, Jorge noted that no one appeared to be paying much attention to him, so he made his way toward the office. He was almost there when someone grabbed his arm. Swinging around, Jorge grew frustrated when he saw Holly Anne Ryerson.

"Mr. Hernandez, do you think I could have an interview with you?" She smiled even though she looked very uncomfortable. "The prime minister suggested that since he considers you one of his top advisors from the business world, maybe my viewers would enjoy learning what makes you tick."

Fucking Athas!

"Well, yes, I would enjoy speaking with you," Jorge gave her a charming smile. "But I must attend to something quickly first. If you do not mind, I must excuse myself to make a call. Then you will have my full attention."

"That would be terrific," She smiled as she moved closer to him, and Jorge, in turn, stepped back. "I will wait here."

Jorge felt his desires deflate. He faked a smile and pointed toward the office.

"I will be right back."

Quickly rushing in the door, he locked it behind him, and he let out a heavy sigh. Paige was sitting on the edge of the desk with interest.

"That's not the reaction I was expecting."

"Paige, you have no idea," Jorge shook his head. "This reporter out there…"

"What about her?" Paige asked as her fingers slid up her thigh, pulling up the smooth material of her dress. "You know, I took the liberty of covering the camera."

Jorge glanced over his shoulder to see a piece of material over the camera. Looking back at his wife, he felt his desires building once again. He rushed across the room, his mouth roughly meeting hers, he suddenly stopped and moved away.

"We do not have much time."

"I don't need much time," Paige whispered as her hand moved toward the clasp on his pants.

Her fingers moved inside his pants, and Jorge's breath increased as he kissed her lips. His tongue moved to her neck as she spread her legs and pulled him closer. He quickly moved inside her, gasping in pleasure as he began to move faster while she wrapped her legs around him. Soft moans turned into loud gasps as he moved deeper inside her as tension released and his body filled with pleasure. Her legs squeezed harder momentarily but finally let go as she leaned back, her face flushed.

They suddenly stopped, and music from the party flowed into the room. They slowly parted, and Jorge managed to compose himself.

"*Mi amor,* that was amazing," Jorge commented as he pulled his pants up while attempting to calm his breath. "I needed that. But later tonight, it will be better."

"Do you think it can get better," Paige asked as she slid off the desk and moved forward to kiss him while pulling down her skirt. "I have to go freshen up."

"I will see you out there," Jorge smiled as he kissed the top of her head. "I must go talk to this nauseating reporter."

A few minutes later, he was sitting at the bar, answering Holly Anne Ryerson's softball questions. That was what he wanted. She asked the standard things, showing that she hadn't done her research, which suited Jorge. Incompetent reporters were the best kind in a situation like this one.

She was followed by others, who stopped to ask him questions. Andrew live-streamed the event, going from guest to guest, focusing on Makerson and Jorge. The crowd seemed to grow thicker as the night went on. Feeling uninterested in being there, Jorge occasionally glanced toward his wife or daughter, usually to see either engaged in a conversation with someone. He was concerned with who talked to Maria but noted that Chase tended to be close at hand, keeping an eye, which made him feel better.

When he finally escaped the reporters, Jorge made his way toward Tony, who sat alone at the bar.

"Aren't you supposed to be working here or something?" Jorge teased.

"Unless I'm serving drinks," Tony pointed toward the alcohol. "There's not much for me to do here."

"Socialize?"

"These people aren't here to see me," Tony reminded him. "I'm just another media guy tonight. Andrew got a handle on things. I've been watching on my phone to see comments and that kind of thing. So far, it's looking pretty positive."

"This here, it is going a lot better than I expected," Jorge commented as he glanced at Makerson. "I was expecting….something else…"

"Book releases tend to be pretty low-key," Tony mused. "Even when the topic is someone as high profile as you. It's just a different medium. We weren't expecting things to get too wild. Plus, everyone is just dropping in, getting their interview, then leaving."

"Following Athas around," Jorge wondered.

"That's what I'm thinking," Tony nodded. "He has an event across town."

"Figures," Jorge muttered, feeling slightly annoyed.

"But this is what you want," Tony reminded him. "Low-key, remember? I saw Holly Anne Ryerson talking to you."

"Yes, she decide to interview me," Jorge commented. "I could barely keep awake."

"Well, she's gone now," Tony glanced toward the door. "Probably to wherever Athas is now."

The two men shared a grin.

"So do I have to make a speech, anything?" Jorge asked as he leaned against the bar and looked at the crowd. It was starting to phase out. "What else is there to these book release parties?"

"Not much," Tony shook his head. "People have food, a drink or two, ask a few questions, see the cover, and go."

Jorge nodded, relieved it was almost over.

"Then this here, it was a success?"

"It appears so," Tony replied as he looked through his phone. "There are some tweets about it, but mostly pictures of you or Makerson, with a short blurb. All and all, this is what we hoped for tonight. Enough attention to make the publisher happy, but not too much."

Jorge didn't reply but nodded. He hated to admit that it was a little disappointing. He had expected much more. Perhaps his popularity was slipping. Maybe he never had it at all.

Paige made her way across the room, reminding him of their earlier encounter. Jorge felt his desires building again as she moved closer, and they shared an intimate smile.

"I think things are winding down," She remarked. "Are we happy with everything?"

"Yes, it was a success," Jorge moved closer to kiss her. "We must remember to have Clara check the bar very carefully tomorrow morning."

"Yes," Paige nodded. "We don't need surprise cameras or listening devices left behind as parting gifts."

Jorge nodded as he noticed Tony's face tense up as he looked toward the door.

Turning around, Jorge quickly saw why.

CHAPTER 11

He felt his blood boil as she walked across the room. It wasn't that Jolene Silva left on bad terms when she officially retired from the *familia* earlier that year. It was that deep down, Jorge knew she would never stay away.

Feeling Paige place her hand on his arm as if warning him to stay calm, Jorge flinched but managed to hold his composure. There was something about Jolene's expression that disarmed him. Quickly glancing around the room to monitor the situation, his eyes met Chase's, who appeared as surprised as Jorge. He quickly realized that everyone in his inner circle was watching Diego's sister with a mix of concern and horror. It was up to him not to overreact.

"Jolene Silva," Jorge said as the Colombian femme fatale approached him, her heels loudly clicking against the floor. "I am surprised to see you here. The guest list was quite short, so I am…"

Before he could even get another word out of his mouth, he saw her lift her hand, preparing to slap him. He quickly grabbed her by the wrist and gave Jolene a warning look. Seeing the fury in her eyes, Jorge felt his anger rise.

"This will not be here," He muttered, squeezing her wrist before roughly letting it go. He once again glanced around to make sure no one saw, but it was only Andrew giving him a wide-eyed stare. His expression was more of fascination than concern. "Go in the fucking office if you have something to say to me."

Jolene didn't reply. Glaring at him, she turned to make her way toward Chase's office. Passing the bar's manager on the way, she ignored him. His mouth fell open as he exchanged looks with Jorge. Beside him stood Maria, who appeared angry. She immediately started toward Jorge, who was on his way to the office with Paige in tow.

"*Papá,* what the hell was that about?" Maria's eyes were full of anger. "Should I come with…"

"No, Maria, I need you to stay out here," Jorge spoke firmly. "I need you to go around the room and make sure that no one here saw that, and if they did, try to play it down."

"OK," She stood up straighter, much like a soldier taking a command. "I will do that. I don't think anyone saw."

"Just make sure," Jorge said as he continued to walk past her. He turned his head back. "You know what to do."

"Stay calm," Paige was catching up to him. "You know Jolene. She's always dramatic."

"Yes, well, you do not do this here," Jorge replied as he rushed ahead. "In the middle of my fucking book launch. In public, and she knows this."

He flew into the office as Paige quietly closed the door behind them. Sitting behind the desk as if she owned the room, Jolene leaned back in the chair, her eyes daring him. To this, Jorge stood in the middle of the room, refusing to sit across from her.

"What the *fuck* was that, Jolene?" Jorge shouted at her.

"You know what the fuck that was about," Jolene leaned ahead on the desk, her breasts almost spilling out of her dress. "You kill my brother and you think I would not find out!"

"What?" Paige jumped in before Jorge had a chance.

"Jolene, this here, I do not know what you are talking about," Jorge shook his head. "Diego is…"

"Do *not* play this game with me," Jolene snapped as she jumped up from the chair, pointing in his direction. "I know you, Jorge Hernandez, and I know what you do and how you hide it. Diego, he say you were upset with him, then he suddenly disappears."

Jorge exchanged looks with his wife.

"I do not know why you would jump to this here conclusion," Jorge shook his head. "But if there was one of the two of you I wanted to kill, it would be *you,* Jolene, not your fucking brother."

His comment seemed to throw her off course for a few seconds, but she quickly found her ground again.

"Then where is he?" She countered with strength in her voice. "And why has he not returned my calls or texts? Why isn't he at his house? Why is he not in the office? Why will no one tell me anything? Tell me that."

"Jolene," Paige began to reply. "It isn't what you think…"

"Jolene," Jorge cut off his wife. "You are always so dramatic. You jump to a conclusion. Why not just ask me where he is? Why do you do this here?

"As if you would tell me the truth!" Jolene snapped back. "I know *you.* I know what you do."

Jorge said nothing. Crossing his arms over his chest, he gave her a warning glare before continuing.

"If you think…"

"Enough of this!" He yelled at her. "Diego, he is fine. And if you *ever* do something like you did out there, in the middle of my book launch party, worrying about your brother will be the least of your concerns. I have warned you, again and again, Jolene, you are a loose cannon. Do not make me second guess my decision to let you go on with your life when you leave this here *familia*. Because right now, I wonder if I made the right decision."

Her lips squeezed together as if attempting to hold the words back. All the lines on her face became pronounced as her face tightened. She needed to be reminded of her place since she had forgotten.

"Your brother is fine," Paige spoke in her usual calm voice. "He's at the safe house."

"Where is this safe house?" Jolene spoke in a more reasonable tone to Paige. "I want to see him. Why is he there? Is he in danger?"

"You cannot," Jorge shook his head. "He is trying to recover from addiction, and this here, he will not be able to do with *you* hanging around."

Jolene's expression fell. Her shoulders drooped.

"What?" Her voice was suddenly full of vulnerability. "Diego, he is…"

"He has a problem, Jolene," Paige stepped forward. "We saw him unraveling recently, and he finally admitted that he's been doing cocaine and drinking a lot for years."

"But if this is true," Jolene appeared confused. "How did I not know this?"

"None of us did," Jorge replied. "We were all shocked."

"How could he hide it?" She glanced around as if attempting to grasp the explanation. "No, this here, it must be a mistake."

"It's not, Jolene," Paige replied and took a few steps forward. "We had to find someone who would quietly help him and work on his issues, the ones that put him in this situation in the first place."

"Oh," Jolene replied and looked down.

"There's a lot of trauma from when he was younger, especially from his childhood," Paige continued. "We talked about it at great length, and I found the right person to help him. I'm sorry we didn't tell you. No one thought of it because everything happened so fast. We had to send him away from everyone, from everything. We couldn't have word get out."

"Can I go?" Jolene asked but automatically shook her head. "No, I see. I mean, I know why not."

"I can see if we can arrange a phone call," Paige offered. "For your peace of mind, but that's all I can do."

"This here," Jolene nodded. "This would be good."

Paige nodded and reached in her purse.

"I cannot believe you thought I would kill Diego!" Jorge felt his anger rise again. "Why would I do this? He is like a brother to me. You know this, Jolene."

"I do not know," Jolene suddenly appeared childlike in her mannerisms. "I just think of all the times...."

"But he is *familia*," Jorge shook his head.

"But when he did not answer my calls," Jolene shook her head. "That is not like Diego. He usually gets back to me."

"Hello," Paige was on her phone and walking toward Jolene. "Could I speak to Diego for a moment? How's he doing?"

She nodded in response to the question.

"Ok," She calmly said and glanced toward Jorge. "That's good. Can he talk for a moment? His sister is here and would like to speak to him."

Paige continued to nod.

"That's fine," She said. "Jolene knows that he can't talk for long. It's just to make sure he's ok."

"Thank you," Paige continued and passed the phone to Jolene, who rushed to grab it.

"*Hola, Diego!*"

She continued to speak in Spanish while Jorge and Paige moved away.

"I do not like what she did," Jorge muttered to Paige. "This here, it was too much."

"I know, but you have to consider that she thought you killed her brother," Paige muttered. "It was an overreaction, but you must see where she's coming from."

"It was an overreaction in public," Jorge corrected her. "What if someone, they see this and word gets out? I do not want the news from this here party to be that Jolene attacked me. I want the focus to be on the book."

"There weren't many people left," Paige assured him. "And I don't think anyone noticed. Also, Maria and the others will do everything to put out any potential fires."

"They better," Jorge commented. "Or it will be her paying for my headaches."

"She does cause a lot of them," Paige confirmed.

Jorge shot her a look as he turned, noticing Jolene finish her phone call. She slumped over with tears running down her face. He stood back and observed as Paige rushed over to comfort her. Crossing his arms over his chest, Jorge just shook his head.

CHAPTER 12

"Woo!" Andrew said when Jorge joined the others in the Hernandez Productions Company boardroom the following morning. "When I saw Jolene walking out of that office yesterday, I said that cat got nine lives *for sure!*"

Tony gave him a warning look, while across the table from Andrew, Makerson ignored the remark as he stared at his tablet. Marco snickered as he looked at his laptop.

"Nine more than she deserves," Jorge bluntly replied as he glanced around the table. "I thought Chase would be here this morning?"

"He got tied up at the bar," Andrew said. "Didn't he message you?"

Jorge pulled out his phone and turned it on.

"So, what the actual fuck was that about last night?" Andrew continued to push. "With Jolene? I thought she was gone for good? Why did she attack you? Or want to attack you? Or like, whatever…"

"She wanted to know where Diego is," Jorge explained as his phone came to life, and Chase's message immediately popped up. Satisfied, Jorge turned his phone off again. "She thought I did something to him since he was not answering his phone."

"That seems like a….bit of a jump," Makerson observed as he turned off his tablet, and beside him, Marco closed his laptop. "I mean, Diego hasn't been gone that long. Besides, didn't he tell Jolene what was going on?"

"He was ashamed," Jorge confirmed. "I mean, this here, he hid for many years. It got worse as time went on. I could see it. Even earlier this year, last year, I notice he was drinking more. My instincts tell me something was wrong, but I did not want to accept it. I guess that is what happens when it is family."

"Jolene has never been someone who takes things calmly," Tony reminded them. "Remember when she worked here?"

"That was holy fucking hell," Andrew jumped in. "Please don't tell me she is coming back."

"That will not be happening," Jorge assured them. "My hope is that Jolene leaves town as quickly as she arrived."

"She still here?" Andrew asked. "Staying at your house?"

"Over my dead fucking body," Jorge shook his head, and Marco laughed. "That there would be a nightmare. No, she is staying at Diego's."

"Isn't it funny how we have so much going on," Makerson remarked. "With the book launch last night, the new show coming out, the election, everything, and yet, Jolene somehow manages to take over the conversation?"

"This here, it is a good point," Jorge replied. "Unfortunately, that is what she does. Jolene takes over."

"Can we stop talking about her?" Tony made a face. "And get back on track?"

"Nothing would make me happier," Jorge admitted and took a deep breath, glancing at a copy of *House of Hernandez* lying on the table. The cover was black with large letters in crimson red. "So, what we got this morning?"

"Actually," Makerson turned his attention to Jorge. "Not much in the media about the book launch. HPC news is one of the few that had anything about it, and well, that's us. Other news outlets barely mentioned us, if at all."

"They're ostracizing us," Tony spoke with reluctance. "They don't consider us part of the club, so they bury the story."

"But it's a book launch," Andrew jumped in. "It got nothing to do with Hernandez productions."

"Well, it *is* about Jorge," Makerson reminded him. "And he's the leader of the pack. That's how they look at it. I thought it would spark more attention. But then again, isn't that kind of what you wanted, Jorge? To not bring too much attention to your life story?"

"What about social media?" Jorge ignored his question, his thoughts jumping around.

"It did get more attention there," Tony nodded. "But it depends on which side of the fence you're on. One side spoke highly of you and your accomplishments, but the other side was more focused on the rumors."

"Was I top of trending topics?" Jorge asked as he looked around the table.

"Well, not really," Andrew finally replied. "Athas was sort of the top for that."

"Why? What the fuck did he do?" Jorge countered. "Make another boring speech and put people asleep?"

"He had some musicians…." Makerson started to explain.

"He had a major rock star play at his campaign thing last night," Andrew injected. "So yeah, he got the attention."

"I see," Jorge grimaced.

"Again," Makerson calmly reminded him. "We want this, remember? You *don't* want much attention going your way, and I don't want to be on a book tour for long. The book keeps the wolves at bay. This is perfect."

Jorge grimaced. The last thing he wanted was for Athas to steal his thunder. If it was anyone else but not Alec Athas! He bit his bottom lip and opened his mouth, but Tony was already speaking.

"It's all because of fangirl," Andrew jumped in. "You know, that Ryerson chick from the news. The one that is fucking Athas. He must be doing her right cause she's in *love* with him. She's the official media following him around, everywhere he goes."

"Yes, if he's trying to escape her," Makerson added and grinned. "He can't now. She was assigned to his campaign trail."

Jorge nodded his head.

"So, I leave for the book tour tomorrow," Makerson continued. "I sent you a list of dates and places. It's going to be fast, major cities, that kind of thing. Just enough to fulfill our obligation, and then I'm back here."

"Just in time," Tony replied. "The next season of *Eat the Rich Before the Rich Eat You* starts when you get back."

"This here is good," Jorge nodded, shrugging off his concerns regarding the book launch. "Let us talk about this here."

The meeting continued, and Jorge didn't think about his disappointing response to the book launch again until arriving home. It irked him that Athas was gaining more attention than him in the media, especially when he was such a spineless fuck. He wanted people to like Athas but not to love him. There was a fine line.

"Maria went on another kick about Jolene this morning," Paige commented as she poured a cup of coffee. "I reassured her that she did good at the party, so no one asked questions. We can handle Jolene."

Jorge grunted and rolled his eyes.

"Leave it to Jolene," He finally responded. "To fuck up something."

"But she didn't," Paige reminded him. "She came along when the place was clearing out, and we took care of her."

"Yes, clearing out, so they could go see Athas," Jorge grumbled. "Did you know he had a rock star at his campaign thing? No wonder no one stayed at my book launch."

"Jorge, I thought we agreed that you wanted this to be low-key?" Paige calmly reminded him, passing him a cup of coffee. "*This* is what we want. We satisfied the publisher by having the party, the book is getting attention, but not too much. No one else will decide to jump on the bandwagon and write another book about you. And we know that someone else writing another one might be more problematic."

"I know," Jorge took a deep breath as he sat at the kitchen table, and she joined him. Running a hand over his face, he shook his head. "But with Athas, I…"

"You need to get over your ego," Paige cut in. "We *have to* keep under the radar. If we don't, *we'll* be at the safe house with Diego for a different reason."

Jorge nodded and looked into his coffee.

"Have you heard anything today about Diego?" Jorge asked, deciding it was time to move on.

"He's the same," Paige quietly assured him. "It's going to take some time."

Jorge nodded, saying nothing.

"It's ok," She continued. "You have someone looking after *Our House of Pot,* and well, Jolene's watering his lime trees."

To this, Jorge rolled his eyes.

"Not that she is staying long," Paige reminded him.

Jorge wasn't so sure. They exchanged looks, but neither said a word. Turning his phone back on, he glanced toward the patio.

"It's a nice day," She pointed toward the clear doors. "You should go out and enjoy yourself.

His phone lit up with messages.

"So much for that," Jorge shook his head.

"They need to stop relying on you," Paige commented. "You keep wanting to step away, but they pull you right back."

"Oh, it is the usual," Jorge shook his head. "You know, Athas, he message me."

Paige didn't reply. He noted her expression.

"I will tell him to call the secure line," Jorge said. "See what the fuck he wants now."

"Be nice!"

"Paige, you know that being nice isn't my thing," Jorge replied as he stood up and reached for his coffee. "Not when it's Athas that I am dealing with."

"Try."

Jorge winked at his wife before making his way to the office. He was getting tired of Athas. It was always a problem with this man, and that day would be no exception.

"What is wrong now?" Jorge said as soon as he heard the anxiety in the prime minister's voice. "You had a rock star event last night. You had lots of positive attention. I see your poll numbers are going up. What is wrong? Did you find a run in your pantyhose? What is it this time?"

"I got myself in a precarious situation," Athas admitted with some hesitation.

"What? Do I have to clean up another body, Athas?" Jorge grumbled. "What the fuck you do now?"

"It could be my body you'll have to clean up," Athas replied. "Because you aren't going to like this one."

CHAPTER 13

"Remember last year when there was a hit on you?" Jorge gruffly reminded Athas as he glanced at the bulletproof window in his office and back at the phone. "Can you remind me again why I did not just let them kill you"

Athas said nothing.

"So, tell me, what is it *this* time?" Jorge continued as he ran a hand over his face and yawned. "This better be good, Athas. I don't got time today."

"Last night," Athas started, but in an attempt to rush things along Jorge cut him off.

"At the party?"

"No, after," Athas replied. "I was staying at the hotel…"

"Do you not have a house in Toronto?" Jorge cut him off.

"Yes, but because of the event…"

"Ah! This is courtesy of the taxpayers?" Jorge nodded his head. "Of course, that is where I wish for my tax dollars to go. You stay at a fancy hotel, and I assume that was with your new girlfriend? The reporter?"

"She's *not* my girlfriend," Athas rebutted. "Holly Anne and I have more of…an arrangement."

Jorge raised an eyebrow as he listened.

"I notice you did not address the hotel remark," Jorge commented. "I guess your bigger concern is that I have your dating status right, not the misuse of taxpayer's money."

"It's not exactly like that," Athas insisted.

"Nothing ever is," Jorge sarcastically responded. "Now, get on to the part I will not like, so I can decide whether or not to call Andrew to go to the crematorium."

"I may have let something slip to Holly Anne," Athas nervously explained. "It was during a particularly…vulnerable moment."

"I have a pretty good idea what *vulnerable* moment that is," Jorge replied. "Why it is you are so *weak,* Athas? This here, I keep wondering. How can you always be such a pussy?"

"I didn't mean to," Athas rushed to explain. "She brought up the topic of Marshalton and how he went missing…"

"And when you weren't saying much," Jorge cut in. "She decided it would be a great time to suck you off while taking breather breaks to ask more questions?"

"Well, it was something like that," Athas replied. "She…"

"Please, spare me the details," Jorge closed his eyes. "There are some visions I do not wish to have in my head. Now, can we get to the fucking point? I don't got all day."

"She asked if I had any thoughts about what *really* happened to him," Athas said. "Holly Anne doesn't think he just disappeared and that something more sinister happened to him."

"Does she suspect that it was you that murdered him?" Jorge bluntly asked.

"No, I mean, of course not," Athas laughed as if it was the most unbelievable thing, causing Jorge to roll his eyes. "But she thought I might be privy to some information from CSIS or the RCMP."

"And she wanted a story."

"Well, maybe, she might just want to know."

"Athas, she isn't licking your balls because she wants to marry you and have babies," Jorge reminded him. "She wants information, and she wants that information to get ahead in her career. Open your eyes."

"I know, but even what I did tell her…."

"What did you tell her?" Jorge snapped.

"I admitted it seems unlikely that he would just disappear."

"Is that it?"

"And," Athas reluctantly continued. "When she implied that you might know something, I didn't deny it."

"So, she thinks that I know something about Marshalton being missing?" Jorge yelled. "The same fucking man *you* murdered? You led her to believe that *I* had something to do with this? You dumb motherfucker!"

"I didn't say you did anything…"

"You put her on my trail," Jorge cut him off. "Is this here not enough? I do not need her sniffing around."

"I think she just thinks that…"

"You *think?*" Jorge cut him off again. "I hope it was a good fuck, Athas because it might be the last one for both of you."

Abruptly ending the call, Jorge seethed in anger. If it hadn't been for Paige, Athas would be dead already, and he would just run for prime minister. As much as Jorge hated the bullshit involved, at least he'd do things right.

Calming slightly, he wondered if he should groom someone else to take the prime minister's spot. Would there be a better person? Makerson? Tony? Paige? There had to be someone in his inner circle that he could get in the top seat without having to deal with Athas again.

Turning his phone back on, he sent a message to Marco.

We need to meet.

How about the VIP room at the bar?

Perfecto.

Jorge let out a long sigh before rising from his chair. Grabbing his phone, he left his office and headed for the door.

"Where are you going?" Paige was behind him. "What happened with Alec?"

"He is a spineless pussy, that's what happened with Athas."

"What?" Paige appeared surprised. "What do you mean?"

"Paige, Athas, is a dumb fuck," Jorge replied as he reached the door. "He tell that Holly Anne reporter that he did not think that Marshalton went missing and that I might know why."

"What?" Paige appeared shocked. "Why would he do that?"

"Because she got him in a *weak* position," Jorge replied, raising his eyebrows as he opened the door. "I will tell you more later, Paige. I have to go meet Marco. I need to see how serious this issue is."

Paige said nothing but nodded.

Once in the SUV, Jorge considered Paige's reaction to Alec's stupidity. It was about time she opened her eyes to what a moron Athas could be. It was always important to take the cards you were dealt and play them to your advantage. Maybe something good could come out of this situation after all.

Traffic was unusually light, allowing him to get to the bar quickly. He parked in his usual spot and made his way to the door. Unlocking it, he walked inside and found Marco standing by the door. His hand was leaning on a bike while he quickly held a finger up to his lips, indicating for Jorge to be silent.

Reaching for his gun, Jorge glanced around. It took him a moment to realize that loud moans were coming from near the bar. His eyes widened, and he shared a look with Marco, who pointed at Chase's office.

"Is this here…" Jorge muttered.

"I think he has someone in there, sir," Marco whispered as Jorge locked the door behind them.

"Either this or he likes his porn very loud," Jorge whispered back.

"I think that's the real thing, sir," Marco said as he started across the bar.

The noises grew louder as they walked towards the VIP room. Once inside, Jorge spoke again.

"Wonderful," He grumbled as he went to sit down. "Everyone is getting laid, and I'm here solving problems. *I* was supposed to be the one stepping away from everything and spending my days in the sun and chasing my wife's ass around the house, and here I am."

Marco laughed at his comment as he sat his laptop bag on the table.

"At least now I know why he was not at the meeting this morning," Jorge continued as he let out a loud sigh. "As long as he is not also fucking Holly Anne Ryerson, we are good."

"I somehow doubt it, sir," Marco made a face. "He is young and handsome. I am sure that he can do much better."

"Well, we may not have Ryerson around much longer, and Athas can't keep his fucking mouth shut," Jorge complained. "He call me today to say that in a *vulnerable* moment, he admit that it was suspicious that Marshalton went missing and then tried to link it to *me.*"

"Oh, sir, it is not good," Marco shook his head. *"House of Hernandez* didn't stir the pot, but Athas did. Why would he do this?"

"She had his dick in her hand," Jorge reminded him. "He will tell her the sky is made of cheese and salsa if this is what she wants to hear. He was supposed to fuck her to get good media attention, not to get her investigating *me.*"

"I will look into her," Marco turned on his laptop. "I was watching anyway, but I have not had time today. I looked at various publishers and media outlets to see if there was any talk on the book. Everything was clean, but now this?"

"I cannot have her poking around," Jorge reminded Marco, who agreed. "This is a problem I do not need."

"Sir, I am looking, but I do not see much here," Marco sat back in his chair. Leaning ahead, he began to type something into the laptop. He sat back again. "Her texts look minor. I do not see much in her web searches. I will search her emails."

"Do you think she has an alternate phone for work? Maybe using another messaging app?"

"It does not appear so."

"Another email, anything?" Jorge wondered.

"I already looked into all that before," Marco replied, and the two men exchanged looks.

"Do you think," Jorge calmed. "Do you think Athas made this up so I get her out of the picture? Maybe he does not want to deal with her anymore?"

Marco thought for a moment.

"Sir, I do not think so."

Jorge bit his bottom lip and exchanged looks with Marco.

"Do me a favor, keep looking. Keep an eye on her. And also, look in on him."

"I will, sir."

"I do have an idea, though."

Grabbing his phone, he sent a quick message to Athas.

I have to see you today.

I'm out of town.

Then get the fuck back in town. And bring your girlfriend too.

CHAPTER 14

They arrived in separate cars but approached the house together. Jorge felt a grin cross his lips as Paige stood behind him to look over his shoulder.

"Is *that* the one?" Paige seemed surprised as she peeked out the window. "She just seems so…"

"I know," Jorge innocently replied. "I guess there is no accounting for taste."

"It's not that," Paige attempted to explain. "It's just…"

The doorbell cut her off, and they exchanged looks.

"Remember what I tell you," Jorge reminded her as he approached the door. "Be ready."

"I won't be far away," She replied as she headed out of the room.

"*Gracias, mi amor.*"

Swinging the door opened, Jorge didn't give them a warm welcome but merely beckoned them to come in.

"I got here as fast as I could, but I…"

"Athas," Jorge cut him off as he closed the door while drinking in the nervousness between both the prime minister and the middle-aged reporter. "I know, I know. You are a busy man. We are *all* busy. Let us go into my office to talk."

"Jorge, this is…." Athas attempted to introduce him to Holly Anne Ryerson as they headed across the room.

"We already met," Jorge abruptly replied as they walked into his office, where he stopped and beckoned toward a hall table. "Leave your phones on the table outside."

They followed his instructions, and Athas looked powerless. Holly Anne's reaction made it clear that she hadn't expected the prime minister to be spoken to in such a manner. Jorge assumed he was the only person that didn't kiss his ass regularly.

"Have a seat," Jorge gestured toward the desk as he closed the door. Stomping across the room, he unsuccessfully attempted to hide his hostility. "We got to talk."

"What…what is this about?" Holly Anne attempted to ask as she sat down. "Is this regarding the campaign? Your book? I would be happy to talk to you another time if…"

"This is neither," Jorge cut her off as he sat behind his desk. "I will get right to the point, Ms. Ryerson. My understanding is that you are trying to figure out what happened with this man, Marshalton? He was an advisor for Athas until he went missing earlier this year?"

"I…well, it does seem rather strange that no one has heard from him," She spoke bravely. "He was getting close to retirement. It didn't make sense why he would do this now. I've met with his family, and things weren't adding up."

"I thought that this was settled," Jorge shrugged. "Was it not on the news, *your* news that Marshalton took government money and run?"

"I'm not in the position to officially verify anything," Athas attempted to jump in.

"Well, the proof was in the pudding," Ryerson attempted. "But something wasn't coming together for me."

"And so you thought I had something to do with this?" Jorge bluntly asked her, watching Holly Anne's face fall. "That is what Athas here, he tells me."

Alec's head titled forward in shame.

"You *told him* I asked that?" Holly Anne turned toward Athas with hurt in her eyes. "Do you tell him *everything?*"

"When a reporter is sniffing around about me," Jorge abruptly answered. "He tell me. Lady, this is my reputation here. I do not appreciate any suggestions that I was involved in something sinister. This here, it implies such."

"I was just being hypothetical," She explained, but more toward Athas than Jorge. "I didn't mean to *imply* anything. I was trying to get to the truth."

"You want the truth?" Jorge snapped at her. "Athas blew his head off, and we disposed of the body."

Jorge wasn't sure who's jaw hit the floor first. Throwing his head back in laughter, he clapped his hands together.

"Your expressions, they are priceless," Jorge continued to laugh. He enjoyed their discomfort. "I needed a good laugh today."

"No offense, Mr. Hernandez, but that is a terrible thing to joke about," Holly Anne grew angry. "What a horrible thing to say about the prime minister! As if Alec would ever *murder* someone! You don't know Mr. Athas as I do, or you wouldn't even joke about a thing like that."

"Well, *clearly,* Ms. Ryerson, I *don't* know Athas like *you do,*" Jorge taunted Holly Anne. "But may I remind you, that it was you sniffing around for another explanation? I am simply offering another possibility. I mean, what else would it be?"

She didn't reply but shared a look with Jorge until finally breaking eye contact.

"The man, he was less than loyal to Athas," Jorge pointed out. "And you know, my experience has taught me that if someone is not loyal, then they can never be fully trusted. That was the situation here, was it not?"

Looking at Athas, he began to nod on cue.

"Yes, Jorge is right," Athas regained his composure. "Although I'm not able to talk about it, we found out that he was working against me more than for me. So, when I learned what he did, I wasn't surprised. We can't reveal everything to the news. This cannot leave this room."

"See," Jorge shrugged. "Perfectly reasonable explanation, but as he said, it does not leave this room."

"Why wouldn't you just tell me that before?" Ryerson asked Athas.

"He was in a *compromising* situation," Jorge abruptly replied as he stood up. "Now, if you don't mind, Ms. Ryerson, I have some business with Athas. I will walk you to the door."

Her face was flustered when she stood up and followed Jorge. Holly Anne didn't have a chance to say anything.

"Now," Jorge continued as he opened the office door for her, glancing toward his wife in the other room, who nodded and started toward them. "My wife, she will walk you out. I do not want to see any stories about me on your channel. Do we understand one another?"

His threatening gaze was enough to cause her shoulders to droop, her body to shrink before him.

"I understand," Holly Anne's voice was small as she left the room. "That was never my intention."

"Good," Jorge was firm as he closed the door behind her and swung around. "Now, Athas, you and me, we got to talk."

"What the fuck was that?" Athas snapped as he turned around in his chair, his dark eyes full of anger.

"Ah, the Greek God is angry," Jorge mimicked him as he headed back behind his desk. "This here is a sad day."

"Why did you tell her I killed Marshalton?"

"She thought it was a joke," Jorge reminded him. "It is because she thinks *you* aren't capable, so do not worry. Or if you wish, I can go get her before she leaves and tell her otherwise."

Athas appeared nervous again. His eyes widened.

"That is what I thought," Jorge replied as he leaned ahead on his desk. "In the future, you will not talk about me to her or any reporter. I'm an advisor. That's all. You keep your fucking mouth shut unless you are making election promises. Marco, he tell me you are down in the polls, then start making promises. You are giving more jobs, more money, whatever the fuck the people want. Don't you have a campaign manager to tell you this? You promise them everything, do you understand?"

"I do," Athas nodded. "But the problem is Frederick Knapp. He's my main opponent in this race, and people view him as more trustworthy than me."

"Oh, why is that?" Jorge was intrigued.

"He's older, to begin with," Athas explained. "He's been in politics longer, and people think I'm too inexperienced. Even though I've been the prime minister for a few years, they don't think I've done enough. We've had riots in Toronto and issues in indigenous communities. They say I spend too much money and I'm not conscious enough about the environment. I mean, you name it."

"Interesting," Jorge nodded. "But what did you think, Athas? That you would have no competition? That you'd stroll back into Ottawa, swinging your cane around?"

"No, I just mean, it's hard to argue the points."

"Really?" Jorge shook his head. "You are working to improve water issues in indigenous communities."

"They say I'm too slow."

"Is there no progress?"

"Not enough," Athas replied. "And people want money thrown at them, but then we have to pay it back. Plus, he said my personal life is questionable because my relationships are short-term."

"Oh, is that so?"

"Well, not in so many words," Athas tried to explain. "He just suggested that I date a lot of women."

Jorge rolled his eyes.

"I know, but he's suggesting it means that I'm not committed or able to commit," Athas said. "It's interesting how he twists things around."

"You need someone to twist things back," Jorge commented. "I will get Andrew and Sonny on it for their show."

"The *Raging Against the Machine* show?" Athas wrinkled his nose. "Oh, I don't know…"

"That show that you look down at," Jorge cut him off. "It gets more views than the ratings for the nighttime news you are catering to, the channel your girlfriend works for, so I would not be looking down at it if I were you."

"Yeah, but is it taken seriously?"

"By the younger age group, yes it is," Jorge reminded him. "I tell you that in a short time, our views are only getting higher each week. You know why? Because they are real people talking. Your Holly Anne, she is not a real person. She's a robot and part of the machine."

"I can't argue with that," Athas nodded. "Ok, whatever you think I should do."

"You really want to know what I think you should do?" Jorge paused for a moment and tilted his head. "I want you to stop cutting your hair so short. You look like a fucking psychopath."

CHAPTER 15

She looked like a pathetic animal, slumped over, exiting the office. Paige pretended not to notice. To show that she did might imply that she cared. Holly Anne Ryerson wanted to expose her husband to enhance her career, and Paige wouldn't have it. She finally spoke when she arrived at the door.

"Your husband," she seemed almost hesitant. "He's quite…direct."

"I wouldn't have it any other way," Paige smiled. "We live in a world where people rarely say what they mean. I think it's quite…refreshing."

"I suppose," Holly Anne shared a smile and stalled. She was attempting to bond with Paige. "You know, Alec told me that he's known you for years. Maybe I should interview you for a more powerful insight for my viewers. You can talk about how you saw him leading up to where he is today, or maybe how you never saw it coming. I think it would be an interesting interview."

Her fake smile displayed the lines around her eyes and lips. Paige could see she either was or had been a smoker simply by the texture of her skin. Holly Anne watched Paige as if she just had to catch her on the nostalgia of the past. But she clenched her fists as if anxious, and she hunched forward like a woman who felt weighed down by the world. Reading people had been her business for many years and what kept Paige alive; other people, not so much.

"I would rather not," Paige said with a sweet smile, watching Holly Anne's face fall. "I don't believe in talking about the past. We live in the present, don't you agree Ms. Ryerson?"

"Yes, but perhaps you had insight back then that Alec was meant to do more," She hurried to explain. "With his social work, especially working in such a rough area of town and..."

"Yes, well, we all have a past," Paige cut her off causing Holly Anne to appear intrigued. "It doesn't mean we must revisit it. There's never anything in the past that implies the future. I was as surprised as anyone when he became interested in politics."

"What was the nature of your relationship?" Holly Anne asked the question casually, but it didn't work with Paige.

"Ms. Ryerson, I have to pick up my daughter," Paige shook her head. "I don't have time for this right now."

To her surprise, the reporter didn't budge. The two made eye contact and the reporter finally looked away.

"If you change your mind..." Holly Anne commented, causing the first ripple of anger to cross over Paige.

"I won't," She assured Ryerson as she opened the door. Paige recognized the unease on the middle-aged reporter's face.

"Thank you," She muttered as she walked out. "You have a lovely home."

Paige didn't reply but closed the door behind her.

"Who was *that?*" Maria's voice came from the top of the stairs as she started down. There was something off. She was quieter and seemed to drag her body down each step as if something was wrong.

"Just a reporter," Paige shrugged it off. "Aren't you working at the bar today? Did Tala pick you up?"

"Yeah," Maria's voice sounded defeated as she hit the final step. "So *Papá* talked to a reporter? Why are those SUVs outside?"

"Alec has a meeting with him now," Paige replied quickly, observing her step-daughter's face. She had been crying. "The reporter was with Alec, but Jorge sent her out. Maria, what is wrong?"

"Nothing," Maria shrugged and avoided eye contact. "Alec is here now?"

"Maria, what *is* wrong?" Paige repeated her question as she reached out to touch her step-daughter's shoulder, causing her to look into her eyes, then quickly look away. "Did something happen at school?"

"I don't want to talk about it."

"Are you ok?"

"Yeah."

"And you don't work at the bar today?" Paige repeated her earlier question, knowing Maria sometimes helped Chase with various tasks when *Princesa Maria* was closed.

"Yeah, I think he didn't need me today."

Something was off.

"And Tala brought you home, not Chase?"

"Yeah."

"I could've picked you up."

"She dropped me off. I just messaged her and she came back."

Paige nodded. She could hear Tala and Miguel upstairs. Usually, they played before dinner.

"Ok, she finally answered. "Well, as long as everything is ok?"

"Yup," Maria replied, just as she heard Jorge's office door open. She looked in the general direction, and Paige turned to see Alec entering the room. He looked as defeated as Holly Anne. Paige looked back at Maria, who was scurrying out to the patio.

"That went well?" Paige asked as Alec headed toward the door. He didn't answer but merely raised an eyebrow before leaving.

"Wow," Paige said to herself, glancing between Maria sitting out on the patio and in the direction of Jorge's office. She decided to see her husband. She would have more luck finding out something from him than Maria.

She entered the room to see him sitting in the chair, his eyes closed. For a moment, Paige panicked, thinking that something was wrong. She rushed across the room. He was laughing.

"What's that about?" Paige asked as she leaned against the back of a chair. "Or do I want to know?"

"Paige, it was a good meeting," Jorge assured her.

"Really?" Paige raised an eyebrow. "Alec didn't look too pleased when he left here."

"Ah, Athas, he is never happy," Jorge grinned. "The man is such a fucking pussy."

"He just tries to be fair…"

"He's a pussy, Paige," Jorge shook his head. "Not that this is a problem all of the time. It is helpful to get him to do what I want, but when it comes to an election, he must learn to be more forceful."

"Well, yes," Paige gently agreed. "You do have a point there. Frederick Knapp is coming across as more solid and stronger than Alec. I thought he did a lot in the last few years, but people still aren't happy. I don't understand."

"He does not ensure trust," Jorge reminded her. "He needs to say more. He needs to attack that fucker. I already have Marco looking into Knapp. He must have something to hide. A whore on the side? An illegitimate child? Pictures of him snorting cocaine? Something."

Paige thought for a moment.

"People think he's a strong family man," She calmly replied. "We have to show he's not."

"Exactly, *mi amor,* we think the same."

"So, when Holly Anne left," Paige thought for a moment. "She was asking a lot of questions. She thought she should interview me since I've known Alec for so many years. I could talk about how I saw him making the path to becoming prime minister."

Jorge rolled his eyes.

"I declined," She continued. "But she was pushy about it."

"She best not push too much," Jorge said. "Or I will push the bitch out a window."

"These things happen," Paige commented. "You just never know what is going on in people's personal lives."

They shared a smile.

"I have to start dinner," Paige started to turn.

"How about I barbecue?" Jorge volunteered as he stood up. "I got those steaks in the fridge. If you want to come up with something to have with them?"

"I can do that," She smiled and then started toward the door. "Maria was acting a bit strange when she got home."

"Teenagers," Jorge shrugged. "They are moody, are they not?"

"Yeah, but she was supposed to work with Chase today," She reminded him as they left his office. "So, it seemed strange. Maybe he sent her home?"

"That may explain if she is upset," Jorge reminded her as they entered the living room. "He *is* her favorite person and…"

Yelling was coming from outside, causing them to end their conversation and rush toward the patio. Paige feared that the nosey reporter had somehow made her way back onto the property to harass Maria, even though it was illogical with the high fence surrounding the backyard. It took her a moment to see who was there and to sum up the situation.

Maria was in attack mode. On her feet, she was pointing at a disillusioned Jolene, who appeared to be dumbfounded, standing in a bikini with everything practically hanging out. Paige glanced at her husband, noting his shared anger with Maria. He pulled the door open and walked onto the patio.

"You're nothing but a *puta* whore!" Maria pointed accusingly.

"Maria," Paige rushed ahead. "Just because her bikini is a little…."

"It's not her bikini," Maria continued to focus on Jolene with pure fury in her eyes. "I *saw* her at the bar. She's a fucking slut! You're married, and you're still *doing* Chase. That's what a fucking whore does!"

"Wait, what?" Jorge looked almost humored but grew serious as his daughter turned to look at him. "Oh, Jolene, this here is inappropriate for my 15-year-old daughter to walk in on! What were you thinking?"

"She was thinking with her *PUSSY!*" Maria yelled as tears formed in her eyes. "Because that's what dirty whores do! Anything to get attention! I guess everyone needs to feel special, even when they're *not!*"

With that, Maria swung around and rushed toward the door. Jolene awkwardly crossed her arms to cover her breasts, and Paige turned to follow Maria, leaving Jorge behind to deal with Jolene.

"What the fuck is wrong with you?" He was yelling as Paige left the patio and headed upstairs. Tala was in the kitchen with Miguel. Both had stunned expressions on their faces. They watched as Paige followed her hysterical step-daughter upstairs.

Maria had to learn there would always be Jolenes in her life. They often taught us lessons we didn't want to learn.

CHAPTER 16

"I....I do not know," Jolene attempted to answer Jorge's question as fear gathered on her face. "I go see Chase sometimes, and we…"

"Are you not married, Jolene?" Jorge shot back, enjoying her discomfort a little too much. "Did you not leave town to marry the love of your life? Where is he now? Did you manage to ruin that too?"

"He left me!" Jolene burst into tears and shook her head. "I…"

"I don't care, Jolene," Jorge shook his head. "I am not interested in this soap opera that you call your life. I do not care for the drama. How did you get in anyway?"

She glanced at the gate between his house and Diego's next door.

"I just want to see my goddaughter, and…"

"Well, she saw more of you than she wished, Jolene," Jorge abruptly replied, pointing at her half-naked body. "And right now, I see more of you than I would like."

"I leave," She pointed toward the gate and wiped away her tears.

"Please do!" Jorge snapped at her. "And if you are seducing Chase, can you do it somewhere besides his workplace? You know, the place your goddaughter works at after school?"

"I am sorry," She said before slinking away.

Jorge turned around and headed back into the house. Tala was giving Miguel a snack.

"Mr. Hernandez, sir, would you like me to start dinner?" Tala innocently asked. "I see Miss Maria, she is very upset."

Jorge stopped and thought for a moment.

"I was going to barbecue, Tala, if you wish to start," Jorge said as he glanced at his son, who was taking it all in with interest. "Tell me, did you pick up Maria?"

"Yes, sir, I drop her off at the bar," Tala explained. "And I barely left the parking lot, and she text me to come back."

"Did she say why?"

"Just that Mr. Chase, he did not need her today."

"Thank you, Tala."

She gave a sympathetic smile.

Jorge headed upstairs with dread in his heart. He was about to have a difficult conversation with his daughter. Maria wouldn't like what he had to say.

Arriving at her door, it was open ajar, and Paige sat beside her on the bed. Slumped over with a blanket wrapped around her, Maria's eyes were red, and her face pale.

"Maria," Jorge spoke in his usual tone but decided he should soften his voice. "I am sorry about what you saw today. This here was *very* inappropriate. No matter who arrived at the bar. But it was most appropriate for someone your age."

Maria said nothing but nodded.

"I would have never given you your key if I knew that this was even a possibility," Jorge continued as he moved inside the room and sat at the end of the bed, glancing at Paige. "But Maria, also, you must realize that even though you care for Chase, he is an adult man, and you are just a teenager and..."

"*Just?*" Maria snapped at him, her eyes full of the Hernandez fury.

"Maria, sorry, I misspeak," Jorge found himself stumbling over his English. "I do not mean that in a bad way. What I am saying is that you are too young for Chase. I know you have feelings for him, and I am not trying to make this sound like it is not important. But Maria, you are 15. Nothing can happen between the two of you."

"I'm not that much younger," Maria whined. "Lots of men date younger women."

"Maria," Jorge calmly spoke, even though his heart was furiously pounding. "If any adult were to try to date you, a 15-year-old-girl, I would have to kill them."

"*Papá!*" She rolled her eyes.

"Maria, this is illegal. And, it is *wrong,*" Jorge insisted.

"Since when do you care if something is legal?" Maria snapped back.

Paige raised an eyebrow as she looked at Jorge.

"Ok, this here is fair," Jorge admitted. "I cannot deny that I do many illegal things, but Maria, he is too old for you. We have had this conversation before."

"Maria," Paige jumped in, much to his relief. "We know you care about Chase, but he *is* too old for you. You're at a different stage of your life, and your maturity levels aren't the same. He's been married and has kids. You're young and just learning about dating, so wouldn't it be better to experience that with someone your age?"

"I don't like boys my age."

"Maria," Jorge decided to take the bull by the horns. "He was with Jolene. And this here isn't the first time. Do you want someone who would have such low standards?"

"Jorge, I think it's a bit more complicated…"

"No, Paige, let us just say it how it is," Jorge shrugged. "I respect Chase from a work perspective, but he lacks in this area. He cheated on his wife when they were together. It was a bad relationship, and since, he has been with questionable women. Nothing ever lasts. I do not think I would want my Maria with him, even if she were closer to his age."

"Really?" Maria appeared surprised. "He cheated on his wife?"

"Maria, he did so many times," Jorge confirmed. "They were too young, yes, but still…I do not think a man who would get involved with Jolene Silva is good enough for my daughter. I know this is not nice, but it is true."

Maria said nothing but appeared to be calm.

"Maybe you're right," She finally said with reluctance. "*Papá,* I don't think I want to work at the bar anymore."

"Well, Maria, this here is your decision," Jorge replied. "But if that is the case, you must tell Chase yourself."

"I don't want to talk to him."

"Send him a letter of resignation," Paige suggested. "That's the adult thing to do, without having to talk to him again."

"But usually," Jorge continued. "Two weeks' notice is preferred."

"*Papá!*"

"I think we can overlook it this time," Jorge admitted.

After his daughter calmed down, Jorge headed to his office. The smell of steaks cooking outside caused his stomach to rumble. He needed some time to think.

In the privacy of his office, Jorge glanced at his bulletproof window as he sat behind his desk. He hated to hurt his daughter, but she had to know the truth about Chase. However, his random hookups with Jolene were disturbing. What did all these men see in her? She was stupid, but perhaps this made them feel powerful. Then again, it was probably just the tits and ass. He was possibly reading too much into it.

Turning on his phone, Jorge saw messages lighting up. Glancing over them, he decided the only one that needed his immediate attention was Makerson. Before calling him, he texted Marco.

We should meet tomorrow morning.

I might have something for you. Did you want to meet at the bar?

Yes, I must talk to Chase.

Very good.

It might not be good for Chase, Jorge considered.

He called Makerson. His message seemed the most urgent.

"Hello."

"Is this a good time?"

"Yes, I'm just getting back to the hotel."

"Is the tour going well?"

"People are asking why you aren't here since the book is about you," Makerson admitted. "I know the publisher was fine with you not coming with me, but the people aren't so pleased."

"I have too much here," Jorge shook his head. "I cannot leave town."

"I tried to explain that," Makerson paused for a moment. "They think you should do an interview talking about your book. Either with a major personality on television or a podcast, or we could have you Zoom in when I go to various stops?"

"That is a possibility," Jorge considered. "I do not want to have an interview just with anyone about my life, you know?"

"You're like royalty," Makerson laughed. "Chances are the queen wouldn't be on a book tour either."

To this, Jorge laughed.

"I do like to think of myself as royalty," Jorge admitted. "But yes, maybe there is a compromise."

"If you had someone big interviewing you, you could insist on pre-approving the questions," Makerson suggested. "That's not unheard of, but Zooming in might work too. Just bring your son into the shot, and it looks more legit that you stay home."

"My family, it is most important," Jorge reminded him. "I would prefer to keep close to home. But I can understand. The people, they want to see me."

"I think we can work something out."

"Anything else?"

"I've been touching base with the office," Makerson continued. "Athas numbers are going down again."

"I saw that."

"We might need to shake things up."

"I have some thoughts," Jorge admitted. "I will be meeting with Marco tomorrow to discuss this more."

"I don't think it's that he's a bad candidate," Makerson commented. "But people think Frederick Knapp is better."

"He probably is," Jorge admitted. "But we need Athas in."

"You'd get nowhere with Knapp," Makerson reminded him. "And he's talking about creating new rules for independent media. That's what I'm hearing. If that's the case, there may be some limitations."

"I see."

"I don't hear good things," Makerson continued. "He's a far better actor than a politician, and he has close ties to Big Pharma."

"I am starting to see a connection here."

"I thought you might."

"Do not worry," Jorge said. "I will sink his ship before it has time to get in the water."

CHAPTER 17

Jorge was up before his family the following morning. He preferred it that way. It was still quiet and peaceful, allowing him to grab a coffee and get out of the house while he could.

But not before stopping by both his children's bedrooms to peek in. Miguel was sprawled out on his big boy bed with two stuffed animals on the floor. Closing the door, Jorge then stuck his head in Maria's room. Much to his relief, she was fast asleep.

She looked peaceful and angelic.

This was her escape from the miseries of the previous day.

He worried about his daughter. He worried a lot.

Gingerly leaving the house, Jorge got into his SUV and hesitated before backing out of the driveway. He sighed when he considered what was ahead of him that day. The more he attempted to untangle himself from his many responsibilities, the tighter they enclosed him. There were always problems. Even if it wasn't a situation, it was with his *familia*. In many ways, those problems were the worst.

He stopped to get a *Taza de Sol* coffee, then continued to *Princesa Maria*. Marco had messaged him earlier that he would be in the VIP room. But of course, Jorge had to deal with Chase first. This wouldn't be a pleasant conversation.

Arriving at the bar, he recognized the vehicle in the parking lot. Chase would be receiving orders or preparing for the day ahead. Marco hopefully had some good news for him, although that seemed rare. Why did there always have to be a problem? And more importantly, why must he always solve it?

The bar was quiet when he walked in. Seeing the coffee was on, he could hear Chase in his office. That would be his first stop.

Jorge found him sitting behind his desk, his laptop opened.

"What a relief I do not find you in here fucking Jolene," Jorge abruptly announced. "Like my daughter did yesterday!"

Not only did Chase's jaw hit the ground, but Jorge also heard someone loudly gasp behind him. He turned to see Marco's eyes widen in shock.

"Marco, I will be with you shortly," Jorge sternly commented.

"Yes, sir," Marco stuttered. "No..no rush, sir."

He hurried away, and Jorge turned back to Chase.

"Jorge, I…"

"I do not want to hear this," Jorge shook his head as he entered the office, not bothering to close the door behind him. "I do not want to hear your excuses or how it just happened. This is Jolene. Nothing *just happens* with her. It's all planned out. But you? I thought you were smarter than this here, Chase. I thought you could find someone….better than her. I don't understand."

"It…I just," Chase stopped and looked down, his face turning red. "I'm sorry. I didn't know. Is that why…"

"Maria, she saw it and was very upset," Jorge said as he glared at Chase. "She come home crying. She said, 'I do not want to work with Chase anymore', and you know what? I do not blame her. Even if she did not have a crush on you, I would still suggest that she not work here anymore. I do not care what you do behind closed, *locked* doors. I do not care what you do in your personal life. I do not care for any of this soap opera that Jolene always gets involved in, but do *not* do it where my daughter can see."

"I'm sorry," Chase repeated, his body slumped over in shame.

"I know you are," Jorge replied. "But this changes everything. It is good that maybe this is the shock that Maria needs to get over this silly crush on you, but I would have preferred it not to be in this way. I am not stupid. I know kids these days, they see everything on the internet, but that there is not the same as what happened here."

"I know," Chase quietly replied.

"Jolene is poison," Jorge reminded him. "I don't care how big her tits are or if she's a good fuck. Jolene is still poison. You already knew this and why you still decided to put your dick in her is beyond me. I do not understand. I will never understand. But it is time Jolene leaves town again because I cannot deal with this drama."

Chase said nothing but nodded.

"Now, I must talk to Marco," Jorge said, and he took a deep breath, noting how hard his heart was pounding. His thoughts returned to Maria, slumped over in tears the previous day.

With that, he turned and walked out of the office. Entering the VIP room, Jorge immediately noted a bottle of his favorite tequila on the table and a shot glass.

"Sir, I took the liberty to get this for you," Marco pointed at the alcohol as Jorge closed the door behind him. "It sounds like you may need it."

"Truer words were never spoken," Jorge admitted as he walked across the room and sat down. Reaching for the bottle, he poured a shot. "This here is how I start my day. So, you can imagine how yesterday ended."

"Sir, it is not good," Marco shook his head. "I looked into Jolene's texts, and she attempted to message Maria, but she blocked her."

Jorge said nothing but nodded.

He grabbed the shot glass and knocked the liquid back. It burned down his throat.

"I cannot believe that Chase, he would do this," Marco continued. "But I guess Jolene, she is very manipulative."

"That she is," Jorge agreed. "She has been back only a few days, and look at the mess she already made."

"There may be more, sir," Marco made a face. "Rumors are surfacing on the internet that she attempted to slap you at your book launch. I did not think they would get out since so few people were there at the time, but it somehow did."

"I will do worse than slap her if she don't keep away from my fucking family," Jorge shook his head. "She is poison, wherever she goes. You know her marriage, it is gone to shit. It has been, what? A few months?"

"I see where they have separated," Marco said as he pointed at the laptop. "He is back in Mexico."

"Some things, they never change," Jorge said as he sat back in his chair. "So, Marco, what else do you got for me? I am almost scared to ask."

"Well, sir, this man, Frederick Knapp," Marco closed the laptop. "I see that he has strong ties to Big Pharma."

"I heard."

"They are donating as much as they are allowed to his campaign and making sure they help in other ways," Marco continued. "They are in his back pocket and plan to push hard to get him in. They have started propaganda against Athas."

"I heard they want to cause issues for independent media, such as HPC news?" Jorge said as he looked around the room, then back at Marco. "The vultures, they are always out."

"But the vultures, sir," Marco shook his head. "They are no match for you. You can take them."

"I do appreciate that, Marco," Jorge grinned. "I just get tired of always taking them on, you know?"

"I know, sir," Marco agreed. "And it is always more of the same. It never ends."

"It does seem that way," Jorge nodded. "But this time it is worse because Athas has put a lot of barriers on Big Pharma, or he is trying to. He sees them as a threat. They are used to people like Knapp who cave to whatever they want."

"So, what would you like me to do, sir?"

"We wait, Marco," Jorge thought for a moment. "Keep spying and let me know what you see. He is a family man, right? What is the best way to bring a family man down?"

"There are many ways, sir."

"The best way to kill a pig," Jorge grinned. "Is to make him feel that he can move into the house easily before you swing the ax. I suspect that Knapp assumes he will win, but we must attack at the last minute. Otherwise, he will have time to rebuild. Let him get comfortable. Let him feel at ease. That is the best time to slaughter your opponent."

"This makes sense, sir."

"Meanwhile, we have to build up Athas," Jorge rolled his eyes. "If that is fucking possible."

Marco laughed.

"His reporter fuck buddy, she is asking too many questions about me," Jorge continued. "Keep a close eye. I gave her a stern warning yesterday, so if she is smart, she will back off."

"Let's hope she is smart, sir."

Jorge left the bar shortly after and headed to the Hernandez Production Company, where he noted Tony's car was in the parking lot. The production house had picked up steam fast, with various streaming services regularly adding new shows, which meant they were also looking for new content. His staff had increased, and he was proud that Canadian talent could create internationally recognized programs. It's too bad that the CRTC was always attempting to get in his way. They could be a problem.

Tony was in his office when Jorge walked in.

"Good morning, Jorge," He looked up from his screen and closed the laptop. "I was wondering if you would be making your way in this morning."

"I had to stop at the bar first," Jorge commented as he closed the door. "Jolene, she created another soap opera for me that I had to end."

"End?" Tony appeared intrigued.

"Well, relocate," Jorge grinned as he sat down. "It is hard for Chase to get any work done when she's there, waving her pussy in his face."

"Oh," Tony grimaced. "I hate to say it, but I'd rather she do it *there* than *here.*"

To this, Jorge let out a hearty laugh.

"Tony, you do not know how much I need that right now," Jorge grinned. "Unfortunately, my daughter sees this and quits her job. I wonder if you have anything here for a kid to do? I do not want her sitting on her phone and getting paid. I mean, *real* work. I do not want her favored over other employees. I do not care if she is my daughter. She has to learn how to work, not like every other kid in her fucking generation."

"Yeah, actually," Tony nodded. "Even a gofer, to do odd jobs around here would be awesome. The more she can do, the more we can find for her."

"This here, it would be perfect," Jorge hesitated. "But, I want her to apply, like everyone else. I will make her write a resume, a cover letter, everything. So, we did not have this conversation."

"We didn't, sir."

"Now, let us go over the numbers," Jorge said. "And talk about how we can make Athas look like a rock star rather than the useless fuck he is."

This time, Tony laughed.

"Well, we can only try, sir."

CHAPTER 18

"*Papá,* I have a job interview!" Maria bounced into his office with a smile on her face. In seconds, it quickly faded away. "Oh, you told them to call me, didn't you?"

"Maria, I did not tell anyone to give you an interview," Jorge looked up from his laptop.

"It's at the production house," Maria slumped over as she walked toward his desk. "So, you told them to give me a job."

"Maria, I *asked* them if there would be anything you could do," Jorge corrected his daughter as she sat across from him. "I did not tell them to hire you. That is up to you. I said I did not want you to have special treatment."

"I don't want to be treated differently," Maria replied as she looked down. "I will miss the bar and Chase, but I just can't go back."

"Well, Maria, it will be your bar one day to do as you wish," Jorge reminded her. "Even if that means selling it. This here is your decision, but it is not a decision you have to make yet."

"I'm still...very disappointed about everything," Maria's voice softened, her vulnerabilities leaked out. "I just can't believe he's that kind of person, you know?"

"Maria, one of the biggest disappointments we have in life is other people," Jorge spoke regretfully. "I am sorry that this happened to you, but you must know the truth."

"I don't know what upsets me more," Maria admitted, her brown eyes expanding as she spoke. "The fact that Chase is not the kind of person I thought he was, or that Jolene…."

"I know, Maria," Jorge gently replied. "People, they will disappoint you. I am not surprised by Jolene, but I *was* surprised by Chase. But as I said, Maria, he does not have the best track record. When we look at people, we must always see the good and the bad, even if we don't want to."

Maria nodded, but the sadness in her eyes broke his heart.

"I think the production house," Jorge continued. "It is a better fit for you anyway."

"Jolene isn't going to go back to work there, is she?"

"Over my dead, fucking body," Jorge abruptly replied, causing Maria to laugh.

"Jorge," Paige was standing in the doorway with Miguel in her arms. "The interview is starting soon."

"Oh yes, this is true," Jorge sat up straighter and glanced at a nearby clock. "Maria, I am doing this Zoom thing about my book. Would you be able to help me set it up? I was trying when you came in."

"Maybe I can be your assistant, *Papá,*" She teased while reaching for his laptop.

A few minutes later, he was live. Although talking about *House of Hernandez* was one of the last things Jorge wanted to do, viewers would never know. His reaction was one of positivity and charm. All the questions were pre-approved, and answers were planned. He could've been an actor at his own production house.

His laptop showed four different views; one of Makerson on the far left, the right was a young lady moderating, the bottom was the audience, and the final square was himself. It was all interesting, but impersonal at the same time. Of course, it was much better than traveling around the country and talking about his life.

"Tell me about how you met your wife," The young moderator read from a tablet, then she looked up. "Many people are intrigued, although you didn't go much into it in the book."

"Ah, yes," Jorge gave his usual, warm smile and nodded. "I guess, to me, something as precious as love is not something you talk about with others. Your relationship, it is a personal thing, and once you start to share too much with the outside world, it somehow...I guess it takes something away."

"So, no hints?" The moderator gently pushed. "In the book, you just say she accidentally arrived at the wrong hotel room."

"Yes, actually, Paige, she accidentally came to the wrong room," Jorge repeated her words. "So, I invite her to stay awhile, to have a drink with me."

There was laughter in the audience, and Jorge joined them.

"Hey, this is how I am," he continued. "I found a beautiful lady at my door, and I did not waste time."

There was more laughter as Jorge discretely glanced at the time on his laptop. Only a few more minutes of silly questions before he could carry on with his day. He noted a tense smile on Makerson's face. At least the Zoom interviews at the book signings took some pressure off the author.

"I know that family is important to you," She continued. "And that is one of the reasons why you aren't able to go on tour with Tom."

"It is difficult, yes," Jorge nodded as his office door crept open, and Miguel wandered into the room while Paige stood in the hallway. "My children, my family, they need me here. I have a lot of businesses that need my attention. There is so much to do. Sometimes we must make decisions based on what is important in our lives."

Miguel ran across the room.

"*Papi!*"

"Oh, I am sorry," Jorge acted embarrassed. "My son, he enjoys barging in doors."

The audience laughed as the child climbed on his knee. Miguel seemed fascinated by the four images on the screen and reached out to touch the live view of his father.

"*Papi!*" Miguel giggled, and Jorge gently pulled him back to sit on his knee.

"So, this is one of your reasons for staying home?" The moderator warmly smiled. "And you also have a daughter?"

"Yes, Maria," Jorge replied. "She is a teenager."

"We don't have an opportunity to see your family often."

This was off-script.

"No, I prefer to keep my private life as private as possible."

The moderator smiled. He could see she was nervous.

"So, having lived in Mexico and Canada," She returned to script. "What are the major differences between the two countries?"

The interview was only a few more questions before ending, much to his relief. By then, Miguel was asleep on his lap, and Jorge briefly considered also having a nap. There was nothing more exhausting than performing. How did people do this every day? So many professions required people to be 'on' at all times. It was draining.

His phone rang, causing Miguel to shuffle but continue to sleep.

It was Makerson.

"So, tell me," Jorge answered. "Did this satisfy the people?"

"I think so," Makerson muttered into the phone. "Having Miguel show up was a nice touch."

"Sometimes people need to see with their own eyes," Jorge replied as his son snuggled closer to him. "We will have this here same lady for the next stop?"

"Yes," Makerson replied. "We'll have to change the questions a bit so it doesn't seem overly rehearsed, but we will touch base on that at the time."

"This here, it works," Jorge nodded.

"But that's not the only reason I'm calling," Makerson continued. "Something else has popped up."

"Why do I feel this here is something I don't want to hear?"

"There's a rumor that the romance between Athas and Ryerson might be off," Makerson muttered. "I don't know if it's true, but it might be a problem for us if it is."

"Great," Jorge sarcastically replied. "Well, if this here is true, Athas has not told me."

"Maybe he doesn't know yet," Makerson sniffed. "He is too wrapped up in his other bullshit."

"Other bullshit?" Jorge repeated.

"Yeah, Knapp is making attack videos," Makerson replied. "He released one earlier today showing images from the downtown riots and how Athas mishandled it. He keeps talking about how Alec is like a deer in headlights whenever anything happens because he was too inexperienced to be prime minister in the first place. The usual political crap."

"And we cannot find any rotten apples in his basket?" Jorge inquired.

"Not yet," Makerson confirmed. "He's always played by the book. Unless Marco can find something else?"

"Not yet."

"I'm sure we'll figure something out."

"I will have to because the polls for Athas," Jorge recalled some numbers he saw earlier that day. "They do not make me happy."

"I got an idea," Makerson said as his reception was affected by the sound of traffic in the background. "You said you wanted to make him a rock star. We must start building that impression online, especially on social media, and see if it catches on."

"Light the fire."

"Exactly," Makerson continued. "Maybe we need fans to follow him around, act like he *is* a rock star. Family men like Knapp are boring. Rock stars are exciting. Politics are sensationalized and dramatized now, so it's not a stretch to think people will react favorably."

"This here is true."

"So, we should find lovesick fans to play the game."

"I like this."

"You can put lipstick on a pig," Makerson continued. "And some people will think it's a beauty queen."

Jorge grinned. He knew what they had to do.

CHAPTER 19

"I don't mean to interrupt," Jorge awkwardly commented after walking into his wife's yoga/meditation room as she stood in what appeared to be a powerful pose. Calming music flowed through the room as she glanced at him, appearing unalarmed by him barging into the room. "I just have a question."

"Sure," Paige gently replied.

"What is that there that you're doing?" Jorge stumbled through the words. "I mean, I know it is yoga, but…"

"The pose?" She asked as she morphed into another pose. "The first one was warrior 1, and this is warrior 2. Is that why you dropped by? To ask what pose I was doing?"

Jorge recognized that she was teasing him and self-consciously smiled.

"No, but this here, it is interesting," Jorge shrugged and smiled. "I do think it suits you, the pose, I mean."

"Well, one might suggest the same for you," Paige stopped and turned toward Jorge. "You should try it. It might be just what you need."

"Oh, *mi amor,*" He spoke seductively while his eyes trailed down her body. "That is *not* what I need."

She grinned and shook her head.

"But I *do* have a question," Jorge got back on track. "And it does not have to do with yoga."

"What is it?"

"Well, we are having a meeting with Athas shortly…"

"Here?"

"*Sí,*" Jorge nodded. "When you see 7 or 8 SUVs pulling up with security to protect that spineless pussy, you know the meeting is about to begin."

Paige shot him a look but laughed in spite of herself.

"We think this campaign needs the rock star approach," Jorge continued. "Knapp is boring. His policies are boring. We need Athas to show him up, and the only way is to make him seem cool somehow."

Paige attempted not to smile as she placed her hand on her hip.

"Don't you mean," She asked. "That Knapp has sensible policies whereas Alec, maybe not so much?"

"His policies are all over the place."

"That's because you're telling them to him," Paige reminded him. "He doesn't even know what he thinks. So now you want to make him seem like a rock star to get votes because if you were running, that's what you'd do."

"Paige, if I was running," Jorge reminded her. "I *would* be the rock star. That is all there would be to it, and I would win. There is no question."

Paige appeared humored as she nodded.

"What I am wondering is how do I find these people without the media learning?" Jorge wondered. "I cannot hire actors because people will know they are actors."

"You mean to follow him town to town?" Paige asked, and Jorge nodded. "Then you get them to sign off on the fact that they won't talk. It's a legal contract, so they have to play the game. I wouldn't get actors, though. That can be traced back too easily, especially here in Toronto. Find normal, younger women who have a lot of time on their hands. Find one of those YouTube stars."

Jorge raised an eyebrow and nodded.

"This here," he said. "This might work."

"Remember, your daughter is close to that age," Paige said as she walked across the room and looked out the window. "She might have some thoughts too. Maybe she knows the places to go and what to say. Talk to Marco too."

"He is on the way."

"I think Alec is here now," Paige gestured outside. "I see a string of SUVs on the way."

"Courtesy of our tax paying money."

"But he has to be safe," Paige reminded him.

"It takes seven SUVs, one person in each, to keep him safe?" Jorge countered as he headed for the door. "I am surprised there are no snipers on our roof."

"Ever since the threats this summer…"

"I know, *mi amor,* I know," Jorge nodded. "Thank you for your help."

She smiled as he walked out of the room.

Jorge felt his demeanor change as he went downstairs and to the door. He found Alec on the other side, with his pathetic bodyguards surrounding him.

"Hey," He spoke in his usual wimpy voice as he entered the house. "Is everyone here?"

"Not yet," Jorge replied. "Marco and Tony are probably getting strip-searched before they make it to the door."

"I know, security has tightened more lately," Athas shook his head. "CSIS thinks I'm in more danger as the election gets close."

Jorge rolled his eyes as he walked ahead of Athas. A knock at the door caused him to stop and swing around, almost running into the prime minister.

"You move too fast for me," Athas joked.

"Too bad your political opponents do too," Jorge muttered as he headed back to the door. He opened it up to find Tony and Marco on the other side.

"I figured it would be easier if I just picked him up," Tony gestured toward Marco. "Then we got tied up when they had to search our laptop bags."

Jorge rolled his eyes again and moved aside to let them in.

"Here, I am vastly richer and more popular than you, Athas," Jorge announced as he closed the door, "and yet, I do not have all this security following me around."

"I'm high profile," Athas attempted to explain.

"So am I," Jorge countered as he gestured for the three men to follow him to the office. "But I also carry a gun."

"I do too now," Athas replied, causing Jorge to halt and turn around. All three men gave him a look.

"Are you sure that is a good idea?" Jorge couldn't help but take a jab at him.

"I don't know," Athas answered. "But, with everything going on…"

"Probably a good idea," Tony offered.

Jorge nodded, and the three men continued to his office.

Once inside and seated, Jorge got right to the point. The sooner he could finish this meeting, the faster this circus around his house could end.

"You do know, Athas," Jorge reminded him. "Having 7 SUVs sitting around anywhere; it sets off more bells of *you* being somewhere. People, they may not notice you…."

"I know, trust me, it's not my idea," Athas shrugged. "Sometimes, I wonder if it's worth it, and…"

"Ok, let's get to the point," Jorge cut him off. "You aren't fucking your little government-owned media tart anymore, so we gonna get a bunch of shitty press now?"

"She has promised to back off the topic completely," Athas awkwardly replied while two seats over, Marco swallowed his grin. "She won't talk about me one way or another, nor will she discuss our relationship."

"It would make her look highly unprofessional," Tony jumped in. "It's of no benefit for her to sing a song."

"Let us hope it stays that way," Jorge said. "What about rumors?"

"No benefit for her to have rumors either," Tony shook his head. "It would make her look highly unprofessional, not to mention stupid. We can always spin it back that she had a pathetic schoolgirl crush on Athas. We got her where we want her."

Impressed, Jorge nodded.

"Sir, I might have something about that…" Marco appeared concerned.

"You mean she's gonna say something about Athas?"

"No," Marco confirmed. "But you will be interested in what she is working on now."

"We will come back to that in a moment," Jorge put up a finger. "Let us finish with what I have planned and swing back."

"Very well, sir."

"So, you want to make a rock star out of him?" Tony said. "I already got some girls in mind. That along with the music, everything…"

"What girls?" Athas wrinkled his nose and shook his head. "What are you talking about?"

"We need to get your sorry ass up in the polls," Jorge insisted. "So, we will make you a rock star with the women 40 and under."

"Or maybe older?" Tony shrugged. "You just never know."

"We want to have some women follow you on tour," Jorge informed Athas. "Build a momentum, is that the word? Make people believe you are like a rock star; exciting, cool, whatever rock stars are these days."

"And where you're single," Tony jumped in. "This is even easier."

"Yes, it makes you 'getable'," Jorge teased, then returned his attention to Tony. "So, you have the girls?"

"Yes, I know who to get."

"Actors?" Jorge appeared apprehensive, remembering what Paige said.

"No," Tony shook his head. "Too conspicuous, but they are young and cool. That's all we need. We'll have them on social media too."

"Make them sign something to keep quiet."

"Will do," Tony replied.

Impressed, Jorge nodded. Looking back at Athas, He appeared skeptical.

"Now, we could get a YouTube star to talk about it?" Jorge wondered. "Maybe comment on it?"

"I was thinking the same," Tony replied, although Jorge doubted it. "I'm sure they could be bought."

"I will get on it," Tony continued, pulling a notebook out of his laptop bag and jotting something down. "I bet Sonny would have some ideas. He's young and knows that world more than me."

"That seems…kind of weird," Athas said. "I mean, shouldn't it be about my policies?"

"It should," Tony agreed, "but it ain't."

"So, Marco," Jorge turned his attention to the IT Specialist. "What else you got for me?"

"Ryerson," Marco spoke up. "She is working on another topic that you may not like."

"What's that?" Jorge appeared somewhat humored, assuming it was regarding Big Pharma or other bullshit.

"You, sir," Marco replied. "She's researching *you.*"

Jorge shared a look with Athas, who looked horrified.

"Well, we will see about that," Jorge commented as he raised an eyebrow.

CHAPTER 20

"I say *nada!*" Jolene protested as Jorge barged into Diego's house and glanced around. It was a mess. Even from the entryway, he could see glasses and bottles cluttering up the bar, and when he looked around the room, Jorge shook his head and started toward Diego's lime trees. "I promise. I say I cannot talk about this!"

Jorge ignored her and stomped toward the sunroom, glancing around at the mess as he made his way there. Swinging open the glass door, he walked through the doorway and pointed at the drooping lime trees.

"You can't even water his fucking lime trees, Jolene?" Jorge yelled at her. "You know how much he loves those trees! And this house is a fucking mess. Clean it or get the fuck out, so I can have someone else clean it."

"I was just so depressed, and…"

Jorge didn't reply, his eyes noticing a nearby water can. He grabbed the hot pink container and walked toward the nearby bathroom, where he filled it with water. Jolene continued to talk, but he was no longer listening. Her voice was infuriating.

Returning to the sunroom, he took great care to water each lime tree while thinking about his *hermano,* Diego. He would soon have to make a trip to visit him at the safe house. It was important he monitored the situation, then get Jolene the fuck out of Toronto.

"….as soon as I find an apartment, I will be…"

"What?" Jorge swung around. "Don't fucking tell me you are coming back to Toronto?"

"There is nothing there for me anymore!" Jolene cried as she pointed toward the wall indicating the city she left. "I cannot go back."

"Like fuck you can't," Jorge snapped. "Clean up this place, Jolene, or I will kick your ass out myself! Diego would be horrified if he saw the state of this house. I am coming back later today, and this house, it better be fucking perfect."

"I clean."

"And you better keep your mouth shut when reporters show up," Jorge returned to why he dropped in as he sat the watering can down. "I don't care how nice Ryerson is to you. If I find out you tell her anything…"

"No no!" Jolene quickly shook her head. "I did not."

"Keep it that way!" Jorge snapped as he headed toward the door.

"Is…Maria, is she still angry with me?"

Jorge didn't answer her question but shot her a look before leaving.

Back outside, he took a deep breath and turned his phone on. He sent a message to Sonny McTea.

We need to meet. Are you at the production house?

Yes. I'm working with Andrew on our next show.

Perfecto. I will be there soon.

Heading toward his SUV parked in the driveway next door, Jorge jumped in and flew onto the street. His head was starting to ache.

As he drove along, he called Paige.

"Did you talk to Jolene?"

"*Si, mi amor,* I do not know how that woman is still alive."

Paige giggled.

"The fucking house, it is a mess," Jorge continued. "I told her to clean it *today* or get out. Even Diego's beloved lime trees weren't watered! She's such a lazy…"

"This doesn't surprise me. Remember her apartment?"

"Oh, and it gets better!" Jorge continued. "She is moving back to Toronto. Isn't that fucking wonderful?"

"Oh," Paige sounded less than enthused. "Why?"

"To torment all of us," Jorge replied. "I am wondering, have you checked in with Diego?"

"He's doing good," Paige sounded upbeat. "Much better."

"I am thinking of going to see him."

"That would be a good idea."

"I think I need to see with my eyes that he is making progress."

"Do you plan to do this soon?"

"I hope so," Jorge replied. "I have to go to the production house to check some things. Jolene has not talked to the reporter, and now, I must make sure no one else does either."

"Do you plan to talk to Ryerson?"

"You might say that," Jorge replied.

He ended the call. Left with his thoughts on the remainder of the drive, Jorge had many things to consider.

Pulling into the parking lot, he took his usual spot. Taking a deep breath, Jorge glanced at the time before heading inside.

As usual, the reception area was always quiet. There was now security at the main door since one could never be too careful. The large, black man buzzed Jorge in automatically.

"Good morning, Mr. Hernandez," The young man with a thick African accent nodded.

"Good morning," Jorge replied. "Everything ok here?"

"Yes, sir, everything is well."

Jorge nodded and headed toward the boardroom. He found Sonny sitting alone, hunched over. His eyes seemed enormous behind the huge black-framed glasses.

"Thank you for meeting me," Jorge respectfully spoke as he walked into the room and headed for the table.

"No problem," Sonny appeared nervous as Jorge took his usual seat at the head of the table. "I didn't say anything."

"Is that so?"

"I know this is about the reporter snooping around," Sonny continued. "That bitch from…"

"Ryerson?"

"Yes," Sonny nodded. "Diego was always clear that we never talk."

Jorge nodded. Diego had taught him well.

"And I wouldn't anyway," Sonny continued. "I know, I mean, we met because…"

"Because you talk about me on your podcast," Jorge remembered. "This here was long ago, and I think we resolved that. You work for me now. You know there are consequences if you talk about me to reporters."

Sonny appeared anxious but nodded.

"But, you have proven your loyalty."

"Look, I won't say anything," Sonny continued. "But as you know, there's a lot of speculation on the internet."

Jorge shrugged. He was well aware of the stories floating around.

"Ryerson only asked me about the book launch," Sonny sat up straighter, his confidence growing. "About Jolene attempting to slap you."

Jorge raised his eyebrows.

"I guess she got wind of it," Sonny shrugged as Jorge carefully watched him. "I told her that Jolene is crazy, and I thought you fired her because of a drinking problem, so she was erratic."

Jorge threw his head back in laughter.

"I mean, I know the drinking part isn't true," Sonny relaxed. "But I had to make up something fast. I know you don't want Ryerson poking around."

"This is true."

"So, I made light of it," Sonny continued. "But, I think she's going to keep digging. She tried with me, but I said there was nothing to know. She reminded me of when I brought your name up in a podcast. Which is weird since I removed those shows from my channel *ages* ago."

Jorge nodded, biting his bottom lip.

"But she was pushy," Sonny leaned ahead on the table as if sharing confidence with him. "I told her that I had been wrong. That I went to investigate it more and there was nothing there. Just internet rumors and I didn't want you to sue me."

Jorge nodded in approval.

"Is there anything you want me to do?" Sonny asked. "I mean, I tried to get her off track, but what else I could say? She seemed skeptical since I work for you."

"No, this here is fine," Jorge shook his head. "Do you know anyone else she talked to?"

"I think she tried to get in here to talk to people," Sonny said. "But security stopped her."

"This here is good," Jorge replied. "Do not worry. You did the right thing. I will be taking care of this here situation now."

Sonny nodded.

"I got another question for you," Jorge changed topics. "We are getting starstruck women following Athas on his campaign, acting like fangirls to make him a rock star. I want to have some YouTube star sing his praises, any ideas who would work?"

"Tony mentioned that," Sonny nodded. "I'd go for Sabrina Supergirl."

"Who?" Jorge was puzzled.

"She goes by Sabrina Supergirl," Sonny shook his head. "I actually think she changed her last name *legally* as Supergirl. She said she identifies as a superhero for other women, specifically those who survived sexual abuse as children."

"Ok…"

"Anyway, I would pick her because she's a *huge* Canadian YouTuber that talks politics."

"Is that so?"

"Yeah, and if Athas were to talk about changing laws that child predators were castrated, she'd be all over his campaign."

"Well, although I do not disagree with this here," Jorge laughed. "It may be considered harsh. But we can work on something with Athas regarding this area."

"If you did that," Sonny tapped his hand on the table. "I guarantee she'd talk him up. And if you can get him on her show, even better."

"We might be able to get a deal there."

"I know her," Sonny confided. "I can help."

"You are not just talking her up because she is a friend?" Jorge grinned.

"I didn't say we were friends, honey," Sonny waved his hand in the air. "I said I *know* her."

"This here sounds perfect," Jorge moved his chair out and hesitated for a moment. "I have one last thing. It has to do with Diego."

Sonny's eyes filled with vulnerability with the mention of his boyfriend's name.

"Would you be interested in coming to see him with me?" Jorge asked.

"Yes," Sonny answered quickly. "Please! I would really like to see him."

Jorge thought for a moment and nodded.

CHAPTER 21

"This is a topic very near to my heart," Athas spoke in his usual subdued tone, causing Jorge to exchange looks with Sonny before returning his attention to the road. *"As a former social worker, I know how childhood abuse, especially sexual abuse, can change the foundation of a child's life. For this reason, after I win this election, I will enforce much tougher laws that will…"*

"You know," Jorge said. "I never thought of the social worker angle, but that there is good."

"Probably not untrue either," Sonny pushed up his glasses and nodded. "I mean, I used to have this friend who was…"

"You know, let us just keep listening to Athas," Jorge cut him off and glanced toward Sonny's phone.

Falling silent, Sonny nodded from the passenger side as if remembering his place. He nervously shuffled in his seat and dropped his gaze.

"We can make this country stronger," Athas continued. *"But we must start at the root of our problems. We must work together."*

"Ok," Jorge put his hand up. "That is enough. I can only handle so much political talk for one day and that was my limit. But you also must turn off your phone until after we leave the safe house."

Sonny nodded and turned it off.

"We will be there soon," Jorge pointed ahead. "But remember, you never saw this place."

"I'm surprised you didn't put a pillowcase over my head like in the gangster cartel shows," Sonny attempted to joke.

"I did not have one with me," Jorge replied, smiling at his nervous passenger. "Look, this here house, it is a secret though. So you cannot talk about it. You never saw it. You don't know where it is, and you're only here because I thought it would do Diego good to see you."

"I'm afraid he doesn't want to see me," Sonny confessed.

"Do not make problems that don't exist," Jorge insisted. "Trust me if I had lived my life like that, I would have been dead long ago."

Sonny nodded and looked down.

"So, tell me, do you think this Sabrina person, she will want to talk about Athas now?" Jorge wondered. "What is it you call her?"

"Sabrina Supergirl."

"And you said she changed this to her last name?" Jorge wrinkled his forehead. "Legally?"

"Yes, I did some research this week," Sonny nodded and pushed up his glasses. "She said it's because she identifies as a superhero to young women, so she felt it was appropriate."

"This here, it seems extreme," Jorge mused. "But I guess if all you do for work is roll out of bed and talk into a camera from your home, you have the time to waste on such things."

Sonny laughed.

"Well, am I wrong?"

"You do other things too, like research," Sonny assured him. "But yeah, you probably have more time on your hands than most. When I had my podcast, it was just a side thing, so it wasn't the same. Some people have sponsors, and they have to find guests. It depends on the show."

"Maybe it is as much work as we do at the studio," Jorge shrugged. "But I still think changing your name legally for something like this, it seems…odd."

"I think it was a publicity stunt," Sonny admitted. "I mean, she built it up, and people got excited about it."

"If my daughter tell me she wanted to change her last name to something like Supergirl," Jorge shook his head. "I would tell her she is crazy."

"Oh, speaking of your daughter," Sonny jumped in. "I heard she has a job with us."

"Yes, and make her work for it," Jorge insisted. "I do not want a lazy kid. There are enough lazy fucking young people out there, my Maria, she will not be one of them."

"I will," Sonny nodded.

The two men fell silent as Jorge continued to drive. Both were left with their thoughts.

"Ok, so we are here," Jorge suddenly broke the silence, pointing at a house.

"That looks...smaller than I expected."

"No, it is behind," Jorge said as he pulled in and followed a small road behind the house and into the woods. They were heading toward a large building that appeared to be for commercial purposes.

"Wow," Sonny was looking around. "You have a lot of cameras."

"And for a reason," Jorge replied. "But you didn't see a thing."

"I didn't see a thing," Sonny repeated while shaking his head.

Jorge approached the building that resembled a warehouse, and the large door lifted opened, allowing him to drive inside. After it closed behind them, Jorge stopped the car and turned to Sonny.

"Now, we will go in," Jorge said. "But I will be talking to Diego alone first. I want to see how he is and monitor the situation."

"Ok," Sonny appeared nervous. "Do I...do I wait here?"

"You can come into the house," Jorge said as he put his hand on the door. "That is fine."

The two men got out of the SUV and headed toward the door. Jorge could sense Sonny's uneasiness and shared it but remained stoic. There could be a whole new Diego waiting inside.

Walking into the safe house, Sonny glanced around. His eyes widened.

"Wow, this is nice," he said while taking it all in. "The funny part is it doesn't look like a house from the outside."

"That there is on purpose," Jorge assured him. "The windows are darkened and mainly in the back, so it looks inconspicuous."

"Hello," Jorge heard a voice coming from the stairs. Looking up, he saw a middle-aged white man walking down to meet them. The man appeared peaceful, calm, and unaffected by the world around him. Jorge observed that he almost seemed disconnected from reality. "You must be Jorge Hernandez?"

"Yes," Jorge nodded as he met the man at the bottom of the stairs. "I am here to see Diego."

"Ok," He nodded, glancing at Sonny. Jorge noted that he didn't introduce himself, something Paige had warned him might happen. "I know he is waiting for you. And this young man?"

"He is also here to see Diego," Jorge replied and glanced over his shoulder.

"If it's ok," Sonny shrugged nervously.

"I will see him first," Jorge said. "And we will take it from there."

The man gave a sympathetic nod, and Jorge headed up the stairs. Although he had some concerns about what he might find, it was still necessary to check up on his longtime best friend, his *hermano*.

Finding the bedroom with a closed door, Jorge assumed this was Diego's room. He gently knocked and held his breath. The silence of the house was unsettling.

"Come in," Diego could be heard from the other side.

Jorge slowly opened the door, a sudden chill of air causing a shiver up his spine. He saw Diego sitting on a chair wearing a suit.

"This here it is formal for my visit," Jorge teased, unsure of what else to say as he went inside and closed the door behind him. The room was neat, a sharp contrast from the condition of Diego's house a few days earlier.

"*You're* wearing a suit."

"Me? I always wear a suit," Jorge reminded him as he walked closer to Diego. "I had meetings this morning. But you, you should be relaxing."

"I want to go home today," Diego looked close to tears.

"Diego, I do not know if…"

"I *want* to go home," He repeated more sternly.

"Are you *ready* to go home?"

He didn't reply. Jorge sat on the edge of the bed across from Diego.

"You know," Jorge continued. "Diego, there is no rush. We are not expecting you to return to Toronto anytime soon. Things, they are being looked after."

"I can't do this," Diego shook his head. "I can't keep digging in my past, looking at my demons, you know? This here isn't helping. I feel worse.

It makes me want to drink or do something to take it away. This is the opposite of what I need."

Jorge nodded and glanced down at his hands.

"So, what does….your counselor say?"

"You mean the prison warden?" Diego complained. "He thinks I should be here another six months."

"And you?" Jorge asked. "You think you are ok?"

"I think I'm ok enough," Diego insisted. "But I can't stay here."

Jorge observed his friend. He was conflicted.

"Diego, you know, I worry," Jorge candidly spoke. "I worry that this here, it will be too much. Maybe it is a thing where you feel worse before you get better, but.."

"Look, I know you mean well," Diego cut him off. "But this, it's not helping. I don't know what to do, but this ain't it. I need to be with my family, not locked away from everyone."

"But if you return," Jorge asked. "I worry…"

"I won't drink," Diego insisted. "And no more cocaine, I promise."

"I know, but it is easy to say now…"

"At least let me go home," Diego insisted. "And after a couple of weeks, I will return to work. I can stay home, tend to my lime trees, hang out with Priscilla…wait, my dog is ok, right?"

"Sonny, he has the dog at his place," Jorge reminded him. "And actually, he is here. He come to see you."

"He did?" Diego quietly asked, causing Jorge to wonder if Sonny would be the key to encouraging Diego to stay in the safe house. However, this moment of hope quickly was deflated. "I don't want to see him."

CHAPTER 22

"So, he cried all the way back to Toronto," Jorge told Paige as he collapsed on the couch beside her. "I do not like this soap opera. I would not have brought him if I knew this would happen."

"Sonny was understandably upset," Paige reminded him. "But Diego, he's not himself."

"He was very agitated."

"What did his counselor think?"

"He say it is too soon," Jorge shook his head. "But Diego, he say if we do not let him out soon, he's going to break out and walk home."

"Well, you know he's not going to walk home," Paige muttered. "But we can't hold him against his will."

"I thought he was doing so well?"

"He was, but it's a process," Paige reminded him. "There's a lot of trauma and stuff from his past that we need to unwind."

"But, do we, Paige?" Jorge asked. "Look at me. I have trauma from my past. I am fine."

"Yeah, with a mini heart attack under your belt and panic attacks," Paige reminded him.

"Paige, that is just life."

"True," she nodded. "I get it. We all need to deal with life. But in Diego's case, he was spinning out of control. I'm just scared if we bring him back too soon, it won't go well. Especially if things are off with Sonny *and* Jolene is still in his house."

"Jolene, she can leave his fucking house anytime," Jorge raised his voice. "That *puta* should not even have the key."

"I agree!" Maria's said as she entered the room. "Why is she *there* at all?"

"Obviously, Diego gave her a key," Jorge shrugged.

"Ughhh," Maria rolled her eyes. "*Papá,* can I throw her out?"

"Ok, let's just calm down," Paige put her hand in the air just as Jorge's phone buzzed. Glancing at it, he took a deep breath and stood up.

"I must take this."

"I'll look into Diego," Paige said as Jorge walked away.

"Why? What's going on with Diego?" Maria asked as Jorge headed to his office.

"*Hola,*" Jorge answered.

"Sir," Marco's voice came through the line. "I think we should meet. I am seeing some issues that we must discuss."

Jorge felt a sinking feeling in his chest and briefly wished he could trade places with Diego. He would love to be back in that quiet house.

"Ok," He replied. "Where are you?"

"VIP room."

"I will be right there."

Jorge headed out with a hand in the air, waving to his daughter and wife as they continued to discuss Diego. He hoped they could figure out what to do because Jorge had no idea. He could handle many dicey situations, but emotional ones were another story altogether.

Once in his SUV, he took a deep breath. He was pulling out of the driveway when his phone rang again. It was Makerson.

"*Hola.*"

"Hey, so are you able to do a Zoom tonight for the event?"

"Shit, that's tonight?" Jorge felt his head spinning. "This here has been such a long day."

"We're almost done," Makerson reminded him. "Only a couple more events, and we both can put this behind us."

"You do not have anything else?"

"I have interviews but no book signings or anything with the public."

"This here, it is good."

"Sales are good. The publisher is happy."

"Good."

"There's interest, but not enough to spark any other….issues."

"This is good," Jorge nodded. "I do not need any more issues."

"Things with Athas are picking up already," Makerson continued. "Recent polls are looking better. His fan club is helping bring things along. The announcement today created a new spark of interest in his party. We're on the right track."

"This here, it is good," Jorge felt slightly reassured. "The people, they want a rock star. And now they have one."

"But we can expect the opposition to strike back."

"We can take them."

"I should be back at the production house next week," Makerson predicted. "Just in time since the election is getting closer."

"We must stay vigilant," Jorge insisted, "especially now."

"What's the deal with that Ryerson chick?" Makerson asked. "Is she completely off the campaign trail? For sure?"

"Lover's quarrel."

Makerson laughed.

"But she is now too busy trying to investigate me," Jorge continued as he eased closer to the bar. "And that, it may be a problem."

"I see," Makerson sounded more serious.

"But it is a problem that I can solve."

"I'm sure you can."

Jorge ended the call. A few minutes later, he arrived at the *Princesa Maria*. Walking in, he met a bashful Chase, who appeared nervous, which was what Jorge wanted. People needed to know their place. The two men exchanged pleasantries before Jorge went to the VIP room, where Marco sat, laptop opened. He quickly closed it.

"Sir, we have a problem," Marco confirmed as Jorge closed the door and sat at the end of the table.

"Ryerson?"

"No, but I am watching her closely," Marco confirmed. "It appears she is growing frustrated because no one will talk."

"Let us hope that this here continues."

"Sir, there are powerful people that do not wish for Athas to win this election," Marco explained. "From Big Pharma, but also from people with money invested in the companies. Athas has already affected their bottom line, and they fear if he's reelected, he will continue to do so."

"*Si,*" Jorge nodded. "This here, I know, but nothing has changed. This has always been the case."

"But sir, they are getting more desperate."

Jorge didn't respond, anxious about what was about to come next.

"They see you as the problem, not Athas," Marco continued. "They feel that they could manipulate Athas easily if you aren't around."

"So, they decided that they will kill me?"

"No, sir," Marco appeared anxious. "There is talk....they want to hurt someone in your family."

"*What*! Who?" Jorge felt his heart race.

"That I do not know," Marco regretfully answered. "They are just talking about distracting you, warning you. They have done this kind of thing before, as you know."

"So, my entire family," Jorge bluntly asked. "They could be in danger."

"Sir, that is what I saw," Marco quickly replied. "Let me show you."

The two men looked at the laptop as Marco showed him a string of text messages he had hacked that spoke bluntly of putting Jorge Hernandez in his place. Although he took it with ease, Jorge could feel the anger burning deep inside him. Someone was going to die, but not his family.

"They talked of your children, sir," Marco slowly explained, his eyes monitoring Jorge as he did. "Then your wife, and sir, they are even talking about making it look like some of your enemies from Mexico did it. They hope to cripple you and at the same time make you look like a criminal."

"Give me names."

"Sir, you…"

"Give me names, Marco," Jorge jumped up and started to pace the floor. "And addresses."

"Sir, you must be calm," Marco spoke with kindness. "You will not think clearly, if you jump in with both feet."

"I need Diego," Jorge felt his thoughts moving quickly. "I need my entire army here to help me out."

"But do not do anything rash."

"I must send my family to the safe house," Jorge decided. "Then I will take on these monsters."

"Sir, yes, this is what to do," Marco reminded him. "You must have a plan."

"I know, but I just want to…"

"Sir, if this was my family," Marco assured him. "I would too. But wait, I am tracking these two men. I am tracking their habits and their weak points. Please, trust me. Your first step is to get your family somewhere safe, and we will take it from there."

"I will, Marco," Jorge calmed himself and thought for a moment. "Who are they?"

"Both are high in the pharmaceutical industry," Marco continued. "They are rich and powerful men."

"Not as rich or powerful as me," Jorge reminded him.

"Of course not, sir," Marco agreed. "It is a father and son. Thomas Dunn and Thomas Dunn Jr."

"Can I see?" Jorge pointed to the laptop.

Marco quickly searched and turned the laptop around. An image of two white men smiling was the first image to come up. The senior of the two was wearing a tuxedo, while the younger man appeared less formal, wearing a suit and tie. More images showed the two men with a young woman with dark hair wearing an elaborate wedding gown.

"Who is this?" Jorge pointed at the woman.

"It would be the daughter," Marco replied as he pointed toward the senior of the two men. "This was just last week."

Jorge had an idea.

Nobody fucked with his family.

CHAPTER 23

"Your enemy is my enemy," Chase repeated as he reached for his gun. "Just tell me what you need me to do."

"I need you to take my family to the safe house," Jorge bluntly replied as he reached for his phone. "Marco, he will give you the details. I must go home and see them first. Be at my house in an hour."

"Will do," Chase remained stoic. "But, will Maria…"

"Maria will just have to get over it," Jorge cut him off. "This is about her safety. This will also be a way to keep Diego there. Take him aside. Tell him he must look after the family. I need him to do this for me. When you feel that everything is ok, return to Toronto because we have some work to do."

Chase nodded.

Jorge headed for the door, turning his phone on. It wasn't until he was outside that the sudden pain in his chest hit him. For a moment, Jorge couldn't breathe. Reaching out, he closed his eyes and grounded himself by reaching for the building as a vibration ran through his body. He had to stay strong. He had to protect his family.

Rather than fight it, Jorge allowed the intense feeling to pass through him. He eventually felt weak yet calmer. He made his way to the SUV and got in. Sitting for a moment, Jorge finally started the vehicle and drove away. Once on the road, he called his wife.

"Hello."

"Paige, I have something important to talk to you about," Jorge said as he made his way through traffic. "Please, keep Maria and Miguel home for now. I will explain why when I get home."

"Is this serious?" She calmly asked.

"I will see you soon," Jorge decided to avoid the question. "But ah… just stay there for now."

After ending the call, his mind raced. He had to send a powerful message that no one threatened his wife and children. It wouldn't be quiet and discrete; it had to be loud and awaken those who thought his family was fair game. He had to make sure nothing like this happened again.

By the time he got home, Jorge knew what he would do. But first, he had to protect the people he loved the most. He was met at the door by Paige.

"What's wrong?" She muttered, but Jorge looked past her to his children in the living room. Maria was playing with Miguel.

"You and the children must go to the safe house."

"What?" Paige appeared worried. "Why?"

"These two fucks named Thomas Dunn and his son, that is why," Jorge muttered. "I will explain."

Paige followed Jorge as he approached his children, and both looked up at him.

"*Papi!*" Miguel called out and ran toward him.

Jorge felt his heart sink as he reached down to pick up the little boy. He was just a baby. Hugging him tightly, Jorge closed his eyes and took a deep breath. When he opened them, he saw a concerned look in his daughter's eyes.

"What's going on?" She bluntly asked. A strength filled her face as she stood up. "You're acting weird."

"What? I cannot hug my children," He reached out for her with his left arm while holding Miguel with the right. "Maria, you are so suspicious."

Pulling her into a hug, Miguel struggled to get out of his arms. Jorge put him down.

"Maria, this here is very important," Jorge spoke calmly. "You, Miguel, and Paige must go to the safe house…"

"Not without you!" Maria automatically cut him off as she moved away from him. "If we are in danger, *you* are *too!*"

"*Danger!*" Miguel repeated, his eyes widened.

"Maria, please," Jorge shook his head. "I do not have time for this now. I will be fine. It is just a precaution…."

"What about school?" Maria cut him off.

"Maria, you can work from the safe house," Jorge turned to Paige. "Just say she is sick. This here, it will not take long."

Paige silently nodded.

"Chase, he will be taking you…"

"NO!" Maria defiantly shook her head. "No way!"

"Maria," Jorge sharply replied. "I am not fighting with you about this here. We do not have time. Please. Go upstairs, and pack up your stuff. Chase, he will be here soon."

"But *Papá*…."

"Maria, please!" Jorge spoke more sharply, causing Miguel's eyes to widen. "It is important that you do this for me. Chase will drop you off and then come back here to help me. You do not even have to talk to him for the drive."

Maria said nothing, but her face turned red.

"Paige," Jorge turned to his wife. "This here is also a way to keep Diego there. Tell him he is to look after my family. He will not try to leave, and you will have time to see the best way to handle his situation."

"Good idea," Paige nodded.

"Now," Jorge glanced between the three of them. "This is very important. I need you to be safe while we resolve this issue."

"Is someone….does someone want to hurt us?" Maria nervously asked.

"Maybe," Jorge replied, then decided to be completely honest. "Yes, Maria, someone does. We are not sure which one of you."

"Why?" Maria asked with such innocent eyes that Jorge felt his heartbreak. "Why do they want to hurt us?"

"Because they are motherfuckers, that's why," Jorge ranted.

"Jorge!" Paige gave him a look, gesturing toward his son, who watched him with admiration.

"Because," Jorge hesitated. "It is complicated, but it is a way to get at me. It is two powerful men from Big Pharma, and they seem to feel that

I have too much influence on Athas. If they hurt someone I love, then it takes my attention away. Maybe it scares me off."

Paige appeared nervous, while Maria was angry.

"*Papá,*" She stood taller. "I want to stay here and help you!"

"Maria," Jorge reached out and pulled her close. Kissing the top of her head, he slowly let her go. "I do appreciate this, but no, I would rather you go to the safe house. I cannot have you as a target. I must take care of this problem without worrying about watching you. These here are dangerous people who only care about money."

Maria appeared to accept the answer and nodded.

"Now, please," Jorge spoke gently this time. "Chase will be here soon. I need you to do this for me."

After his family headed upstairs, Jorge went to his office and closed the door. Walking to his desk, he sat down and closed his eyes. His heart was furiously pounding, but it was important he remained calm. His family needed him.

Reaching for his secure line, Jorge called Athas.

"Hello."

"We gotta talk."

"Ok."

"We got a problem. Are you alone?"

"No."

"You can talk."

"Sort of."

"Do you know a Thomas Dunn? A father and son team?"

"Yes," Athas replied quickly, "unfortunately, yes."

"They feel I have too much influence on you."

"I think I heard that before."

"Did they say this to you?"

"Yes," Athas continued. "I said it was a non-issue."

"Well, they do not believe this," Jorge continued. "And they put a target on my family."

"Wait, what?" Athas sounded concerned. "You know, this isn't worth…"

"Calm down," Jorge cut him off. "They are going somewhere safe. And I plan to take care of my problem."

"Ok," Athas replied. "I just feel…"

"I did not ask you how you feel," Jorge cut him off again. "This here, it is not about your feeling. It is about you being aware that some wolves are at the door. They are at the door because they know you're going to win, and this here scares them. But we must scare them more

"So," Athas paused for a moment. "You have it under control?"

"I soon will."

"And I should expect…."

"You should expect that father nor son will be an issue again."

"They own a lot of people," Athas muttered, including some in the media."

"Soon, they will own nothing," Jorge insisted. "Because, where they're going, you can't take it with you."

"I assume you mean the crematorium," Athas muttered, his voice lower this time.

"I mean hell."

CHAPTER 24

"My son," Jorge said as he ushered Marco into his office, attempting to appear calm. "He wanted to pack his suitcase full of toys. When Paige wasn't looking, he threw his clothes out and put in his stuffed animals and cars."

"Oh sir," Marco gave a strained smile. "They are fun at that age. You never know what they will do."

"This is true," Jorge said as he headed behind his desk, and Marco took his usual seat. "I assume you are here because you have something for me?"

"Yes, sir, I do," Marco grew serious. "I found more information on Thomas Dunn and more communications between him and his son."

"I see," Jorge remained stoic even though his heart raced. "What is it you find?"

"This time, sir, I listen in on their phone."

"On their conversation?"

"Sort of," Marco replied as he sat his laptop bag down. "It is more like the microphone on their phone. I can also hack that, sir. But to be honest, most people are pretty casual about what they put into texts and messaging services. They are *ridiculously* easy to hack."

Jorge nodded.

"Except ours," Marco reminded him. "I have a steel gate for our messenger service."

"It is always better to be safe than sorry," Jorge confirmed. "But Marco, you must tell me what you learn."

Marco took a deep breath and hesitated before continuing.

"They wanted to hurt Maria, sir," Marco quietly spoke as if delivering the news in a softer tone would somehow make the information more digestible. "At first, they talked of Miguel, but they say no, he was too young. A young lady, though, that is another story."

Jorge grimaced but listened.

"They had thought of trying to take her from school because they knew there was no way they could get near the house," Marco continued. "Sir, I can play this for you if you wish?"

"Marco, I think I would rather you deliver this news," Jorge admitted. "I think my head will explode if I hear them talking about my Maria."

"I understand," Marco nodded. "I would feel the same if it were my daughter."

"So, they wanted to kidnap her from school?"

"They knew that would be difficult," Marco continued. "Unless they paid off someone or grabbed her as she was leaving. They knew there weren't many opportunities. Maria, she is highly protected."

"This is true," Jorge replied. "But most people, they have a price."

"They were thinking the same," Marco continued, then hesitated. "They said that kidnappings are common in Mexico. It would look like a cartel, so you would want to keep it quiet. You would not want people to think you are still involved in that lifestyle."

"But I do not understand," Jorge shook his head. "How were they planning to let me know it was them?"

Marco looked down.

"Marco, please…"

"Sir, I do not wish to upset you," Marco spoke emotionally.

"Marco, this here is important…"

"I need you to stay calm," Marco insisted. "Sir, this is really bad."

"I can take it."

"You can take it when it is not your children, sir."

"Please," Jorge said with emotion in his voice. "There is nothing I have not heard before."

"The plan," Marco hesitated for a moment. "They wanted to kill Maria…"

Jorge nodded for Marco to go on.

"They said, you know, Mexicans they…"

"Please, Marco, do not stop now."

"Sir, they wanted to make it look like a suicide but let you know that it was not," Marco struggled with the words. "With a message to drop Athas, to step away, to retire and spend what time you had left with your remaining child."

Jorge nodded and bit back his anger. His heart pounded so hard he thought it was about to explode. He clenched his fist as rage filled him.

"Sir, I am sorry to…"

"Marco, this is not you," Jorge shook his head. "I just…I cannot believe that all of this is to keep the integrity of a company."

"A company that has no integrity," Marco reminded him. "This is all about money and shareholders."

"And power," Jorge added. "It is all about power."

"Yes, sir, you are right," Marco nodded and put his head down. "Sir, I just do not know what is wrong with people. This is so disturbing…"

"Marco, there is nothing I have not heard already," Jorge insisted. "I have done such things as you talk about, but never to a child. I refused. And it has taken me this far. I have threatened, *si*, but that was just words."

"Maybe this is too?" Marco appeared worried. "Maybe it is just talk."

"It might be," Jorge nodded. "But it will be their *last motherfucking words.*"

Marco nodded.

"Now, you must tell me a few things," Jorge felt a wave of calamity pass through him. "Tell me about his daughter and where I can find her."

Marco nodded.

Later, when he was alone, Jorge started to process all the information he had just received. His heart couldn't take it if anything happened to his children. It would be the end of him. The fact that someone else was using it to gain power over him was infuriating. He wanted to murder both men with his bare hands.

But he had to be calm.

If Paige were there, she would insist that meditation was the answer. It was a method he had attempted in the past but failed. His brain wouldn't stop. Life had taught him that you always had to be on guard and alert. Meditation pulled him away from the constant thoughts that saved him. But he knew she was right. You had to be calm to do something that required your emotions not to take over. He had a plan, but first, he had to stop his heart from racing. He had to ease the fury within.

Jorge opened his laptop and found some meditations Paige put on his computer. A few years earlier, a well-known publishing house hired her to be the voice for these meditations. Her tone could take you to another place, where you felt safe and calm. No one knew this better than Jorge. It was one of the first things he noticed about her when they met. Her voice had brought him back down to earth so many times.

Closing his eyes, he listened, focusing on her every word. He felt himself get pulled in, taken on a journey as his body relaxed. First, his shoulders dropped, then his head drooped over as energy flowed through his limbs, and peace filled his heart. It was beautiful and tranquil until the vision of his daughter flowed through his brain. Her smile, her eyes, as she grew younger and younger.

Then he saw his brother, Miguel. His son's namesake was looking at him with the same fear his daughter had that day. A wave of emotions suddenly filled him, erupting into a force of tears that caused Jorge to open his eyes again and reach for the tissues on his desk. His entire body shook in despair. The memories were so powerful.

He would never forget the day his younger brother died. The date, the time, what Miguel had been wearing, but mostly, the look in his eyes still haunted Jorge. Miguel had innocently trusted him, and he died. Would his children be the same? Would all his efforts be for nothing?

The tears finally stopped, and Jorge sat back, exhausted. Maybe it was time to step aside. Maybe, it was time to enjoy his family and what was left of his life. Who knew how long that would be? Maybe, it was time to retire.

His phone beeped. It was Chase.

Everything is fine.

Where are you now?

I'm on my way back to Toronto.

Come here when you return.

Will do.

Sitting back, Jorge glanced at his bulletproof window. He had bought this house to keep his family safe. Security experts had assured him of such, yet, you couldn't protect them everywhere, all the time. You had to teach them to protect themselves. His daughter had already had these lessons. Eventually, his son would too. That was the one thing he could give them far more precious than money.

By the time Chase arrived at the door, Jorge had a plan in mind. He wasn't sure if he was ready to share all the details. You could only eat an elephant one bite at a time.

"Chase," Jorge welcomed him at the door. "Please, come in."

"I dropped them off," Chase jumped right into the conversation. "It was a bit of a tense drive, but Maria had her earbuds in and ignored me, so it was fine."

Jorge grinned as he shut the door behind him.

"I checked everything carefully, made sure no one was following us," Chase continued. "I talked to Diego. Of course, he's prepared to protect your family. He almost seemed like...he was back to his old self."

"Maybe he needs this here to get back to who he used to be," Jorge commented as he pointed toward his office. "And what really matters."

"I think you're right," Chase agreed as he followed Jorge. "He said he can help with whatever you need."

"Right now," Jorge replied as they walked into his office. "He is where I need him to be."

"He wants to fire his counselor guy."

"Paige can decide on that."

"So, what are we doing?" Chase asked as Jorge closed the door. "I assume you have a plan."

"I have a plan," Jorge replied. "And it will shut these motherfuckers down. For good."

CHAPTER 25

"So, you don't follow the book reviews?" The moderator was a blonde lady on the other end of a Zoom conversation. She was in a room with Makerson and a group of people wanting to meet him on the book tour. On the opposite side of his office, Jorge could see Marco and Chase diligently working while he continued the conversation as if it were an average night for a family man. "You aren't the least bit curious?"

"No," Jorge answered honestly, noting his relaxed manner on a corner image of his laptop. Wearing a suit and tie, not a hair out of place, and a smile on his lips, one would never guess that he was mentally preparing to murder someone later that night. "This here, to me, would feel slightly narcissistic. It is not my business what people think of me or my life."

The crowd laughed while the moderator joined them in a lighthearted moment. Jorge took the cue that he should do the same, even though he was thinking about how he wanted to slit Thomas Dunn Jr's throat for being the person who came up with the plan for Maria. He had excitedly shared it with his father, like a pathetic little boy who sought his father's approval. Some people's cups would never be full no matter how much was poured in because they were empty from the beginning.

"But you must acknowledge," The young woman went on. "That there's been a lot of interest in this book. I'm sure Tom has told you that?"

More laughter erupted in the background, another cue for Jorge to join in.

"Yes, well, there is that," Jorge nodded and grinned. "Of course, we talk about such details, but the specific reviews do not matter to me. Some people will like me, like my story, and others will not. That is just a reality. To take the time and energy to go through such details to measure the success of this book is pointless. How I look at it is that I enjoyed the book. I feel it is well done. To me, that's a success. If others enjoy it as well, that is great. If they do not, well, that is fine too."

"So, you probably don't read social media comments either?" The moderator asked. "Were you aware that you trended on Twitter for several days now…"

"What is Twitter?" Jorge joked, then burst into laughter, causing the audience to do the same. Across the room, Marco let out a giggle. "I joke. I know what Twitter is, but I do not participate in social media. To me, this here can be a dumpster fire and a waste of time wading through remarks about me from people who do not know me. No one should worry about what others think of them. It consumes too much time and energy."

"Words to live by," Makerson chimed in as the interview finished up. "Jorge's attitude is a big part of why people find him so fascinating."

"I did not get to where I am in life," Jorge continued. "By sitting on Twitter, Facebook, or wherever, monitoring what others think of me, this book, or my businesses. I instead put in hard work and tried to do better. That is all we are here to do, after all, not to worry about our image."

"That is indeed great advice," The moderator nodded and sat back. "And on that note, we're coming to the end of this Zoom call…"

Ten minutes later, Jorge was off the call, loosening his tie as he stood up. "We ready?"

"I checked the cameras, sir," Marco's eyes were on the laptop. "Thomas Dunn is at home, alone. I sent him a text, supposedly from his son, saying he had to drop in to discuss an issue. His son also got a message asking him to drop in at his father's house. Junior is so worried about pleasing his father that he will drop everything. He was in the middle of a dinner date and sent the lady home."

Chase shared a look with Jorge and rolled his eyes.

"These men who do not connect with their children," Jorge said as he walked across the room. "They create an empty shell that seeks something they will never find."

"Unfortunately, this is the case here," Marco agreed. "But sir, this works out well for us."

"Do not worry," Jorge assured him. "I have no compassion for him. His life was over as soon as he said what he wanted to do to my daughter."

He noted that Chase's eyes softened while Marco looked down and nodded.

"So, we going?" Chase asked as he stood up.

"We are going," Jorge replied.

"I'll turn the cameras off," Marco assured him as he got to his feet, holding his laptop open.

Jorge nodded.

"We just gotta…"

"I know," Jorge said with some reluctance. "Unfortunately, I know."

While the other men headed out to the SUV, Jorge made his way next door to Diego's house. Walking up the step, he was already regretting what he was about to do. Ringing the doorbell, Jolene answered right away. She wore a skintight, skimpy dress that showed off all her curves. Her makeup and hair were perfect as she stepped forward in cherry red high heels.

"Let's go," Jorge gestured toward his house. "The others are waiting."

"*Si.*"

Once in the driver's seat, Jorge looked past Chase and Marco and directly toward Jolene.

"Realize that this here," Jorge sternly commented. "This is just a one-time thing. You will not be rejoining the *familia.*"

"I understand."

"Don't fuck up, Jolene."

"I will not fuck up."

"You know what to do?"

"*Si.*"

"Sir, I can see his son's GPS, and he is getting close."

"We'll be there first," Jorge started the SUV, briefly glancing back at Marco. "Ladies, Hold onto your purses."

Jorge tore out of his driveway, headed down the street, and jumped on the highway. He wasted no time making his way to Thomas Dunn's house. Fury ran through his veins as he drove. Although the others chatted on the drive, his mind was a million miles away as Jorge flew through traffic like a madman. All he wanted was for his family to be safe. But he had to send a message.

Arriving on the street of the pharmaceutical oligarch, Jorge parked a few houses away and glanced around. Everything was dark, quiet, with almost no signs of life. The large estate was overkill for one man living alone, his wife having passed years earlier. He now had a much younger girlfriend that dropped by from time to time. Tonight, he would have a different guest.

"His son, he is getting close, sir," Marco reported from the backseat.

"You want me to go?" Jolene asked in a childlike voice.

"Yes," Jorge nodded as he chewed on his bottom lip. "He will think it is his son at the door."

"I go," Jolene said as she opened the door.

Jorge was silent as she got out of the vehicle and quickly walked toward the mansion. Marco was tapping on his laptop while Chase finally spoke.

"Are you sure this is a good idea?"

"No," Jorge answered honestly. "But I am willing to take the chance."

Jolene's heels clicked against the pavement as the mic on her phone played back each second. She cleared her throat as she walked to the entrance. They watched her ring the bell. Finally, the door opened.

"Who are you?" Thomas Dunn barked when he opened the door. "I did not order a girl tonight."

Marco let out a giggle.

"Of course, he thinks she is a whore," Jorge shook his head.

"Do we not have a date?" Jolene sounded confused, innocent. "I was told we have a date."

Thomas Dunn's libido must have kicked in because he seemed to hesitate, then relent.

"I…no, but, you know….maybe you should come in so we can sort this out," he seemed to back paddle. "I mean since you are…."

There was some shuffling, and the door closed.

"I'm expecting my son, so if you want to…"

"Shut up, old man," Jolene's voice grew sharp. "You listen to me!"

"The son is here…." Marco spoke up from the backseat as they watched a car pull into the driveway.

"Let him go inside," Jorge said as he reached for his leather gloves. "We will follow."

They watched Thomas Dunn Jr. walk up the step, while on the other side of the door, Jolene demanded that the older man remain calm and let him in. Within seconds Jolene was yelling at the two men to go to the next room. This was the sign for Chase and Jorge to head inside. Glancing around the neighborhood, Jorge noted it continued to appear dead. They couldn't be conspicuous.

"Let us go in," Jorge muttered, reaching for his gun as he and Chase got out of the vehicle and made their way to the house. Jorge continued to monitor their surroundings as they walked up the driveway.

Pushing the door open, Jorge immediately noticed that both men were sitting in the next room while Jolene pointed a gun at them.

"….want? Money? Are you robbing us? I don't understand," The older man shook his head, confused, while his son stared at Jolene's breasts.

"Let me help clarify some things," Jorge's loud voice barked at them as he closed the door behind him and Chase, and they headed toward the next room. "She is here for me. And me, do you know why I am here?"

Neither man responded, but terror filled their eyes as they watched Jorge approach them. Jolene continued pointing her gun in their direction, and like a good soldier, her attention was focused. The older man was white as a ghost, while his son looked like he was about to cry. Some with more compassion might feel sorry for them, but not Jorge Hernandez.

It was just the beginning.

CHAPTER 26

"Have you ever had a Zoom meeting?" Jorge casually asked the two pharmaceutical giants, who sat side by side on the couch. Behind Jorge, both Jolene and Chase pointed guns at Thomas Dunn and his son while Jorge spoke to them in a calm voice. He glanced around the room, noting an expensive piece of artwork. "You know? With the computer? It is interesting. Me, I prefer to meet people in person, but I could not do so because I must stay in Toronto to look after my family from psychopaths like you."

"But with computers these days," Jorge shook his head. "There is almost no limit to what people can do. I mean, you can talk to people on the other side of the world, learn so many things, even find people you went to high school with."

Both men continued to look like they were in shock, although Thomas Sr. was starting to appear irritated.

"But who the fuck wants to find someone they went to high school with?" Jorge shrugged and sat across from them on a large, solid oak coffee table. "I mean, who wants to see those fucking people again? Am I right?"

Neither man said a word. The older man now appeared confused.

"But you can do so much more," Jorge continued. "With computers these days, you can spy on people. You can learn that they are making evil plans. You can turn off their security system or turn off the cameras in their house. It is amazing. Some people, they can do anything with computers."

"Me?" Jorge continued as he looked from one man to the other. "I like being able to do such things. It gives me a chance to learn about people. For example," Jorge turned to Thomas Dunn sr. "I learn that you like to pop a Viagra and call up the high-class whore house to send over a woman who would never fuck you if you had no money. Probably not even on your best day."

"And you," Jorge continued as he turned his attention to the younger man. "I learn that you get off on something very different. You get off on trying to impress your father by solving problems. Unfortunately for you, it does not matter what you do because this man, your father, he will never give you what you need. He cannot because he has no heart. He is not able to appreciate you. So your plan to murder my daughter, to keep me out of politics and stop fucking with your company, it will not work."

"I...I wasn't..."

"Shut the fuck up!" Jorge yelled. "I see the messages. I see the texts. You think watching some Mexican cartel shows that you know anything about me, or my life, about what will happen. I will tell you what would happen..."

Jorge grew more agitated, which in turn caused both men to flinch.

"If you kill my daughter, I would kill everyone in your fucking family," Jorge sharply glared at him. "I would kill them in front of your eyes. I make it painful. I would torture them, and then I would torture you and murder you. You may have watched a cartel show and learned something, but you did not get to the episode where the Mexican retaliates."

"I didn't..."

"Shut the fuck up!" Jorge yelled again. "I did not ask to hear from you."

Jorge stood up and began to pace, loosening his tie.

"Did you think I would not find out?" Jorge asked as he glanced between the two men, his heart pounding. "Did you not think I would catch you before you pulled off your plan? You can pretend you were shooting the shit, but I know you had someone lined up to hurt my daughter. The reason why he backed out was that he knew me. He knew what I would *also* do to him and his *familia* if he hurt mine."

Thomas Dunn almost appeared impressed as Jorge talked, while his son started to break down, his body shaking.

"You see, back in Mexico, I had a bit of reputation," Jorge continued, stopping in the middle of the floor and standing in a powerful pose. "They called me *el diablo* because I was the motherfucking devil. I killed a lot of people. I killed anyone who got in my way. These days, I have slowed down. I have a family. That is my priority. I am getting close to retirement, you know? But I do make exceptions. And one of those exceptions is if someone hurts or threatens anyone in my family."

"Truth be told," Jorge continued as he watched the son crumble. "Even if I were to walk out right now, these two behind me," he stopped and pointed toward Jolene and Chase. "They would kill you. Do you want to know why? Because we are family. We are about loyalty. Jolene, she is my daughter's Godmother. Chase, he is also close to my Maria. Neither of them would let you live."

"That was him," The older man spoke up, pointing toward his son. "That had nothing to do with me."

"See this here," Jorge pointed toward the older man, while the son appeared horrified by what his father said. "This is not loyalty. I would *never* sell out my daughter like that. If a man had a gun on my child, I would stand in front of it. Not push them ahead in the line. That right there should tell you everything you have to know."

The two men exchanged looks.

"I told you, you were playing with fire," Thomas Dunn said to his son. "But you wouldn't listen."

"But you didn't try to stop him either," Jorge reminded the older man. "You did not care, as long as he could pull it off."

"Now, that's not what I said," The older man began to stand up, and with one swift move, Jorge pulled a gun out of his pocket and shot the pharmaceutical giant in the head. Beside him, the younger man fell into hysterics. He appeared almost unable to breathe as he looked at all the blood and what was left of his father's skull. Leaning over the side of the couch, he vomited while continuing to cry in hysterics.

"See," Jorge calmly continued. "You do not have the stomach for this here lifestyle. Maybe you think it looks exciting on television. Not so much fun in real life, is it?"

Thomas Dunn wiped his mouth and shook his head, attempting to make himself small. He was in shock.

Jorge reached in his pocket and pulled out his phone.

"Now, let me read your exact words," Jorge tapped on his phone with one hand while holding the gun with the other. "Because you were pretty specific about what you wanted to do to my *teenage* daughter, who is still technically a child."

"Please don't hurt my children," Thomas Dunn hurriedly said, his voice shaking. "Please, I will do anything. Please!"

"I will not hurt your children," Jorge shook his head. "It did occur to me to make your father think I would kill your sister, his real pride and joy, but in many ways, I am not as evil as you. You see, I do not hurt people who don't deserve it. I don't make drugs that hurt people, that kill people, but you do. I also don't torture and kill children. But you were going to. So I think that makes us very different people, wouldn't you say?"

Thomas Dunn looked slightly relieved but stared at Jorge in admiration. Peacefulness crossed his face.

"Now, I see here," Jorge returned to his phone. "Where you say, 'Let us do like the Mexican cartel shows. Jorge Hernandez should be familiar with that. We could kill his daughter and make it look like a suicide. We could cut her head off. We can have someone rape and torture her. We can set her on fire. I saw all this on a series I watch. Any of these things would destroy him. He would see that Canadians play the same games as his Mexican counterparts. In fact, to the world, it will look like someone from back in Mexico seeking revenge, but he will know. And he will finally relent, letting us control Athas and spend time with his other child."

"I was..I," Thomas attempted to explain. "I...I didn't mean..."

"Like I say earlier," Jorge cut him off in an almost comforting tone. "I know you were attempting to hire someone, so this here story, it won't work. You were making a plan. You were trying to impress your father. But he was never going to be impressed by you. He was just a miserable old fuck who only liked money and whores. What did he know?"

Thomas looked down.

"But you have studied all of this," Jorge continued as he put his phone away. "You already know the importance of sending a message. In the same way, you had hoped to send a message to me, to scare me, I must do the same thing to people in your industry because I am *tired* of dealing with you soulless pricks in Big Pharma. You don't give a fuck about people. You care about money. But here's the thing with money, something I learned a long time ago. You can't take it with you. You cannot take it with you to your cold grave. The man beside you, the one who no longer has a head? He is burning in hell right now. He cannot buy his way out of there, and you know what? Neither will you."

"Don't make it easy for him," Chase spoke up. "A bullet in the head, it's too fast. We need him to suffer."

"He did just see his father's head being blown off," Jorge shrugged. "But then again, that does not hurt him."

"Cut off his fingers," Jolene suggested. "Rip off his fingernails. Cut his throat. Make him suffer for what he wanted to do to Maria."

"What if this hitman had agreed to do it?" Chase jumped in. "We might be too late now."

"These here are good points," Jorge nodded. "But we need to make a big statement."

"Maybe he write a public message saying they are criminals, and he commits suicide?" Jolene suggested.

"Yeah, kind of like what he has planned for Maria," Chase added.

"We could do that," Jorge nodded. "But we do not have to. See, Marco, he is already working on a plan to humiliate Junior boy while we are here, taking care of business. See, this fuckup grew frustrated with his father and killed him…..and then he killed himself….."

"I can do…." Jolene said.

"No, it will have to be from my gun," Jorge insisted, then turned to Thomas. "But don't worry, my gun. It is untraceable. No one will know. There will be no fingerprints. And of course, the police, they work with us, so it would not matter. No one will ever know the truth….see *that,* that is how the cartels work, *amigo.* You should have watched more of your series, or you would know that."

Thomas was pale, quiet as if accepting his fate.

Minutes later, both men were dead. Jorge and the others were in the SUV and driving home in silence.

CHAPTER 27

"*Police continue to investigate the gruesome murder/suicide of Thomas Dunn and...*"

Jorge was barely paying attention to the mainstream media report. Instead, he focused on Miguel, who had difficulty coordinating his cereal with his spoon. The little boy patiently picked up the blobs of cereal and placed them on the spoon before lifting them to his mouth.

"He seems to be making more work for himself," Maria observed from across the table. "Miguel, let me help..."

"No, Maria," Jorge shook his head. "Let him do this himself. That is how he will learn. One of the problems with kids these days is that everybody does everything for them. Then they get into the real world, and they expect it. They become lazy fucks."

"Jorge," Paige called out from across the room. "He's picking up everything now. We can't have him swearing in preschool."

This caused Maria to laugh while Miguel watched his father with interest.

"Yes, you are right, Paige," Jorge nodded. "Miguel, do not swear."

Miguel thought for a moment, picked up a piece of cereal, and extended his arm, as milk dripped on the table. "Look, *Papi, cer*ee*!*"

"*Papá,*" Maria pointed toward the laptop on the table. "Why would that guy on the news kill his father and himself?"

Her question appeared innocent, but her eyebrow rose in interest. Jorge gave her a warning look. Miguel continued to watch him with interest.

"Maria, I do not know," Jorge attempted to brush it off. "But remember, many families are not close like we are. That is one thing I pride myself on. A strong family unit is important. Loyalty is important. That is what I always say. This man, his family, they clearly do not have this."

"The police are still investigating…." Maria started, but her voice drifted off.

"The police," Jorge turned to her, his voice stern. "They will find nothing."

She nodded in understanding.

"You never know what is going on behind the scenes," Paige calmly added as she crossed the room and sat beside Maria, a coffee in hand. "I guess that's the lesson here."

Jorge raised his eyebrows and nodded.

"Maria!" Tala called out as she walked into the room. "We must leave soon or you will be late for school."

"Ughh," Maria rolled her eyes. "I don't care."

"I pay a lot of money for you *to* care," Jorge referred to her pricey private school. "Try to at least pretend."

"They just keep harassing me all the time," Maria complained.

"Harassing you?" Paige turned to her stepdaughter.

"They keep bothering me since I started that Facebook page," Maria rolled her eyes. "They still think it's a cult."

"Maria, this here, it is not good," Jorge shook his head.

"The last time I looked," Paige appeared concerned. "You had spiritual quotes. Did I miss something?"

"No," Maria shook her head. "That's all it is."

"Maria?" Tala smiled and pointed toward the door. "I am sorry, but we will be late…"

"I know," Maria slid off her chair, pushing her coffee cup aside.

"Maria, dishwasher," Jorge gestured toward the cup. "It is not our job to clean up after you."

"I know," Maria repeated as she picked up the cup and headed across the room.

"I will be outside in the car," Tala called out as she headed for the door. "Mrs, are you sure you do not mind taking Miguel to preschool?"

"I have to go out anyway, Tala," Paige assured her. "Thank you, though."

"*Adios!*" Maria waved her hand as she passed the table and reached for her backpack in the middle of the floor.

"Be good, Maria," Jorge instructed as she headed for the door. Once she was gone, he turned to Paige. "Should we be concerned?"

"It's probably just the school being overly cautious," Paige shook her head. "It all seemed pretty innocent to me."

"Let us hope," Jorge skeptically replied. "Let us hope."

"Is it this morning that Mark Hail is coming over?" Paige made reference to the local police officer that often communicated with Jorge. "Or is that later today?"

"This morning," Jorge replied as he closed the laptop, cutting off the live stream of news. "I have some things to do so, please, send him in when he arrives."

The doorbell rang, and the two exchanged looks.

"I guess he is here now?" Jorge shrugged and rose from his chair, crossing the room. He glanced out through the peephole before moving aside, shaking his head. Opening the door, Diego was standing on the other side.

"*Buenos dias!*" Diego walked in the door without an invitation. "I smell coffee!"

"Diego, it is nice to see you," Jorge commented as he gestured toward the other side of the room, but his friend was already heading for the coffee pot.

"Morning, Diego," Paige called out, to which she got a quick wave.

"I'm on a mission," Diego stated as Jorge closed the door and returned to his chair. "But good morning!"

"Do you not have coffee in your own house?" Jorge teased.

"I do," Diego replied as he reached for a cup. "But I also have Jolene, and I can't deal with one without the other."

"That's fair," Paige nodded.

"I would say it is more than fair," Jorge muttered.

"Is she a visitor or a permanent guest?" Paige called out as her eyes glanced toward Diego.

"It better be a short-term visitor," Diego replied as he poured coffee into his cup. "Cause I ain't got much more patience for her."

"Oh, it's been interesting having her around," Paige commented.

"Yes, my favorite time was when my daughter walked in on her and Chase fucking at the bar," Jorge commented, quickly noting the expression on his wife's face. "I am sorry, Miguel, please do not repeat my language."

The child started to laugh. The parents shared a look, and Jorge shrugged.

"What!" Diego's mouth was hanging open, and his eyes widened. "Are you kidding me right now?"

"Nope," Jorge shook his head. "I wish I were kidding you."

"Just when you think she's hit a low point," Diego commented as he crossed the floor and sat at the other end of the table. "Jolene, she finds a new low."

"Send her packing," Jorge suggested. "It's your house."

"I will," Diego confirmed. "We already had that discussion. But is that true? Did Maria…"

"She was going into work," Paige replied. "That's what she found."

"Ughh," Diego made a face. "She has no shame."

"So, Diego, tell me," Jorge cut him off. "How is life back at home, Jolene aside?"

"I want to go back to work."

"Are you sure?" Paige countered. "I mean, you're still getting back on your feet. What if that's too much?"

"I'm fine," Diego assured her. "What I need is to get back into my routine and get Jolene out of my house."

"And what about Sonny?" Paige asked.

"What about him?" Diego shrugged. "It was never serious."

"Then why do I hear him crying on the way back from the safe house that day I take him there?" Jorge countered. "He seems to take *you* pretty seriously."

"That's not my problem," Diego countered. "I can't help how others feel."

"Maybe you need to have a conversation with him," Paige suggested. "Or maybe it's too soon."

"Conver...satan!" Miguel shrieked from the other end of the table.

"Oh great," Jorge muttered. "We'll be getting another call from the preschool."

"Conversation," Paige corrected the little boy, who giggled and shook his head.

"So I wanna get all up to date on everything," Diego insisted. "Starting with this whole Big Pharma father/son thing."

"Not now, Diego," Jorge shook his head. "You, you need to get Jolene the hell out of your house and rest for a few days before you jump back into the game. We do not want you to be overwhelmed."

"I agree," Paige chimed in.

"I'm fine," Diego insisted. "I've lost too much time already."

"Just listen to us, please," Jorge insisted and noted that Diego relented. "We are only interested in your well-being. You will get back up to speed soon."

"Very soon," Paige insisted. "But you should take care of your...mess over there."

She pointed toward his house.

"You will never keep your sanity with Jolene living with you," Jorge added.

"No joke," Diego shook his head. "It's already a little shaky."

"Well, then you gotta sort that out before anything," Jorge suggested as he stood up, reaching for his laptop. "Trust me, if you don't..."

The doorbell rang.

"Trust me," Jorge insisted as he headed for the door. "I know what I am talking about."

"Danger!" Miguel randomly yelled out before shoving a piece of cereal in his mouth.

Jorge glanced at his son and grinned while the others laughed.

He opened the door to find a young, black man on the other side, wearing a leather jacket and sporting some 70s sunglasses.

"Come in," Jorge said and stood aside. "We can go to the office."

"This won't take long," Mark replied as he removed the sunglasses and walked in the door. "I have some news, and you're not going to like it."

CHAPTER 28

"You make it sound like Maria has a whole secret life," Paige gave a nervous smile, glancing back at Jorge, who appeared stunned by the news. "It doesn't make sense."

"Perhaps it's because you're too close to the situation," Mark Hail suggested as he cautiously glanced around the table. "Kids today, with the internet and…"

"Don't give me that bullshit," Jorge cut him off. "Kids are kids. The only thing that has changed is that parents let them do whatever they want, but not my Maria. This stops now."

"Wait a minute," Diego spoke up from the end of the table. "How do we know this is even true? People make up shit and…"

"That's the thing," Mark Hail shook his head. "With school shootings in the US and gangs around Toronto, schools often work closely with the police department and report anything they feel is amiss. They felt that about Maria's group and reported it to the police."

"This here is a way to target me," Jorge grumbled. "Maria is going to be taken out of that school…"

"Wait," Paige put her hand in the air. "All he said is she's being monitored, it doesn't mean anything. As I said earlier, I've looked at the Facebook group, and it looks pretty innocent."

"The thing is that's not what they're looking at," Mark shook his head. "They're looking at things they associate with gangs. Maria has a small group of Mexican/Canadian children she hangs out with, and…"

"So, because she is Mexican, she must be in a gang, right?" Jorge cut him off.

"No, but it's the fact that they call themselves *Los Poderosos* that set off some alarms," Mark began. "And…"

"The Powerful Ones?" Paige cut him off this time. "That's just what they call their Facebook group. All their quotes are about feeling powerful in the face of life."

"Well, if that were all," Mark continued, shrugging. "I'd agree, but it's hard to argue with random violence."

"My daughter?" Jorge laughed. "My, what? Ninety-pound daughter is out beating up people now?"

"There are reports that she may have attacked someone at the mall this summer," Mark hesitantly continued. "No proof, but there were rumors around the school. There have also been several students who witnessed her being aggressive at school."

"Anything on camera?" Jorge automatically asked.

"No."

"Then you got nothing," Jorge shrugged. "Just some kids starting trouble. If there's no proof, it didn't happen."

"That might work in your world," Mark reminded him. "But these rich schools are another thing altogether."

"So, what I gotta do?" Jorge asked. "Donate money to something or another to shut them the fuck up?"

"Well, we had that one meeting at school," Paige reminded him. "Mr. Anthony didn't seem to be too concerned. He certainly didn't mention the police."

"Yeah, I gotta admit it's sneaky as shit," Mark nodded. "They do that a lot these days, go behind parent's backs with the excuse that they're worried about a school attack. They assume parents won't see their problem child."

"Are we not seeing *our* problem child?" Paige directed her question at Jorge.

"Of course not," Jorge shook his head. "This is an attack on me, not Maria. Nothing you have said says she is in a gang. It just says she is a teenager."

"They also say she has uttered threats," Mark continued.

"Who hasn't?" Diego shrugged, twisting his mouth in an awkward pose. "I don't get it."

"Hey, don't kill the messenger," Mark put his hands in the air. "Like, literally, don't kill me. I'm just telling you what I found out. How you handle it from here is none of my business, and we didn't have this conversation. I just dropped by today because I heard about some break-ins in the area."

"Really?" Diego sounded alarmed.

"Diego, you got guns and a baseball bat," Jorge shook his head. "Not to mention an alarm system, a batshit crazy sister, and me as your neighbor. I would be more worried about the motherfucker breaking in."

"Jorge…." Paige muttered and glanced at Miguel as he played with a toy car on the floor.

"Paige, he does not care about what we are talking about," Jorge insisted. "But hey, maybe that will be next. He will start a gang in preschool. Who knows with these dumb fucks."

Paige shook her head.

"Anyway," Mark rose from the chair. "I gotta go, but I wanted to give you the heads up."

"Thank you," Jorge rose from his chair and followed Mark to the door. "I do appreciate this."

"We'll be talking," Mark said before giving everyone a quick wave and walking out the door.

"So, what do we do about this?" Paige asked as Jorge made his way back to the table.

"We go talk to that fucking principal again," Jorge insisted.

"Maybe we should talk to Maria first," Paige suggested, "before jumping the gun."

"Paige, it does not matter," Jorge shook his head. "Whether she has done this or not, they approached the police, and the last thing I want is to have Maria on the fucking police radar. They went behind our back, and this stops now!"

"I gotta agree," Diego nodded. "Put a fork in this one."

"I will put a fork in something."

"I'm coming with you," Paige insisted.

"No, this here, it will be fine," Jorge insisted as he grabbed his phone and headed toward the door. "You two take care of Jolene. I will take care of this myself."

Paige appeared concerned, something Jorge ignored as he walked out of the house. Rushing to his SUV, he jumped in and flew out of the driveway. Some things had to be taken care of immediately before they got out of hand. This was one of them.

Arriving at the school, he found a security guard at the door.

"Name and reason for your visit today, sir?"

"I am here because my daughter is a student," Jorge sharply replied. "I need to see Mr. Anthony regarding a concern."

"What time is your appointment?"

"I don't have an appointment."

"Oh, but you must make an appointment to…"

"I pay a lot of fucking money for my daughter to go to this here school," Jorge gestured to the building behind him. "I will talk to the principal whenever I wish."

"Hey, it's not me," The young man spoke defensively as his body shrank in size. "We just have to…"

"Do you have a list of appointments with you?" Jorge glanced at the empty-handed man.

"No," He admitted. "I usually…"

"Then I have an appointment," Jorge cut him off. "You saw me here before. You recognized me, so you had no reason to doubt it, right?"

The security guard swallowed and nervously stood aside, allowing Jorge in the door.

"*Gracias.*"

Jorge was well aware of the route to the office. The empty hallways were sparkling clean as a sweet scent filled his lungs. Muffled voices came from behind the closed doors. Everything seemed peaceful, if not welcoming. He made his way to the office, only to find an overweight, white woman at the reception desk.

"Hi, can I help you?" She spoke cheerily.

"I would like to speak with Mr. Anthony."

"Do you have an appointment?"

"No."

"You have to make an appointment," She tilted her head to the side, reaching for the cross around her neck. "Otherwise, I…"

Irritated, Jorge stomped past her toward the principal's door.

"He's with someone now. You can't go in."

Jorge ignored her and barged into the room. Mr. Anthony hurriedly zipped up his pants while a heavy-set Mexican girl blushed as tears formed in her eyes.

"What the *fuck* is this?" Jorge asked, while behind him, the secretary gasped.

"Oh my God!" He could hear her say before Jorge entered the room and slammed the door shut.

"I…what….we don't have an…"

"Fuck off," Jorge cut him off and turned to the girl. "How old are you?"

"Fifteen," She replied as tears rolled down her cheek.

"Go," Jorge pointed toward the door. "Get that lady, the secretary, to help you."

"This isn't how it looks."

"Like fuck it's not," Jorge turned his attention back to the principal. "Do not tell me you are a pedophile, working as a principal. You better not have *ever* tried anything with my daughter."

"You completely misunderstand…"

"Oh yeah?" Jorge raised an eyebrow before turning to walk to the door. Pulling it open, he stuck his head out, gesturing for the secretary, who was comforting the hysterical teenage girl. "Lady, come here. Just to confirm, she is a student at this school?"

The same woman ready to kick him out moments earlier moved close to him in confidence. Her eyes were tearing up.

"She is."

"Who oversees this asshole?" Jorge asked as he gestured toward the office. "Get that person here, now. This is an emergency."

"Ok," She replied and sniffed. "This is *so* wrong."

"I know, but we will take care of it," Jorge assured her in a comforting voice. "Call the person who oversees this asshole, then look after the girl."

She gave him an appreciative nod and hurried away.

Turning around, Jorge glared at the principal as he shut the door behind him.

"You and I, we gonna talk, motherfucker."

CHAPTER 29

"It's not what it looks like," Mr. Anthony repeated as Jorge turned his attention to the principal. "What happened…"

"I don't give a fuck what happened," Jorge sharply cut him off, watching the man automatically shrink in size. "I don't give a fuck what kind of sick, twisted fuck you are, because that there, you will have to take up with your boss…or the police. I do not care."

Mr. Anthony didn't reply but nodded.

"Now, sit the fuck down so we can talk," Jorge gestured toward the desk. "Because I got something to say to you, and you're going to listen."

"Yes, of course," Mr. Anthony rushed behind his desk, head down, while Jorge took over the room.

"My daughter," Jorge started as he stood over the desk. "Maria Hernandez? I do not want the police to get a report about her behavior. I do not want the police to even know her fucking name, do you understand?"

Mr. Anthony nodded.

"I know you have been reporting things to them," Jorge continued. "That will stop *now*. That means you pick up the phone and call whoever you speak to about these matters. You tell them there was a mistake. You tell them there was a misunderstanding. You tell them to back the fuck off my kid, or when your boss comes here, I may have seen a lot more than I did today. And you know what? I got an active imagination and I got an even bigger fucking mouth. So, unless you want your life to get even more fucking miserable, I suggest you pick up that phone, and you sort this out now."

"Right now?" Mr. Anthony appeared confused.

"Is that not what I fucking said?" Jorge sharply asked as he leaned forward, challenging the principal with his eyes. "I know my English, it is not always so good, but I think I was pretty clear when I spoke just now."

"Yes, I mean, yes…"

"Do it!" Jorge nodded toward the phone. "And put it on speaker phone. I want to make sure you aren't fucking with me."

"I…I will…"

Twenty minutes later, Jorge was in his SUV and back on the road. He phoned home.

"Hello," Paige answered the phone on the first ring.

"*Mi amor,*" Jorge started as he drove through traffic. "It is all sorted out."

"Everything is fine?"

"Yes, we will have no more issues," Jorge replied. "I will talk to you when I get home."

He ended the call, and his phone rang. Glancing toward the number, Jorge was hesitant to answer.

"Jolene, what do you want?"

"I need a place to stay."

"I don't care."

"Diego, he kick me out," Jolene continued. "I help you. We are family and…"

"We are *not* family," Jorge cut her off. "Jolene, you help us recently, and that does not automatically earn you a seat at the table."

"Well, I need a job."

"Jolene, I…"

"I will work at the crematorium," she hurriedly added. "I will."

"That is a switch," Jorge commented as he stopped at a light. "You hate it there."

"I appreciate any opportunity," She spoke slowly, almost as if she were reading.

"Is that so?"

Jorge would never trust Jolene.

"I can do what you want."

"I'm surprised you don't ask to work at the bar with Chase," Jorge decided he would torture her. "You know, so you traumatize more employees when they catch you fucking…"

"I tell you," Jolene jumped in. "I am sorry about that. I just…"

"I don't care, Jolene," Jorge cut her off. "I really *don't* care."

"So, you give me a job?"

"Yes, but finding a new place to live," Jorge shook his head. "That's on you to do. But Jolene, it won't be at my fucking house."

With that, Jorge ended the call. The phone rang again, causing him to automatically answer it with impatience, assuming it was Jolene calling back. The woman was clueless.

"What do you want now?"

"I…." Alec's voice rang through the SUV. "I just wanted to update you on a few things."

"I am on my way home."

"This, it should be ok," Athas stumbled on his words. "We don't need the other line."

"Ok," Jorge took a deep breath. "What you got for me?"

"I'm up in the polls," Athas replied. "The things I'm talking about are resonating with people. The clean water for indigenous communities, cracking down on Big Pharma…."

"*Cracking* down," Jorge repeated and let out a laugh. "There is that…"

"Also," Athas continued. "Tougher laws on people who hurt children."

"You might want to look into my daughter's school now."

"Why is that?"

"There might be a principal resigning very soon," Jorge commented. "I had a little talk with him over an issue with Maria. A non-issue they were trying to make into an issue, and I came across something unsavory while there. I talked with his boss before I left the school. They are quietly letting him go. Why is this man even a principal in a school at all? And Athas, I pay a lot of money for this school."

"Wow…"

"I would say much harsher penalties," Jorge continued. "I got what I want, so maybe the story gets leaked. You could pounce on it like a dog in heat."

"Well, it's a privacy issue and…"

"No names will be given," Jorge insisted. "But it pushes what you recently announced. Plus, do you got that Supergirl lady supporting you yet?"

"I was going to mention that," Athas replied. "Sabrina Supergirl, and yes, she's mentioned me a few times in her podcast, which has helped a lot. She's even endorsing me, which apparently means something when you're a bubbly podcaster who talks about social issues one day and make-up the next."

"Hey, do not complain," Jorge insisted. "This here, it is reaching a new audience for you, people who wouldn't normally vote. If you got Toronto, you got the rest of the country."

"Well, it's not exactly…"

"I gotta go, Athas," Jorge cut him off. "I got another call coming in."

"Ok," Athas stuttered. "So, about the school thing…"

"I will get back to you," Jorge replied, immediately switching to the other call. "Hello?"

"Sir, are you available to come by the bar?" Marco was on the other line. "I have something I need to discuss with you?"

"I can stop there on the way home," Jorge replied as he looked around. "If I can ever get through this motherfucking traffic."

"It is bad, isn't it, sir?" Marco was laughing.

"I guess that's why you got a bike," Jorge replied and took a deep breath. "Although, at this point, I think I could walk faster."

"Well, sir, that was the issue that made me start to bike," Marco giggled. "I do not have time or patience for traffic."

"I will be there soon, Marco."

Ending the call, Jorge welcomed the silence. Collecting his thoughts, he called Makerson.

"Hello."

"We might have a story coming down the wire."

"Really?" Makerson replied. "What's this regarding?"

"A school principal that was…inappropriate with a student."

"Wow, that would tie in nicely with…"

"That is what I was thinking."

"Keep me posted."

"I gotta let the dust settle first," Jorge replied. "But that should not take long."

"I'm back in Toronto and ready to go live anytime."

"*Perfecto.*"

Jorge ended the call just as he arrived at the bar. Glancing around, he parked in his usual spot. He hesitated for a moment before getting out and heading inside.

Chase was behind the bar and gave him a quick nod but seemed subdued for some reason.

Jorge stopped and observed him.

"Jolene ask you to live at your place yet?"

"I…" Chase appeared shocked as he stumbled on his words.

"That's what I thought," Jorge cut him off before heading for the VIP room. "She'll keep your dick happy while you slowly go insane."

Marco was smothering a giggle as Jorge walked into the VIP room and closed the door.

"Sir, that is probably very true."

"What do you know about it?" Jorge bluntly asked as he sat down. "Were you talking?"

"I may have overheard a conversation, sir," Marco confirmed. "I think she might be moving in with him."

Jorge shook his head.

"Sir, people, they do not learn," Marco confirmed. "But that is not why I needed you to come here. I have something that may trouble you."

"What is that?"

"The legacy media," Marco said as he turned his laptop around. "They are about to release this picture."

Jorge felt tension fill his body when he saw it.

He may have won the battle but had yet to win the war.

CHAPTER 30

"I haven't seen this picture before," Paige studied the photo on Jorge's phone. "Gees, that must be over 20 years ago. Where did they even find it?"

"That is a good question," Jorge nodded as he leaned in closer to his wife. "Do you think that Athas may have…"

"What?" Paige began to laugh. "Right! Like he wants to explain why there's a picture of him and Jorge Hernandez's wife together. That was so long ago. I don't know what kind of scandal they think will come out of this."

"It is not about the scandal," Jorge reminded her. "It is because they want to torture me."

"They can't do that unless you let them," Paige reminded him, just as the secure line rang in his office.

Neither saying a word, the couple walked toward the darkened room in the corner of the house.

"All I know," Jorge said as they entered the room and he closed the door. "Is that whoever is posting this…"

"Let's just wait and see what happens," Paige suggested as she took her usual seat and Jorge rushed behind the desk, answering the call.

"Athas, you are on speaker," Jorge answered as he sat down. "Where the fuck did this picture come from?"

"I was about to ask you the same thing," Athas replied. "Maybe Paige knows…"

"I'm here," Paige cut him off. "I have no idea where or *when* that was taken. So, I don't know who took it or how it got out."

"Wow, you know," Athas spoke slowly. "That was such a long time ago, but we can't deny we were a couple because you can tell by the picture. Plus, others will jump to verify it."

"Does it matter?" Paige directed her question at Jorge. "I mean, who cares? It's not like I had a child with an international dictator or something. It was like 20 years ago, and it looks innocent enough."

"Well, the story is out," Athas confirmed. "And even though it seems like a non-issue, it's enough to start a scandal. It's obvious the only person benefiting from this is Frederick Knapp's camp."

"And the journalist who write it," Jorge reminded him. "That person, they have something that is going to get views, to get clicks, or whatever the fuck they want these days. That is all anyone cares about anymore. Not the truth or what really matters."

"So, who wrote the story?" Paige asked.

Athas let out a deep sigh.

Jorge rolled his eyes.

"Just tell us," Jorge demanded. "Stop being so dramatic."

"It's Ryerson," Athas replied. "I just found out."

"Again, I don't think this is such a big deal," Paige jumped in. "So what? We were practically teenagers. Who cares?"

"The story she wrote," Athas continued. "Suggests that our connection has been strong over the years and that basically, Jorge is controlling my whole campaign."

"I am merely advising you," Jorge stated. "I have said this all along."

"But she makes it sound like there's something sinister because of my connection with Paige," Athas continued. "I will send you the article, but there's a lot of innuendos in it."

"Suggesting what?"

"That we planned this for a long time," Athas continued. "That you groomed me to take on this role for years. Even when I was doing social worker, it was leading to creating an image."

"Oh, for fuck sakes!" Jorge complained. "I did not even know you back then."

"I wasn't even talking to you then," Paige reminded him. "I wasn't even in Canada, and I hadn't even met Jorge yet."

"I know, but she's desperate to connect the dots," Athas said with a loud sigh.

"What a stupid *puta*," Jorge said, "does she not realize this could be a mistake on her behalf."

"She just wants clicks on the article,' Athas reminded him. "It's a game."

"Life," Jorge sat ahead in his chair, directing his attention to the phone. "It is all a game if you have not noticed yet."

"I just want to make the country a better place," Athas spoke dreamily.

"And I just want to give my daughter a fucking unicorn for her birthday," Jorge sharply replied. "But we both would be living in a fantasy world there."

"Ok, let's just calm down," Paige spoke up. "Let's get this into perspective. Her story won't prove true. Unless she has proof, she has nothing."

"She just says 'sources say' throughout the article," Athas replied. "We could take her to court, but if that were the case, it would still be too late for this campaign."

"You could just say she is bitter because you broke up with her," Paige suggested, causing Jorge to raise his eyebrows. "I mean, it does come across that way."

"Then I have to admit to *being* with her," Athas sounded discouraged. "I would rather not do that."

"That's fair," Jorge nodded. "I can imagine that when I turn my phone back on, I will have lots of messages about this here article."

"Talk to Makerson," Paige suggested. "Do an interview and point out that you didn't know him until you met me and that you *do* advise him, but for stuff like water in indigenous communities and child abusers getting stricter punishments."

"No one can argue that these are good suggestions," Athas replied. "If you can do an interview first, I will follow your lead, whatever you say."

"I will call Makerson right away," Jorge said. "And Ryerson, I will be taking care of."

"Do I want to know?" Athas asked.

"No," Jorge shook his head. "You do not."

"No, let *me* take care of her," Paige sternly replied. "I think her time is up."

The two exchange looks.

Jorge's prediction that several messages would be waiting for him when he turned his phone back on was correct. Glancing through them, he did his best to acknowledge each before calling Makerson.

"We need to do an interview."

"I was thinking the same thing."

"We need to do it right away."

"Can you come to the production house?" Makerson asked. "We can set things up. I'll post on social media that you'll address these accusations."

"I will be there soon," Jorge said, already standing up. His eyes met with Paige's before he looked away to end the call.

"Think before you talk."

"Paige, you know I always do."

"But I also know," She stood up. "That this is a sensitive topic for you. And so does Ryerson. That's why she brought it to the forefront. It's not a coincidence."

"I know this too, Paige," Jorge nodded. "Do not worry. I know what I will say."

"And I will take care of her."

"Let us just wait a minute or two," Jorge put his hands out and laughed. "Paige, she cannot suddenly have her throat slit. It will look suspicious."

"But she might have an accident."

"Go talk to Marco," Jorge suggested. "Let us see what you can learn."

"We'll talk later," Paige headed for the door, with Jorge behind her. "Let me know when your interview is going live."

"Of course, *mi Amor,*" Jorge reached for her hand and squeezed it as she opened the office door. "I was thinking…"

"What the *hell* happened at school today," Maria was on the other side, forcing Jorge to readjust his thoughts. "I heard you were there. I didn't do anything this time. I was…"

"Maria, this here is fine," Jorge shook his head. "I do not have time to talk right now…"

"Then why were you at school today," Maria countered as she pushed her laptop bag up, as it started to fall off her shoulder. She was still wearing her jacket. "Mr. Anthony has it out for me and…"

"This is over," Jorge cut her off. "I have taken care of the situation, trust me, he will not give you problems anymore, or anyone else, for that matter."

"*Papá,*" Maria leaned in and lowered her voice. "Did you kill him?"

"Maria, no, of course not," Jorge couldn't help but laugh. "But he no longer has a job at your school."

"Why is that?"

"I do not have time to talk about it now," Jorge attempted to pass her. "I have a meeting to attend."

"No meeting starts without you," Maria reminded him. "So, why did you go there today? Did he call you? Did you have him fired?"

"Maria, I go there," Jorge decided it was easier to explain, or she'd never let him out of the house. "Because I hear that he reports your behavior, this group you are in, to the police. I went to sort this out, and I find him in a compromising situation, which he was fired for. I cannot get into details now, but that is all you need to know."

"Oh," Maria appeared surprised. "That sounds sketchy and gross."

"Your principal," Jorge nodded as he eased past her. "He was sketchy and gross, Maria. But I will tell you more later. The point is that you will no longer have issues, but please, do keep yourself under the radar. I do not want to go to that school again unless it's for your graduation."

Maria nodded and shared a look with Paige. Jorge headed for the door and jumped in his SUV. Pulling out of the driveway, all he could think about was ruining Holly Anne Ryerson's life.

CHAPTER 31

"This here," Jorge spoke assertively in response to Tom Makerson's question. "It is a non-issue. I do not know where this picture came from, but it has no relevance. It was at least twenty years ago."

"Were you aware of your wife's relationship with Alec Athas in the past?" Makerson asked the preplanned questions.

"Oh yes, of course!" Jorge faked a smile. "But I mean, again, this was twenty years ago, so I was not so worried."

Makerson laughed.

"Look, my wife, she dated Alec Athas many years ago when they were both barely out of their teens," Jorge attempted to downplay the relationship. "They remained friends over the years. When he got involved in politics, I offered to advise him, and here we are. There is nothing very unusual about this story."

"Does he follow many of your advisements?" Makerson tilted his head in interest.

"Some," Jorge lied. "He takes some of what I say and, you know, leaves other things. And this here is fine. Again, I only advise, I do not instruct. Prime Minister Athas makes his own decisions, and I do the best to support him."

"So the reports of," Makerson glanced down at the iPad on his lap. "You 'ruling the show from behind the scenes' are inaccurate?"

To this, Jorge let out an abrupt laugh, his head falling back.

"Do you not think," Jorge finally regained himself. "That if I had that kind of power, I would not use it to my advantage? That I would not change laws to suit my own companies? You do not see this here. Look at what Alec Athas has done in his years in office. He has helped to put stricter guidelines on pharmaceutical companies and worked with indigenous communities to improve their water. Although I feel these are great policies, they certainly do not affect me personally. I did support and encourage them, but you know, does this affect me on a professional or personal level? I would have to say no."

"Even the pharmaceutical changes?" Makerson challenged. "Wouldn't stricter laws help you out at *Our House of Pot*?"

"No, I mean, people still will use pharmaceuticals if that's their choice," Jorge shook his head. "This ensures that they are safer for the people. That is my concern. It should never be profit over safety."

"As his advisor," Makerson continued. "Are there any specific changes he's made or announced that you are particularly pleased with?"

"Although I am happy with much of what he has decided to do," Jorge considered for a moment. "I like his recent announcement about getting tougher on people who abuse children. As you know, I am a father, which is my most important job. I would do anything for my children, for my family, and I know this is how most parents feel. However, we often feel powerless in the world we live in. These new changes that Athas wants to make ensure all child abusers are punished. This here pleases me a great deal. We, as a society, talk a lot about how important our children are, but then these terrible people are arrested for hurting them, and what do they get? A slap on the hand? What message does this send to children? What does it say about their value? It tells them that we do not mean what we say."

"And you feel this new law will help to change that?"

"I know it will," Jorge nodded. "With what Athas is proposing, child predators, child abusers, anyone who hurts a child will be properly punished for their actions. This is necessary because a minor punishment tells the child, the abuser, and our society as a whole, that it's not such a big deal. It says, we advise you not to do this, but we won't punish you if you do. This here, it is wrong."

"Were you behind advising Athas on this issue?"

"Well, yes, I did advise it," Jorge spoke honestly. "As I said, I have children. I want nothing but the best for them. In my life, I have seen people who have suffered from abuse and how it changes them, changes who they are. It can be quite devastating. This here, it is not acceptable."

There was a brief flicker of concern in Makerson's eyes when he looked at Jorge, but he blinked it away.

The interview came to a smooth landing shortly afterward, as a peacefulness filled the room. It was only after the interview concluded that Makerson hesitantly asked Jorge a question that heavily sat in the room, invisible to the viewers.

"That sounded pretty personal," Makerson hesitantly offered as he stood, iPad still in hand.

"This is because it was," Jorge admitted as he stood, shuffling around uncomfortably. "It was a different time. People back then, they were not like today. That is the only explanation I can give that keeps me sane. And to tell you the truth, I'm not even sure it worked."

Makerson gave him a sympathetic look.

"But, you know, life moves forward," Jorge continued. "And we must move forward too. I cannot change the past, but I can do whatever I can to influence the future."

Makerson nodded as if unsure of what to say.

"Anyway," Jorge decided to break the tension in the room. "My daughter, she starts here soon?"

"In a few days," Makerson replied.

"Make her work hard," Jorge insisted as he started for the door. "Let her learn that this is important."

"I will."

"I must go," Jorge reached for the doorknob. "There's somewhere I gotta be."

After he was out of the room, he could finally breathe again. His body felt light as he made his way down the hallway. He didn't get far before the boardroom door swung open. Andrew was sitting in an office chair, giving him a thumbs up.

"We got it."

"All of it?"

"Right till you walked out the door."

Jorge nodded.

"That should help," Tony spoke from inside the room as Jorge slowly moved toward the exit, and Andrew pulled his chair back. "We cut it abruptly as if it were a mistake that your conversation went live, but people are reacting. You're winning them over."

"Then my plan," Jorge replied as he turned on his phone. "It did work."

Another door opened, and Makerson stuck his head out. He didn't say anything, but the two men shared a smile.

His phone rang. It was Maria.

"I must take this call," Jorge said as he started to move away. "I will talk to you later."

Walking toward the exit, Jorge answered the call.

"*Hola.*"

"*Papá*, you were live and…"

"I know, Maria."

"But…"

"It was on purpose," Jorge muttered into the phone as he walked out the door and headed for his SUV.

"But why would you…"

"Maria," Jorge cut her off. "Why do you think? I want you to take a moment and think about everything that happened."

"Well, Paige told me about the picture."

"Which I addressed," Jorge said as he got into his vehicle.

"And you said that you only advised Athas."

"*Sí.*"

"And that it was only advisement," Maria continued. "That it had no benefit to you."

"Yes."

"But *Papá,* I think you have some benefits," Maria continued. "Like the changes to Big Pharma…."

"Maria, what is important here," Jorge cut her off again. "Is that the people they think Athas and me are trustworthy. So many politicians today, they read from a script. They lie. My association with Athas, it affects him. I need to be as trustworthy in their eyes as he is since I have influence. I have left them with an impression, an image of me. Yes, I influenced this change to the law, but I was also a victim at one time."

"So, by hearing you talk off the record…."

"It shows who I am."

"And you never talked about it publicly," Maria said and paused. "I think I understand."

"I did not air my dirty laundry as many others do," Jorge replied. "But that does not mean I don't have any."

Maria fell silent. She finally took a deep breath and continued.

"People are talking online."

"And what are they saying?"

"They're saying how brave you are," Maria replied. "That you never publicly spoke of your abuse, but instead, tried to improve the laws for other people."

"Maria, trust me," Jorge gently spoke. "You will see, this accidental slip will have many benefits."

"No one is talking about the picture anymore," Maria observed.

"No, and no one will," Jorge insisted. "They are like vultures, always looking for a new carcass to feed off."

"But don't you want to avoid attention?"

"This here it is fine," Jorge replied. "It is intriguing enough to change their train of thought but not scandalous enough to keep their interest long. Trust me, this story it will help Athas and help me too. Maria, most things that are 'leaked' are *not* really leaked. Add that to your book."

Maria giggled. He referred to the red book where she had been writing all the lessons she had learned from her father. These lessons would help her one day lead the family.

"I will, *Papá*."

"Now, I must go," Jorge spoke gently. "I have some other business to take care of."

Ending the call, he started the SUV and pulled out of the parking lot.

Now, he had to figure out what to do about Holly Anne Ryerson.

CHAPTER 32

"I tried to reach out to your people…." Holly Anne Ryerson attempted to explain herself before Jorge abruptly cut her off.

"I don't got people," Jorge stood at the end of the boardroom table at the *Princesa Maria,* hovering over the reporter. "And I don't got a story for *you* either."

"I just thought…"

"You thought wrong," Jorge replied as he sat down, continuing to glare at the middle-aged woman. "But you knew if you came here and harassed Chase, he would find me for you."

"I wasn't sure where else to go."

Jorge glared at her but didn't reply.

"Can we talk?" Ryerson continued as she leaned ahead, then pulled back. "It's not like I have my phone or anything on me to record what you say."

Jorge glanced behind him, where Chase stood.

"I took her phone," Chase confirmed. "It's at the bar, and I checked her for listening devices."

"How thoroughly?" Jorge countered. "She could have one stuck up her twat. This here wouldn't surprise me."

"I…I would rather not…"

"Chase," Jorge turned and shook his head. "This here is fine. Have you spoke to Marco?"

Jorge nodded, which indicated that the IT specialist was on his way.

"Very good," Jorge turned his attention back to Ryerson. "We are fine here, Chase. Let me talk to Miss Ryerson alone."

"Ok," Chase replied and left the room, closing the door behind him.

"Now, it is interesting that you show up here looking for me," Jorge commented as he watched Ryerson with interest. "Because I was thinking about talking to you as well. I am curious where you found a picture of my wife with Athas, and even more so, I am curious about why you would share it?"

"Well, obviously, there's a strong connection between your wife and Alec," She spoke innocently enough as if she had no motives. "It goes back for too long to not be meaningful. I'm more curious why you chose to hide it."

"No one hid anything," Jorge shook his head. "But it wasn't relevant enough to mention."

"I disagree."

"And I don't care."

"I think you are controlling the government," Ryerson said. "You're telling Alec what to do and how to do it. I probably am just scraping the surface. Who knows how entrenched you are in all of this?"

"You," Jorge pointed at her. "You have an active imagination. But remember, you report the news...facts, not make-believe drama. And that's all this here is."

"And this new revelation," Ryerson continued as her confidence grew. "That you were an abused child and therefore, you suddenly care about the well-being of all children, well, that's just..."

"You don't believe me, lady?" Jorge sharply cut her off. "Are you saying you think I am lying about being abused?"

"Well, I think that..."

"Have you ever been beaten with a belt?" Jorge cut her off again. "Across the back until you almost passed out?"

Holly Anne fell silent. Her face fell.

"I do not mean the light S&M that helps get you off," Jorge pushed harder, leaning closer to her while she sat back. "I mean *beaten*. Beaten to hurt you. Beaten out of anger, out of hatred? Have you ever had this happen to you, Ms. Ryerson? Have you? Have you ever had someone attack you?"

All the color drained from her face, and she shook her head no.

"Then do *not* speak to me about how I *suddenly* care about the well-being of children," Jorge sharply retorted. "*I* have been that child. *I* have children. Not everything, Ms. Ryerson, is a political game. At least, not for me. Do you understand?"

"I'm not denying that *maybe* you…"

Jorge jumped up from the chair, pulled up his suit jacket and shirt, turning around. Knowing the scars on his back were quite visible, he wasn't surprised when he heard her gasp. Pulling his shirt and jacket back down, Jorge turned back around.

"Now, lady, do you *still* not believe me?"

"Ok, but what about all the other stuff?" She stuttered, although it was clear to him that she was losing ground.

"What other stuff?" Jorge snapped as he fixed his shirt and sat back down. "Tell me, I am curious."

"Well, for example, they say that your production house's new cartel show was based on your life," Ryerson started, "that you used to be in the cartel, and you came here to take over the government."

With that, Jorge's head fell back in laughter.

"Lady, you must be crazy to believe this," Jorge finally composed himself. "If I was in the cartel, do you think I would be here? In Canada? Working a legit business? I understand that here in Canada, you only know cartels from what you see on television and movies, but I assure you, many of these people end up in prison or dead."

Intrigued, she nodded.

"I am very much alive," Jorge calmed down. "And I am not in prison."

She didn't reply.

"The cartel, they do not let you go so easily," Jorge continued. "This I know."

"But *how* do you know that?'

"Because I spent most of my life in Mexico," Jorge reasoned with her. "I hear things. Our news is not as gentle as your news here in Canada. If you were a reporter in Mexico, lady, you would report on mass murders because of the cartels. You would report on innocent people getting caught in the crossfires and tourists getting murdered when they go to the wrong places."

She nodded in understanding, her defenses down.

"That is," Jorge continued. "If you report on anything at all because a lot of nosey reporters in Mexico, they are murdered."

She stiffened, and they shared a look.

"Ms. Ryerson, does that not make you happy to be a reporter in a safe country like Canada?"

She flinched.

"How lucky you must feel," Jorge spoke in a condescending tone as he stared into her eyes. His cruel glare spoke volumes.

"Ok," She finally replied. "I guess then…"

"There is no story here," Jorge cut her off. "The only story is the one you make up, and I would not recommend you do this."

She nodded and slowly stood up.

"Did I say you could leave?" Jorge continued to glare at her.

Without replying, Ryerson sat back down.

"Now, lady," Jorge continued. "Let me be clear about something. There is no story about my wife and Athas. There is no story about my supposed influence on the government. There is no story about my past. There is no story about me being in the cartel. So, I suggest you stop looking under the hood because you do not know what you are even looking at."

"I understand," She said in a quiet voice. "I just thought…"

"*Think* about something else," Jorge cut her off. "But not me, and not Athas, because this ends here."

He finally let her go. After hearing the door close, he stood up and went to where she sat. Reaching under the table, he checked for a listening device but found nothing. He turned his attention to the chair. It was clean.

After adjusting his shirt, Jorge left the VIP room and headed for the bar. Both Marco and Chase were in their usual spots.

"I never saw a sober person almost trip over their own feet on the way out that door," Chase pointed toward the exit. "Until just now."

At the end of the bar, Marco giggled.

"Well, we had a stern conversation," Jorge replied. "She knows to keep her fucking mouth shut."

"I thought she was going to forget her phone. She was in such a hurry," Chase continued as he leaned against the counter. "But she managed to hobble over here."

"Marco, did you find anything?" Jorge asked the Filipino, who was already nodding.

"It was easy to get in, sir," Marco replied. "I am able to spy on her phone, and she will never know."

"You kind of do that anyway," Chase reminded him.

"Yes, but sir, there are some limits if you don't have physical access to the phone," Marco reminded him. "I saw a lot while she was in the VIP room."

"She had a plan?" Jorge asked.

"Yes," Marco nodded. "She wanted to push you to find out information about your past, but also she was planning to 'Me too' Athas."

"Oh, is this so?" Jorge asked with interest as he sat at the bar. "You got a coffee for me there, Chase?"

"Coming up," Chase turned around and reached for the coffee mugs on the counter.

"Sir, I do not think she will be doing this now," Marco said as he glanced at his laptop. "I already see where she is contacting her boss, saying that the 'plan is off'."

"It better stay fucking off," Jorge muttered as Chase passed him a coffee. "That is all I will say."

"Sir, this here is almost guaranteed."

"Yeah, she wanted to say Athas used his power to force her to have sex," Chase shook his head. "As if he were going to do that, he'd pick her."

"Yes, lots of hot reporters," Jorge shook his head. "But he chooses this one? This here makes sense."

Both men laughed at his comment.

"Keep an eye though, Marco," Jorge continued.

"Her messages, sir," Marco shook his head. "She is nervous."

"Well, it better be the end of this bullshit," Jorge insisted. "Or it will be the end of *her.*"

CHAPTER 33

"I still can't believe you put that out there," Maria commented to Jorge over dinner that night. The aroma of garlic and pasta filled the air. At the end of the table, Miguel stuck his hand into a bowl of spaghetti. Paige made a face and grabbed a napkin while Jorge focused on Maria. "*Papá,* you always say to keep family business quiet."

"*Sí,* Maria, but there is a reason I did so," Jorge reminded her as he reached for another slice of garlic bread. "The people, they must believe you. Public figures, such as politicians, they lie. So, you must give them a reason to believe that you are real and truthful."

"But you aren't a politician," Maria reminded him. "I mean, you're in the public eye, but…"

"Yes, but I am advising a politician," Jorge reminded her. "And also, I am the head of an empire. People, they do not trust rich people, especially those in business. And really, Maria, they have every reason not to trust these people. Few have gotten to the top by being ethical, that I know. They play a role, but behind closed doors, it's another story."

"But *Papá,*" Maria leaned in, lowering her voice. "You've got to the top."

"Maria, we both know that I have done so by some unethical means," Jorge reminded her with a grin. "But this here is the past. The point is that your image is important."

Maria fell silent. Jorge could see she was considering his words.

"In the end," Jorge continued as he looked around the kitchen table. "Nothing I do is by accident. Everything it is all just another chess move."

In the days that followed, podcasters and reporters discussed Jorge's accidental confession. Most saw it as genuine, while others were skeptical it was truthful. In the end, Makerson suggested that Jorge release a statement to the media, giving as few details as possible but confirming that he was an abused child.

"Make it short and sweet," Makerson suggested from the other side of the boardroom table. "But I wouldn't get into many details. Just give them what they have to know."

"This here, it makes sense," Jorge agreed.

"I already wrote up something," Makerson passed him the iPad. "I need you to approve it or make changes, whatever you think."

Glancing at the screen, Jorge squinted and read the statement. Nodding his head, he looked back up.

"Does it sound ok?"

Jorge looked down again and read it aloud.

"Recently, private information about my childhood was released to the public. Although I will not deny that I grew up in an abusive home, I do not wish to discuss it in further detail. For the sake of my family, I prefer to keep my personal life private. Child abuse fundamentally changes those affected: and for that reason, I fully support Alec Athas in his plans to create harsher laws toward abusers. This is a community problem, and as a community, we must work together to solve it."

"Anything you wish to add?" Makerson asked as Jorge slid the iPad back to him. "Or change?"

"No, this here, it is perfect," Jorge nodded. "I like it."

"I thought we should address it since it came out of this office," Makerson turned the device off. "But I will say, it's working in your favor. People find you more authentic since this information came out. You've been discussed in various podcasts, including Sabrina Supergirl's channel."

Jorge rolled his eyes.

"I know, but for what you want to do," Makerson nodded. "This is a good thing."

"The world is becoming a crazy place," Jorge shook his head. "How you are viewed on social media, it is somehow important. Things have gotten so complicated. I worry about my children. Growing up in this world now is difficult."

"Well, Maria has been here two days," Makerson gestured toward the boardroom door. "And already, she is fitting in, so there isn't any need to worry."

"People know she is my daughter."

"Yes," Makerson said. "But don't worry, they're giving her work. I was clear that she is here to work, not to sit around on her phone all day."

"This is good," Jorge nodded. "Too many, they do not teach their children the value of hard work."

"That's because most people don't know it themselves," Makerson suggested. "They have no loyalty."

"You know how I feel about loyalty," Jorge took a deep breath. "And Maria does too."

"I also wanted to mention," Makerson continued. "We're watching social media closely to see how Athas is doing. I see a definite uptake in the last few days, but the election isn't over yet."

"It's getting close, though," Jorge said as he and Makerson stood up. "Athas could run into a burning building on the first day of the campaign and save a baby, but people forget fast. They only know what is right behind or in front of them."

"Unfortunately, that's true."

"This can be good for a politician sometimes," Jorge continued. "And not so much other times."

"Well, if we have to," Makerson reminded him. "We can always arrange for him to run into a burning building at the end of the campaign."

Jorge grinned as he turned to walk out of the door with Makerson in tow.

"Do not think I had not thought of that," Jorge muttered as they walked into the hallway. Hearing a familiar voice nearby, he stopped. "Is that Andrew?"

"Him and Sonny are prepping for the next episode of *Raging Against the Machine*," Makerson tilted his head to the right.

"I gotta talk to him," Jorge said, and Makerson nodded.

"We'll be in touch," Makerson pointed the other way. "I gotta get ready for the show tonight."

"Very good," Jorge said and headed in the opposite direction. Finding the room where Andrew's voice was coming from, Jorge knocked on the glass door to capture his attention before walking in.

"You got something for me, or what?" Jorge asked as he glanced between the two men.

"I heard rumors that a local private school principal was caught in a compromising situation with one of his students," Andrew boldly remarked as Jorge closed the door behind him. "But I don't name the school."

"Speak of it as if it could just be a rumor," Jorge suggested.

"I plan to," Andrew nodded, and Sonny nodded. "The idea is that we want to talk about how often this shit happens. You know, camp leaders, church leaders, bosses, anyone in power over kids. I mean pedos look for situations where they can be around kids. It's fucked up."

"And I'll discuss," Sonny added in, "that there are a lot of hoops for people to jump through to work with children. We plan to go back and forth on it. It gives people food for thought."

"But we aren't mentioning Athas at *all*," Andrew insisted. "Because that would be too fucking obvious. We're just saying how the way it is now, these fuckers pretty much get away with it and are on the street to do it again."

"And as a gay man," Sonny added in. "I'm talking about how my community often is victimized."

"And we're gonna talk about that rich fuck who was pimping out kids," Andrew pointed toward his laptop. "You know, it was all over the news…"

"Then suddenly disappeared," Sonny added. "Even though he had some big names associated with him."

"I like this here," Jorge nodded. "Any chance we can find any holes in the opposition stand on this issue?"

"Good point," Sonny nodded. "They haven't been saying much about any of this."

"Probably cause they ain't got much to say, period," Andrew snickered. "Those fuckers are falling in the polls and fast!"

"*Perfecto!*"

"If you try to argue against being harsher with child abusers," Andrew said. "Then you might be a *motherfucker.*"

"There is that," Jorge grinned.

"And I heard Jolene is moving back to town," Andrew continued. "Please tell me you aren't bringing that lunatic here."

"No, that lunatic will be nowhere close to this place," Jorge confirmed. "And if I have my way, that lunatic will be out of the city soon."

"Like, permanent?" Andrew held his fingers up to his head as if to shoot himself.

"No, not in that way," Jorge shook his head. "Although it is tempting, isn't it?"

"But, I know, it's Diego's sister," Andrew turned toward Sonny, who was cringing. "Oops, sorry, I said that name I am not to speak of."

"I didn't say that," Sonny corrected him. "I just prefer we don't talk about him."

"You need to fucking go to his house and…"

"I don't go where I'm not wanted," Sonny sat up straight. "If he doesn't want me there, then…"

"Ok, this here soap opera," Jorge shook his head. "I do not want to hear about but, if you wish to speak to him, he is home."

Andrew turned to Sonny, who made a face and shook his head.

"Anyway," Jorge attempted to get the conversation back on track. "I will be watching later. Let me know what people are saying."

Before Jorge even had a chance to leave the building, he got a text from Paige.

I think something is going on next door. Hurry home.

CHAPTER 34

"Who the fuck is this?" Jorge asked when arriving at Diego's house to find him standing near the entryway with a baseball bat in hand. On the floor was a muscular, white man. Paige stood wide-eyed behind her husband. "Is this here one of your boyfriends, Diego? Did you have an argument?"

"No," Diego shook his head, squinted his eyes, and twisted his lips. "No, this is some random fuck looking for Jolene."

"Oh, so one of *her* boyfriends?" Jorge nodded as he walked in the house. "Now, this here makes sense. Leave it to Jolene to leave a mess for us to clean up."

"I'm not her boyfriend."

Jorge looked down at the man on the floor as Paige closed the door behind them. He was attempting to sit up.

"And don't hit me again!" He directed his comment toward Diego.

"You come to my house and show me a gun," Diego replied. "Then I hit you with a baseball bat, and that's because I couldn't get to my gun fast enough."

"Ok, let us calm down," Jorge put his hand in the air. "What exactly happened here?"

"Diego sent me a text," Paige jumped in. "That some random guy was at his door."

"I got a bad feeling," Diego explained. "Then this fucking idiot comes asking for Jolene. I said she don't live here anymore, and he made a point of showing me his gun when he asked if I was sure."

"Trust me, if she were," Jorge said. "We wouldn't hold you back."

"She made a mess of my fucking house while I was gone, and…"

"Diego," Jorge cut him off. "We will talk about that another time. First, I want to know why this guy was looking for Jolene. What kind of shit is she into now?"

"She owes me money."

"For what?" Diego skeptically asked.

"I did something for her."

"Could you be a little more specific," Paige piped up.

"She got me to follow her boyfriend or husband or whatever he is around," He replied while attempting to stretch his leg out. "You know, I think you broke my fucking leg. I can barely move it."

"Threaten to call the police, and I will break more than your fucking leg," Diego shot back.

"Why were you following Jolene's husband?" Paige asked.

"She thought he was cheating."

"Too much drama!" Jorge complained. "So, let's get to the point, she owes you for your services?"

"Yes."

"Why didn't she pay?" Diego asked suspiciously.

"I suspect 'cause she didn't like what I had to say," He shook his head. "They never do. They hire me to see if their husbands are cheating on them, then get mad when I prove that they are."

"So, her husband was cheating?" Diego asked with interest.

"Yeah, with this frisky little lady," He said while carefully stretching out his leg.

"He got a type," Jorge muttered.

"Yeah, well, she flipped out and refused to pay me," The man continued. "Said I was lying. I wasn't lying. I got pictures, but she refused to look."

"I guess the cheating only goes one way with Jolene," Jorge commented and reached out to help the man off the floor. "What does she owe you?"

"You aren't really going to pay him, are you?" Diego countered. "Let Jolene pay her fucking bills."

The man stood up slowly, hesitant to put weight on his leg.

"Diego, *you,* you're paying him," Jorge insisted. "You're the one who lost his mind and hit this guy. Plus, it's your fucking sister."

"He had a gun," Diego insisted.

"I need a gun," The man started. "It's pretty dicey out there. You gotta be careful."

"Diego will settle your bill, and I will pay you extra if you got any shit on Jolene," Jorge said as the man finally stood upright on his own.

"I don't got much, really," He insisted. "The lady was frantic when she thought her man was cheating on her. Like, a little desperate, which surprised me because she's hot, but you know, crazy."

"So far, you ain't telling me anything I didn't know," Jorge shook his head.

"There isn't much to tell," He shook his head. "She came to me, asking for help, and I did what she asked, and well....she took off and didn't pay. I tracked her down, and here I am. There's not much else to tell."

"Where's your business?" Jorge asked.

"Everywhere," He reached in his pocket and pulled out a card, his gun fully exposed as he did. "If you ever need to reach me."

Glancing at the card, Jorge nodded.

"Thank you, Mr. Ritchie," Jorge said. "I will keep this in case I need your services."

After he left, Jorge turned to Diego, who was halfway to the kitchen.

"So you, find your fucking sister and tell her to be a little smarter if she's not gonna pay people," Jorge reminded him. "You don't need her problems on *your* doorstep."

"This is Jolene," Diego reminded him as he reached into the cupboard for a bag of coffee. "Her problems somehow always become all *our* problems."

"Well, you can talk to her about reimbursing you, at least," Jorge insisted as he turned to his wife. Her eyes were full of concern.

"Jorge, you need to calm down," Paige gently said as she reached for his hand. "Let's go home. The house is empty and quiet..."

"The house is empty, *mi amor?*" Jorge raised an eyebrow and squeezed her hand.

"Maria's at school, and Miguel is in daycare. Tala is in her English class…"

Jorge didn't reply at first, as he looked into her eyes. He finally turned his attention back to Diego. "Are you ok here?"

"I'm ok."

"You're not going to beat the fuck out of anyone with a baseball bat once we leave?"

"I can't promise that," Diego reminded him. "I take it one minute at a time."

"Go talk to Jolene."

"Oh," Diego frowned. "I will be talking to her all right."

"Adios," Jorge grinned as he headed for the door. "We will talk more later."

Once outside, Paige turned to him.

"You get too upset with…"

"No one's home, you said?" Jorge asked as he studied her face. "We have the house to ourselves?"

"Yes."

"Are you sure?"

"Positive."

"No surprise returns home early?"

"I don't think so."

"Then maybe," Jorge said as they entered the house, and he pulled her close. "We need to take advantage. I will turn my phone off, and we will have some alone time…"

She answered by leaning in and kissing him.

The couple headed upstairs to their bedroom, where Paige closed the door. They quickly undressed, and Jorge wasted no time pulling his wife close and reaching for her naked breast. His lips met hers as he massaged her left breast slowly until her nipple grew hard, and his other hand slid down her back to cup her hip. He maneuvered her toward the bed, moving her down onto the mattress, where he joined her.

"This here, we haven't had enough of lately," Jorge muttered as he pulled her close. His tongue slid down her neck, leading to her breast, where he greedily pulled it into his mouth. His fingers made their way between her legs, causing her to moan and lean back. She began to move.

He felt her tighten around his fingers as his thumb rubbed the soft skin on the outside, causing her breath to increase until a soft moan escaped her lips.

Feeling his excitement intensify, he quickly removed his hand to lay on his back. Paige found her position on top of him as she straddled his body. Jorge grasped her hips as her body slowed but quickly picked up the pace, leaning forward. Jorge squeezed her hips and pushed his torso up, causing her to let out a loud whimper.

"Oh, God!" She was crying out as she moved faster as Jorge's eyes transfixed on breasts bouncing, her eyes closed as she leaned back, with a vulnerable expression on her face. This is what he loved.

Things intensified until Jorge felt pleasure ringing through his body, followed by a sense of comfort. His heart continued to race to almost a level that scared him, but he could die at that moment, and it would be worth it. He took a deep breath as Paige snuggled up to him. Jorge opened his eyes and leaned in to kiss her.

"The magic, it is not gone yet," He teased as his body relaxed.

"That's because it's real," She replied. "Not like Jolene's relationships."

"Well, that there," Jorge shook his head. "Is a disaster. There are no other ways to see it."

"She makes it a disaster."

"But still, as long as there is Diego," Jorge commented as he pulled her closer. "She is, unfortunately, a part of our *familia.*"

"She creates undue stress."

"For her and everyone around her," Jorge calmly replied. "But that man, do you think he came this far over a few dollars?"

"I was wondering the same."

"I feel that there is more."

"Maybe he just wanted to find *her.*"

"He was kind of young, maybe her type, no?"

"I was thinking the same," Paige replied. "This is getting way too complicated."

"That is how she likes things," Jorge replied. "Complicated like a *telenovela.*"

"Jolene needs to start *watching* soap operas," Paige said as she sat up. "Not *live* them. I guess the positive side is that Maria has got over her crush on Chase."

"Yes, I agree, *mi amor,*" Jorge nodded. "That was starting to concern me."

"Well, she announced yesterday that she was ready to 'move on', so..."

"Wait, what?" Jorge was suddenly alert. "What do you mean by 'move on' exactly?"

"I think she has a boyfriend."

CHAPTER 35

"And what's *that* supposed to mean?" Maria prodded as she walked through the school hallway. Students brushed past her with little interest in the petit Mexican-Canadian girl, most involved in their conversations and dramas. Cameron backtracked on his earlier comment as they headed to their next class.

"I just mean," he started, as if stalling to pick his words carefully. "You had that *thing* for Chase and…"

"That's over," Maria abruptly cut him off. "I don't want to talk about Chase."

"I know," Cameron gently touched her shoulder, causing Maria's defenses to fall, if only slightly. "I'm just saying that it takes time to move on sometimes. It's normal. Remember when I had that thing for Daniel."

Daniel had been Cameron's piano teacher that he was crushing on. He obsessed over the twenty-something in a way that was borderline stalker, but Maria didn't have the heart to tell him. It wasn't the same as her deep feelings for Chase. Especially considering Cameron's instructor was a straight, married man. At least Maria knew Chase liked women. Although, his recent choices caused Maria to lower her opinion of him.

"But I've known Chase since I was ten," Maria couldn't help but remind him.

"I know," Cameron continued to show understanding. "But it sounds like, maybe he wasn't such a good guy…at least, not morally speaking. I mean, this Jolene woman…"

"I told you she's not a woman," Maria shook her head. "She's a whore."

"Ok," Cameron nodded. "But sometimes, men are like that. You know, they care about sex more than someone that's a good person."

Maria looked away, wanting to abandon the conversation. They had talked this one to death, and no matter what, nothing made her feel better about it.

"But Niko, he's different," Cameron touched her arm as if to get Maria's attention again. "He's your age, and he seems to really like you. It's been a couple of weeks now, right?"

Maria had met Niko at the rollerskating rink. It had been Cameron's idea to go. Maria had been slightly intrigued but probably wouldn't have gone if her best friend hadn't pushed her. As it turns out, Cameron's insistence that it would take her five minutes to catch on had been an exaggeration. But there was something exciting about the atmosphere; the lights, the music, the disco vibe, and the kids gliding by her in a mix of dancing and skating.

Of course, after seeing others fly past her, Maria decided to pick up speed and fell on her ass.

She was humiliated. Maria wanted to cry, she refused to show such a vulnerable state.

"Oh, sweetie!" Cameron was quick to lean over, reaching for her arm. "Are you ok?"

An unfamiliar voice chimed in. Maria looked up to see a cute guy leaning down on the other side of her, reaching out to help her up. Although the lights were low, she could see he was at least half Filipino, but there was something else there. He was cute, with kind eyes and smile. Her heart began to race as a song about love at first sight ironically played in the background. She'd later learn it was by Madonna and would secretly listen to it over and over.

"Thanks," Maria shyly replied as the two boys helped her to her feet. "I'm…kind of new at this…"

"It's ok," the boy with the kind eyes smiled at her. His hand seemed to linger on her back, as if he expected her to fall again. "Is this your first time here?"

"It is," Maria replied as she stared at the boy. "Thank you for helping me."

Later that night she'd learn that his name was Niko. He made a few more visits throughout the night, only to linger longer each time. Maria noticed he flitted between some Filipino kids and a couple white guys, but continually made his way back to her and Cameron.

"I think he likes you," Maria's best friend commented at the time.

Of course, Maria disagreed. She insisted that Niko was only being nice. Cameron was reading too much into it. By the night's end, her friend's prediction was proven correct. During a rare moment alone, Niko inquired about the social media platforms he might find her on. Things just happened from there.

"Yes," Maria finally answered Cameron's question as they headed to their last class. "It's been almost three weeks."

"What did your dad say?" Cameron asked with wide eyes. "I mean, I know he's so overprotective."

"Yeah," Maria nodded. "But I didn't tell him yet. Paige said she would sometime when he's relaxed and calm."

"Really?" Cameron made a face. "Your dad is *that* bad. It's not like you're pregnant."

"God, no!" Maria shook her head. "Things aren't going that fast."

"That's good," Cameron confirmed. "At least you know he really likes you. And he's not just some dirtbag....like Chase."

Maria gave him a look but couldn't help but laugh.

"Really," Cameron continued. "You think your dad will be all crazy about that?"

"He just thinks I'm too young to date," Maria replied. "He worries...a lot."

"As if anyone who knows your dad would ever do anything bad to you," Cameron sniffed. "God look at The Nazi..."

"Well, he's gone now," Maria reminded him. "I heard we might have a new principal next week."

"Did your dad know we called Mr. Anthony that, BTW?"

"Nah," Maria shook her head. "But it's probably not true 'cause I heard the girl he was trying to be pedo with wasn't a white girl…"

"Really?"

"Yeah, I dunno," Maria shrugged. "I mean, I might be wrong."

"There are rumors…"

"I think I heard the same rumors."

"But you know," Cameron said as they entered their final class of the day. "I think your dad would like Niko. He's a nice kid."

Maria didn't reply.

Her *Papá* brought up the topic while the family sat around the dinner table a few days later. Maria was embarrassed. He picked one of the nights Tala joined them for a meal. She usually opted to cook her own food in the luxurious basement apartment of the house. Maria couldn't blame her. It probably felt like she was never off the clock if she was stuck having dinner with them too. Still, she wished her father had brought it up in a more private discussion rather than around the table.

"So, Maria, I hear you have a boyfriend?" Jorge spoke bluntly, while wearing a forced smile.

She nearly choked on her food.

"Jorge," Paige started before Maria had a chance to reply. "Maybe that's a bit private to…"

"Nonsense!" Jorge waved his hand in the air. "We are family. There are no secrets. I'm just starting a conversation."

"It's ok," Maria shrugged. "It's a boy I met the night Cameron and I went to the rollerskating rink."

"Is that for kids?" Jorge asked.

"All ages," Maria replied and shrugged. "Sometimes they have a night just for kids too."

"Be careful, Maria," Jorge automatically warned. "Sometimes people, they go to these places because…"

"Jorge," Paige cut him off and shook her head. "I think it's fine."

"It's fine, *Papá*," Maria insisted. "They have security and stuff there."

"So, who is this boy?" Jorge continued.

"His name is Niko, and he's from another school."

"Which one?"

"A public one," Maria shrugged. "He's just normal, not rich."

"Is he a nice boy, Maria?" Tala gently asked.

"I think so," Maria shrugged. "He's half Filipino, Tala. His mom was from the Philippines."

Tala smiled and nodded.

"Half?" Jorge asked. "What's the other half? White?"

"You say that like it's a bad thing," Maria accused her father.

"Maria, I am married to a white woman," Jorge reminded her and pointed at Miguel at the end of the table, chewing on a piece of chicken. "The baby, he is half white..."

"He doesn't *look* very white," Maria reminded him.

"He's very much a Hernandez," Jorge sniffed.

"Actually Niko said the other side of his family," Maria said. "Is like half Portuguese and white."

Her father listened but showed no emotion.

"How old is he?" Paige asked, even though they had already discussed the topic of Niko on several occasions.

"Fifteen like me, almost sixteen."

Her father continued to be expressionless as he returned his attention to the food on his plate.

"Well, Maria," Jorge finally spoke up. "All I am going to tell you is to be careful and not to rush into anything. You are still very young. Don't lose sight of the things you want in this world. And for God sakes, do not become boy crazy."

"*Papá,* it's *one* guy!"

A glance toward her father revealed he was teasing. Giving his daughter a wink, Maria couldn't help but blush and look away.

She would later text Cameron to tell him the news.

Papá knows about Niko. He was fine.

You worry over nothing. It's not like your father can stop you from dating.

Maria said nothing but set her phone aside and laid back on her bed. Reaching for her journal, she stared at the word *Los Poderosos* and smiled.

CHAPTER 36

"You usually have an upsurge of book sales when you're doing public events," Makerson shook his head as he glanced at his laptop before returning his attention to Jorge on the other side of the table. "I'm guessing it's the revelation that you were an abused child that's caused an added interest in your life."

"People, they see a car accident, and they want to stop and stare," Jorge reminded him as he reached for his cup of coffee. "It is human nature."

"I hadn't thought of *House of Hernandez* sales at the time," Makerson confessed. "I guess that's a bonus."

"As long as it doesn't encourage too much interest in my past," Jorge reminded him. "I do not want these people digging further into my history."

"I don't think that will happen," Makerson confirmed. "You gotta also remember that people have short attention spans."

"This is what I am counting on," Jorge admitted. "But it is interesting that people find me to be a…fascinating public figure."

"It's working too," Makerson reminded him. "The election is coming to an end soon, and advance polls start this weekend. I think Athas has it unless he really fucks up between now and then."

Jorge raised his eyebrows.

"That's the scary part," Makerson continued. "Most people make up their minds at the last minute. This isn't the time to color outside the lines."

"Let us hope Athas knows this," Jorge shook his head. "Because the man is incredibly naive for someone running a country."

"I hadn't noticed," Makerson joked, causing Jorge to laugh.

"The debate on Monday," Jorge pointed toward the laptop and reached for his phone. "It went good."

"Athas did ok," Makerson agreed. "He could've been stronger though. That's the part I worry about. He's good, but he needs more power behind him. He sometimes comes across as too soft."

Jorge didn't say anything but turned on his phone.

"He got a few good swings in at Knapp," Makerson continued. "But unfortunately, Knapp got some swings in at him too. Maybe he'll do better in the next one."

"It is all theatre," Jorge insisted as he glanced at his phone as it came to life. "It is for entertainment purposes. In truth, we have seen what Athas has done already, but people have a short memory."

Makerson nodded but remained silent.

Jorge glanced over his messages and let out a loud sigh.

"I must go," Jorge stood up and reached for the paper cup labeled *Taza de Sol*. "There is some emergency or situation at the bar that I must take care of. Is there anything else I need to know before heading out?"

"I think everything else is fine," Makerson stood up. "I mainly wanted to talk to you about the book sales and Athas, but everything else is running smoothly."

"Maria, she is doing ok?" Jorge asked.

"I got her working," Makerson confirmed. "She's not sitting around. She doesn't have the time."

"*Perfecto.*"

A few minutes later, Jorge was in his SUV and pulling out of the parking lot. He knew Chase wasn't likely to call him over unless it was important, but they also had to be careful of how much they said through text. Although Marco had their messages encrypted and was adamant about their security, one could never be too careful. Fortunately, the *familia* had keywords that alerted him to any problems. Chase's message suggested they may have an unwanted visitor on the property.

That could mean a lot of things.

Driving toward the *Princesa Maria,* Jorge decided to call home to check in.

"Hello," Paige answered the phone in her usual tone.

"Hey, *mi amor,* is all fine?"

"Yes," She hesitated for a moment. "Is there a reason it mightn't be?"

"Nah," Jorge decided to brush it off. "I just worry, you know me."

"Anything else going on?"

"I have a visitor at the bar."

Silence.

"I am not sure who," Jorge calmly continued. "But I am told someone wants to see me."

"Do you need me to…"

"No, no," Jorge insisted. "I think this here is fine. I want to make sure all is well there."

"Yes, just sitting outside with Miguel," Paige confirmed. "Your crow is hanging around, and Miguel seems to think he can catch him, but that's not going so well for him."

To this, Jorge laughed.

"It is *my* crow," Jorge joked. "No one will ever catch him."

"Let me know what happens," Paige continued. "If I don't hear from you, I'm going over."

"This here, it is fine," Jorge insisted. "Do not worry, Paige."

"I do, though."

"It is fine, *mi amor,*" Jorge said as he turned onto the street behind the bar. "I will message you soon."

Arriving at the *Princesa Maria,* Jorge took his usual parking spot and glanced around. An expensive car sat nearby, indicating the potential visitor was waiting inside. He considered having Marco look into the plates but decided it would take too much time. Checking for his gun, he headed for the door.

Carefully opening the door, his eyes scanned the room. No one was in the main bar, but Chase stuck his head out of the VIP room and tilted his head, indicating the visitor was waiting inside. Jorge took a powerful stance as he headed across the floor, swiftly walking into the room. He found a man close to his age sitting at the table. He was a Mexican, also dressed in an expensive suit.

"Mr. Hernandez," The stranger rose from his chair, causing Jorge to reach for his gun, but suddenly stopped when realizing this was a gesture of courtesy, not an attack. "Thank you for meeting me today."

Jorge studied him for a moment and glanced at Chase.

"I'll be at the bar."

Jorge nodded as Chase left the room, closing the door behind him.

"So, I do not know who you are or why you are here," Jorge bluntly spoke as he walked toward his usual place at the table. "I was only told that someone was here to see me."

"Yes, I had a difficult time finding you," the man continued, unnerved by Jorge. "I did not mean to barge in without a meeting, but I was told you didn't take meetings…"

"I don't," Jorge cut him off, watching him with a cold stare.

"I had to meet you," the man continued, appearing nervous. "because of my daughter."

"Your daughter?" Jorge was confused. "I do not understand."

"My name is Juan Perez," he hesitated for a moment. "It was my daughter you found in Mr. Anthony's office, at the school…"

"Oh," Jorge felt his defenses drop as he reached out to shake his hand. "Oh yes, yes, I do understand. Please, sit down."

Jorge sat across from him.

"I had to meet with you," Juan continued as he sat back down. "I cannot thank you enough for stopping that sick man from whatever he was going to do…"

"I cannot take much credit," Jorge spoke humbly. "If I can be honest with you, I barged into his office to give him shit about something else, and your daughter, she just happened to be there."

"Did she…." Juan started. His face showed vulnerability. "I mean, she said nothing happened, but…I worry you know?"

"Of course," Jorge nodded in understanding. "I would be the same if it were my daughter, but from what I saw, I arrived before anything *could* happen."

Juan Perez showed some relief, if not sorrow, as he nodded.

"I can understand your concerns," Jorge continued, quickly reading the situation. "Sometimes the kids, they do not tell us everything, but I do not believe there was any reason for concern from what I saw. I promise you, if there had been, there would be hell to pay."

Juan gave an appreciative nod.

"It is terrible when you work hard to make something of your life," Jorge continued. "To put your children in the best of schools, only to find out they are run by the same fucking assholes that ran the public ones."

This caused Juan to laugh and nod.

"My parents worked hard to get to this country," Juan confirmed. "And even harder to get me through university. My family and I have done well, but it was not without sacrifices, and yet, here we are. Money, it seems, can only buy so much."

Jorge nodded. "This is true. I would trade everything I have to be sure my children were safe, that they would be happy, but it just does not work that way."

"*Si,*" Juan nodded. "It is not easy."

"So, what is happening with Mr. Anthony?"

"I was told very little," Juan confirmed. "But I can promise you he will not get away with what he did…or tried to do with my daughter. You do not mess with a man's family."

"I can appreciate this," Jorge nodded as he sat up straighter.

"Your media company," Juan continued. "They let the cat out of the bag, and that is good. They would otherwise try to hide it, push it under the rug."

"That won't be happening," Jorge confirmed. "I know what I saw, and I will not keep quiet."

"I appreciate this too," Juan said as he moved his chair back. "I must not take any more of your time. I only wanted to come to thank you in person, on behalf of me, and my family."

"I did not do much," Jorge reminded him. "But if you need anything more, do not hesitate to ask."

"Well, I think I got it covered," Juan admitted. "But we will see."

"So tell me," Jorge casually spoke as they headed for the door. "What kind of work do you do, Mr. Perez?"

CHAPTER 37

"When I was younger, I wanted to be one of Madonna's backup dancers," Diego confessed to Maria as the two sat side by side at one of the patio tables. Across from them sat Miguel, appearing intrigued by the conversation. "But I was never really much of a dancer."

"Well, Diego, it's never too late," Jorge teased as he stepped outside and looked around at his *familia;* everyone was there: Marco and his family, Makerson, Tony, and Andrew. Chase and Jolene kept their distance while Sonny attempted to help Paige and Tala with the barbecue. He found it interesting to see where people situated themselves at a social event. Fortunately, the patio was large and had more than one table in front of the pool.

"Oh, I think it's too late for me," Diego said with laughter in his voice. "I do good to stand up in the morning and not get a kink in my leg, let alone trying to dance for hours."

"I do recall you doing some dancing in your day," Jorge reminded him as he walked closer to the table while his eyes continued to glance around. "Sometimes right till dawn."

"It was a different time," Diego reminded him. "A very different time."

Jorge noted that Sonny was casually trying to eavesdrop. Chase and Jolene looked uncomfortable. It would be interesting to see how things played out.

"Dance," Miguel spoke up as he slithered around his chair, as if unable to get comfortable.

"Miguel!" Jorge turned to his youngest child. "Show us how you dance!"

The excited toddler was helped off his chair and started to shake his bum, causing everyone to laugh.

"Maybe Miguel will be a backup dancer one day," Maria laughed.

"Maria, where is your new boyfriend today," Jorge teased. "I thought you would have him here to introduce to everyone!"

"No," Maria's face turned crimson. "He's busy today."

"You have a boyfriend, Maria?" Jolene piped up as if seeing this as a way to start a conversation, but it was with little success.

"Yes," Maria answered abruptly and turned her attention back to Jorge. "I invited Cameron too. He might come later."

"I like Cameron," Diego nodded. "Good kid."

"Hot dogs and hamburgers are ready," Paige called out. "If the kids want to come over."

"Come on, Miguel," Maria stood up and reached for her baby brother's hand. "Let's go get something to eat."

"Hot dog!" Miguel screeched and grabbed his sister's hand.

"Hey," Diego gestured for Jorge to sit beside him. "I gotta ask you something."

"What is it, Diego?" Jorge asked as he sat in Maria's chair. "If this is work, I do not want to talk about it now."

"Nah, that's going fine," Diego admitted. "I'm getting back in the saddle, as they say."

Jorge raised an eyebrow.

"I wanted to ask about that guy who showed up at the bar the other day," Diego lowered his voice. "Chase said he had something to do with the situation at Maria's school?"

"His name is Juan Perez. He is the girl's father who the principal was trying to…"

"A Mexican?" Diego twisted his lips and nodded.

"Yes," Jorge continued. "He come to thank me for stopping things. I explained that I did not do anything, at least not on purpose."

"That's it?" Diego was suspicious.

"So far," Jorge nodded.

"You think there's more?" Diego asked.

"I have not seen the last of that man," Jorge guessed. "I suspect he will be back, and soon."

"He wants revenge?"

"I do not know," Jorge wondered that himself. "But I can tell I have not heard the last of him. He went to great efforts to find me. And yes, it was probably to know what I saw, out of fear that his daughter, she wasn't telling him everything. But I don't know, Diego. Something tells me there's more."

"I'm surprised when you walked in and saw a Mexican." Diego teased. "You didn't shoot first and ask questions later."

"Until I knew why he was there," Jorge admitted. "I was suspicious. Maybe a ghost from my past had appeared, but fortunately, this was not the case."

"So, what does he do?" Diego asked. "He got money if he has a kid in that school."

"That's the funny thing," Jorge began to laugh. "He tell me he runs that coffee company, *Taza de Sol*. I laughed and say, 'I had one of those cups in my hand earlier today!'"

"Oh wow," Diego thought for a moment. "Ironically, you claim to have started from a coffee company in Mexico, and this guy *did*. Kind of a coincidence."

"Yes, well, I was thinking the same," Jorge considered. "Coffee, you can sell it at huge markups, which I assume would make it so easy to launder money."

"I wondered the same."

"It could be legit."

"It *could* be legit."

The two men exchanged looks just as Maria returned to the table with Miguel. Already, the toddler had mustard all over the front of his t-shirt.

"Miguel," Jorge said as he stood up. "Look at your shirt. I think you have the whole bottle of mustard on there."

"Don't even ask!" Maria shook her head as she helped the child back on his chair and handed him the hot dog. "He even had mustard in his hair!"

"This here, it does not surprise me," Jorge commented as he glanced at the others making their way to the barbecue. "At least today, the weather is nice. Barbecue season, it is pretty much over for this year."

"It was cold this morning," Maria commented before biting into her hamburger.

"Winter is coming," Jorge muttered and exchanged looks with Diego. "I must go see about my steak."

On his way, Jorge stopped by Marco's table to talk to him and his family before heading toward Makerson and Tony. Both men were enjoying a steak while talking shop.

"Work can wait," Jorge cut them off as he sat down. "It's the weekend. It's a beautiful day. Do not worry about work."

"We were just thinking," Makerson began to explain. "HPC should have a special a few days before the election, but it might be too late to put it together. Andrew went over to run it by Sonny too."

"If we want to talk to the candidates," Tony shook his head. "We'll never get them now, but we can always do some kind of feature. I'm just not sure how to go about it."

"The goal is to get people to vote," Makerson directed his comment at Jorge. "Athas can have the biggest fan club ever, but if they don't get out on election day, then does it even matter?"

"Good point," Jorge nodded. "But maybe it is better if it's a bit insidious. A little at a time, day-by-day, rather than making it too obvious that we are involved."

"We have been doing that," Makerson commented. "But we feel we need to do more."

"Maybe Athas needs to announce something closer to the election," Tony suggested. "Something that will make people *want* to vote. Most people think their vote means nothing, and tell you the truth, I see why they feel that way. Sometimes it does feel that way. Plus, politicians lie. They say what sounds good during the campaign than do the opposite once they are in."

"Then, I think you need a feature showing what Athas promised last time he ran," Jorge suggested. "Followed by the results. We know that he did do some of what he said. Let that be your focus."

"We can do that," Tony nodded. "That actually might work."

"He's still good in the polls," Makerson confirmed. "But that's been the case before then things took a 180 at the last minute."

"We cannot have this happen," Jorge reminded him. "I think it will be fine."

Noting that everyone had their food, Jorge made his way to the barbecue and insisted that Tala, Sonny, and Paige sit down and he'd take over.

"But your steak," Tala began to object.

"This is fine," Jorge gestured toward a table. "I can cook my own food. Paige makes me do it all the time."

His wife turned around, and he winked at her. Tala laughed.

"Ok, sir, if you are sure?"

"I am sure," Jorge insisted as he found his place behind the barbecue. Glancing around, he noted that Maria was rounding up the children and taking them inside, leaving the adults to have a drink. Diego held a bottle of water as he talked to Paige and Tala. Jorge planned to keep an eye on him, just in case.

Conversations took place all around him, most of which he only half heard. He noted that Chase and Jolene stuck to themselves until Maria went inside the house, but even then, they didn't socialize much before leaving. Both had been oddly quiet for the entire evening. This was something else he was going to keep an eye on.

Everything was calm and relaxed when Makerson and Tony suddenly jumped up and rushed toward the door.

"We gotta go," Makerson called out.

"Hey, what's going on?" Jorge rushed behind them.

"We don't know," Makerson called back, "something with Athas downtown. The police are on the scene. That's all we know."

Jorge exchanged looks with Paige as the two men dashed out of the house.

CHAPTER 38

"You aren't going to get anywhere near him," Tony's voice echoed through Jorge's SUV as he glanced around at the traffic surrounding him. He felt claustrophobic, his body growing increasingly tense. "Security is crazy."

"So, we do not know what happened?" Jorge asked as his eyes scanned the area. "Gunshots?"

"That's all we know," Makerson confirmed. "There are rumors that he was shot."

Jorge didn't respond.

"But, that could be just rumors," Makerson continued. "His security was all over him so fast that no one could see. I did hear there was blood. But I don't know if that's true and if it is, if it's even *his*. There's a lot of unknowns at this time."

"Legacy media isn't saying anything either," Tony jumped in. "Just that there was an incident downtown, that's about it."

"Ok," Jorge finally spoke. "Let me know if you hear anything more."

"Will do," Makerson replied before ending the call.

Jorge attempted to call Athas again on his personal cell phone, but there was still no answer. He decided to call Marco.

"Hello, sir," Marco answered on the first ring. "I am still at your house. Paige put me in your office, and I am trying to find something."

"Anything yet?"

"Not really," Marco paused for a moment. "Things are quiet. That makes me nervous."

Jorge didn't reply.

"I also went on Twitter," Marco continued. "There are people saying Athas was shot, but others saying it is a stunt."

"If it was a stunt," Jorge insisted. "I would know about it. This here, it is no stunt."

"I do not know, sir," Marco insisted. "But I will keep looking."

"Thank you," Jorge said before ending the call.

What if Athas was dead? As much as he disliked the Canadian Prime Minister, there was something very shocking about the prospects of assassination. Where was his security? Weren't they highly trained to catch any potential dangers? Regardless, this sent a powerful message.

Jorge's phone rang, interrupting his thoughts.

"You won't even be able to get near the fucking downtown hospital if you try," Andrew's voice rang through the SUV. "Security and cars every fucking where!"

"He must be there," Jorge thought for a moment. "How did you get there so fast? You left after all of us."

"Hey, I don't drive like you old men," Andrew reminded him. "I got here. Don't worry about the details. I'm snooping around, but I can't get near this fucking place. No one is saying a word. I talked to one guy who works here, and he said he didn't even know what was going on. And he works in the emergency department!"

"But you think Athas is there?"

"I would bet everything he is," Andrew thought for a moment. "Unless this is just a way to distract us. Maybe he's somewhere else. Have you called him?"

"No answer."

"That could be for different reasons."

"Most of which probably aren't good."

"There is that," Andrew agreed. "I will get back to you if I hear anything else."

"Do me a favor?" Jorge replied. "Let Makerson know. He and Tony are stuck in traffic too."

"Yeah, traffic is a clusterfuck right now," Andrew agreed. "I will let them know."

Growing frustrated, Jorge decided to go home.

At one time, this situation would've sent an explosion of excitement through Jorge's body. He would've passionately sought the truth, a sick thrill would've lit up his heart despite the morbid possibilities, but instead, he felt a heaviness in his chest. It was not due to any concerns for Athas but a general apathy. Everything was always the same, but it now felt quite different. What was the point? What if Athas was shot? What did that mean? What if he was fine? Did any of this matter?

Finally moving his SUV along enough to find a spot where he could get out of the traffic gridlock, Jorge made a turn just as his phone rang again. Hitting the button, he answered.

"Hello."

"Where are you?"

It was Paige.

"On my way home now."

"Does that mean…"

"Paige, it means nothing," Jorge cut her off before she could jump to a conclusion. "I am tired of sitting in traffic, and I do not know where Athas is."

"I heard he's at the hospital."

"He could be," Jorge nodded. "But that could be a decoy."

"I heard it mightn't be good."

Silence.

"Well, Paige, do not pay attention to rumors," Jorge attempted to console her. "We still do not know anything."

"If he were ok, he would call us."

"His security, they may not allow it," Jorge reminded her. "Or if he is in surgery. Paige, there are so many possibilities. We cannot jump to conclusions."

"You're right," Paige agreed. "Please let me know if you hear anything."

"I will, *mi amor,*" Jorge's voice lowered. "This will be ok, I promise."

He ended the call with a heavy heart. He didn't care about Athas, but he did love his wife and didn't want her to worry.

He called Makerson.

"You got anything yet?"

"I'm just hearing he was shot," Makerson said. "But there's no confirming, and I don't know the severity."

"Or if it's even true," Tony spoke up. "But someone who was close claims he was shot and rushed away before anyone could see."

"Ok, well, hopefully, we hear more soon," Jorge commented.

"For what it's worth," Makerson added. "People are very concerned. There's an overwhelming response online even from the opposition."

Jorge rolled his eyes.

"Well, that there may not be so sincere."

"It seemed legit," Tony commented. "But then again, maybe they're all good actors."

"Ok, keep me posted," Jorge said before hanging up.

He continued to move slowly through traffic, but at least he was moving now. His thoughts continued to jump all over the place. Should he take the family to their safe house? Were they in danger too?

Marco would find out. He would be hacking phones to see what he could learn.

His phone rang. It was Maria.

"*Papá,*"

"Maria, how are things there?" Jorge asked.

"Everyone is pretty worried."

"I see."

"Tala was crying," Maria's voice was full of sadness. "She went to her apartment to pray."

"Well, that is nice, Maria."

"She said she prays for us all," Maria continued. "And what a nice man Alec is, that she hopes he is ok. Is he going to be ok?"

"Maria, I do not know yet," Jorge gently replied. "I am heading home now and hope to learn something soon."

"I know you don't like him," Maria continued. "But I hope he's ok. He's not a very good prime minister, but that doesn't mean he's a bad person."

"Well, Maria, yes," Jorge agreed. "There is a distinction. You are right."

"Anyway, I just wanted to check in."

"I will be home soon, Maria."

He ended the call with anxiety in his heart. He was suddenly very aware of how much the potential death of Athas could affect people. Jorge had spent so much of his life acting and reacting that it wasn't his natural inclination to stop and take notice but to plan his next move. He had to accept that if Athas were dead, it would affect his family and those around him, but in many different ways.

He was almost home when his phone rang. This time it was Marco.

"Hello, Marco," Jorge spoke with no passion in his voice. "What you got for me?"

"Sir, your secure line rang," Marco began to speak with some hesitation. "And I was not sure if I should answer it…"

"Yes!" Jorge cut him off. "Of course, please do! If it rings again…"

"No, sir," Marco cut him off this time. "I did. I was not sure if this would be fine with you, but I knew if it rang, it must be important…"

"Yes," Jorge felt some relief, as well as anxiety. "Of course, Marco. I trust you. Please tell me, was it Athas?"

"Sir, it was," Marco replied, causing Jorge to feel some relief. "Sir, he *was* shot, but he is ok. His security saved him. The bullet grazed him. At first there was so much blood that they weren't sure."

"Yes, this here makes sense," Jorge took the information in stride. "So, he is at the hospital now?"

"Sir, I think they are treating him at an undisclosed location," Marco spoke in a low voice. "Whatever that means."

"And he is fine?"

"He is fine, sir," Marco confirmed. "Are you on your way here?"

"Yes."

"I will have more information when you arrive."

They ended their call, and Jorge felt his body fill with relief. He took a deep breath and continued home.

CHAPTER 39

"So, he's ok?" Maria asked after Jorge delivered the news to both her and Paige. "Like, he was shot, but he's fine?"

"Yes, Maria," Jorge confirmed while glancing at his wife, who nodded in understanding. "He is fine. This here, it is not serious."

"The way they talk on the news..." Maria didn't seem convinced.

"The news, they love this," Jorge waved his hand in the direction of the television. "People are watching them for a change."

"Eww," Maria made a face and suddenly shook her head. "Oh, I gotta go tell Tala. She was worried."

Maria rushed away, and Jorge exchanged looks with his wife.

"If that's all he got," Paige shrugged. "He'll be fine, but the real question is who did it?"

"Someone is in custody," Jorge replied as he took a deep breath. "The real question *is* who paid this person to do it. Someone wanted to get Athas out of the game."

"Because he was winning..."

"They'll blame it on this random person, someone with mental health problems," Jorge insisted as he pulled his phone out of his pocket. "As if everyone does not have mental health problems."

"Most people don't try to shoot the prime minister when they do," Paige reminded him. "If they wanted him dead, they wouldn't have made it so public, and they wouldn't have just grazed his arm."

"I think the point was to scare him into dropping out," Jorge said. "And knowing Athas, they might be successful."

As it turns out, Jorge had misjudged the Greek Canadian. Rather than be fearful, the Canadian prime minister was full of rage when Jorge spoke to him a few hours later.

"They say it's some random guy," Athas raged through the secure line while Jorge sat back in his office chair and listened. "You know the type, plays violent video games in his mom's basement, says shit on social media...."

"Yes, because that is the kind of person that worries about politics," Jorge quipped. "You know that this person was most likely manipulated, in some way."

"I tried to say that," Athas complained. "But CSIS, the RCMP, they don't want to listen to me. It's not like I'm the fucking prime minister!"

Jorge grinned at his comment and let him continue to rant.

"That bullet was meant to scare me," Athas continued. "'Well, it didn't work. Now that the worst thing that could happen to me in this job... happened, I'm scared of nothing. Bring it fucking on!"

"Well, Athas, that is not the *worst* thing that could happen to you," Jorge smirked. "But if you are dead, I guess none of this will bother you either."

"Well, yeah," Athas backtracked. "I mean dying would be worse, or going to prison..."

"Athas, you are the prime minister," Jorge shook his head. "As if you could ever go to prison! You could haul out a gun and shoot random people and get away with it. I've told you this before. There is a certain level of power where you do not pay for your actions."

"You would know about that."

"As would *you*," Jorge sharply reminded him. "I remember cleaning up a mess you had not long ago."

"I used to have nightmares about that," Athas confessed. "But after what happened today, I feel justified. At least I'm not too much of a coward to pull the trigger myself."

"There is that," Jorge continued to be humored by the rant. "So, any thoughts on who sent this kid to shoot you?"

"I have ideas," Athas seemed to calm down. "But as I said, they aren't being taken seriously."

"Do these police not work for you?"

"I thought they worked for us all."

Jorge laughed.

"Can we be serious now, Athas?"

Athas sighed loudly, causing Jorge to roll his eyes.

"Ideally, they work for us all," he finally replied. "But, the longer I'm in this position, the more I see they work for the corporations."

"And which corporation are they working for today?"

"Today, I would have to say it's for Big Pharma in general," Athas slowly replied. "That would be my guess."

"Well, let's see," Jorge thought for a moment. "Your election platform is to help indigenous communities, be stricter on child abusers, and to…. make harsher laws against Big Pharma. So, yes, this might be the case."

"Plus, the opposition wants to give medications for free."

"Not free. Our taxes pay for it," Jorge reminded him. "But Big Pharma benefits greatly."

"That's what I mean," Athas insisted. "So, they make me look like a pariah because I won't give people free medication, but they don't realize that taxes will have to increase to pay such a massive bill. Also, Big Pharma may decide to gouge us by raising the prices."

"People, they are short-sighted, not to mention on too many pills," Jorge complained. "Everyone wants a fucking pill to solve their problems."

"Plus," Athas fell silent for a moment. "I was invited to an event recently. Until I was there, I didn't realize that this so-called fundraiser was a big scam."

"What do you mean?"

"Picture a fundraiser supposedly to help fund a center that supports children of abuse," Athas started. "With a bunch of beautiful women, wearing skimpy outfits giving out the drinks and flirting. It seemed a little…off."

"This here happened?" Jorge asked.

"Yes," Athas replied. "And the women were very…handsy, if you know what I mean."

"Athas, I may be married, but I am still familiar with the term," Jorge laughed.

"It was getting a little weird," Athas continued. "There was talk of how these women were giving private massages, and when I questioned why a waitress would be doing this, they said one of them was studying to be a masseuse…plus, she looked quite young."

"Of course, she was," Jorge quipped. "She was ready to massage your dick, get some pictures or video and sink your ship."

"That's what I was kind of thinking," Athas sighed. "It was disappointing to have wasted my time at an event that was a scam. Then, I found out that it was sponsored by some guy on the board of one of the pharmaceutical companies."

"Nothing here that you have said surprises me," Jorge remarked. "So, when this didn't work, they had to pull out the big guns. Literally, it seems."

"That's what I think," Athas cleared his throat. "But when I told that to the investigator, he brushed it off. He said, 'there's no proof they are connected' and moved on."

"There may be no proof," Jorge reminded him. "But that doesn't mean they aren't. The fact that you've had many battles with Big Pharma in the past isn't exactly a secret. That party sounds like they wanted to trap you in a rat cage and that handsy lady was your cheese."

"That's what I thought," Athas mused for a moment. "But then again, maybe I'm wrong. Maybe I'm just paranoid at this point."

"You are *not* being paranoid," Jorge insisted. "They want you out. You're not playing the game. You are not doing as they wish. The powerful, they do not like this. Do you think you are the first leader of a country shot because he did not listen to the oligarchs? And if they wanted you dead, you would be dead now. They want you scared. They want you to pussy out. But you are not going to do this. You are going out like a bull. And no one fucks with a bull."

"How did things get this off track?" Athas suddenly showed a vulnerability. "When did the government get so corrupt?"

"Do not be so naive," Jorge countered. "It has always been corrupt."

"But do not worry," Jorge continued before Athas could speak. "I have my best people on this. We will find the information your RCMP and CSIS won't find because they are not looking. Right now, they're creating a story that will satisfy you and satisfy the public."

"I can understand the public," Athas sighed. "But, I want to know the truth…"

"And you will get it," Jorge assured him. "But it will be from me, not them. And we will fight back against the Pharma cartel…and believe me, it is a cartel, and your friend Frederick Knapp of the opposition, he is part of it."

"That's for sure," Athas agreed.

"I am telling you, this here is a war," Jorge said. "And luckily for you, I am very experienced with war. Just leave it to me. I will sort this out."

Immediately after ending the call with Athas, Jorge phoned Marco.

"You got anything for me?"

"I might," Marco replied. "There are some challenges this time, but I'm getting there."

Jorge nodded.

"Have you spoken to Athas?" Marco continued.

"We had a thought-provoking conversation," Jorge said. "The police, they have some…interesting ideas. Nothing that surprises me."

"The usual ideas, sir?"

"Of course," Jorge replied. "They aren't being paid for their creativity."

"I'm not so sure about that, sir," Marco replied. "I'm doing some research, but what are your plans for the morning?"

"It depends," Jorge replied. "What are *your* plans?"

"I'm going to be at the VIP room at the bar first thing in the morning."

"Then that is where I will be as well."

CHAPTER 40

"You're trending on Twitter, sir," Marco announced as soon as Jorge walked into the VIP room of the *Princesa Maria,* with a *Taza de Sol* coffee in hand, "and not in a good way."

"Really?" Jorge seemed unfazed by the comment as he sat across the table from Marco. "You mean it is not because Oprah put *House of Hernandez* in her book club?"

"Sir, is that still a thing?" Marco asked as he started to turn his laptop around. "Is it not other celebrities now?"

"We only care what celebrities think, Marco," Jorge spoke sarcastically. "So, does it matter?"

"This is what I am seeing," Marco appeared concerned as he refocused his attention on the laptop. "There are comments on here about everything. Some people about your book, while others about your companies. Your connection with Athas…actually, sir, that's the majority of comments on here. The people are saying that Athas was shot because of you."

"Because of me?" Jorge sat back in his chair, not bothering to read anything on the screen, "That is interesting. So, did I shoot him and suddenly become a bad shot, or was someone trying to send a message to me? I do not understand, but I am curious."

"People on here," Marco pulled the laptop toward himself and glanced at the screen. "Are saying things like '*It's not news that Alec Athas is connected to Jorge Hernandez, who everyone knows is connected to the Mexican cartel'* and that's the most prominent of comments."

"I see," Jorge nodded. "Anyone saying anything good or is it just that I'm the anti-Christ."

"Oh, sir, it's Twitter," Marco shook his head. "No one says anything good about anyone on here."

"A dumpster fire?"

"Pretty much," Marco nodded.

"Tell me again," Jorge stopped to take a sip of his coffee. "Why is there so much importance on social media at this time? On Twitter? All these other sites? Why should I care about what they say?"

Marco paused for a moment before commenting.

"Well, sir, I can see how you would wonder why any of this is relevant…"

"This is what I am thinking," Jorge nodded. "Why does anyone even care? These here are not news reports. Am I right?"

"To a degree," Marco thought for a moment. "It is like modern-day marketing. It is like our newspapers now or television."

"Except all the comments on this here," Jorge pointed toward the laptop. "They are by everyday people?"

"Well, that is the other thing, sir," Marco shook his head. "I think many of these are by bots, not even real accounts. This makes me think that someone is behind this sudden burst of comments. It's a way to attack you at a sensitive time when people are upset over Athas being shot."

"I see," Jorge took this in stride. "Well, Marco, I do not care much about social media, but I would think that maybe the best option is to ignore it. Either that or have people attack those making the comments."

"Sir, I think they aren't real accounts anyway," Marco admitted. "I could hack their accounts, but there are so many."

"I would be more interested in finding who is behind it," Jorge commented. "Although, I have a funny feeling I already know."

"That's the other thing I wanted to talk to you about, sir," Marco shook his head. "This here, it was something I just discovered after we talked on the phone. It wasn't even the original reason I wanted to see you."

"What is that, Marco?"

"Sir, I was researching since Athas was shot," Marco continued. "I was trying to find out who did it, who paid for it, who this kid was that shot him. I have been going in circles because things are locked up tight, but I think I may have unraveled something."

Jorge nodded.

"I was able to find out the guy they say *shot him*," Marco tapped on his laptop and turned it around, showing him an image of some ratty-looking kid. "Had no interest in politics. If he did, I see nothing indicating it in his online searches, social media, none of that, which is highly unusual for someone passionate enough to shoot the prime minister."

Jorge nodded as he drank his coffee.

"So, I looked a little further," Marco continued. "I wanted to get a sense of who he was, what he did. From the looks of it, he didn't do much. He worked part-time in fast food and played video games all day."

"This here doesn't surprise me."

"But here's the interesting part," Marco continued. "Not shooting games, as you'd expect. He played games centered on going into space, that kind of thing."

"I did not know this was a thing."

"Neither did I, sir," Marco shook his head. "It wouldn't be my first choice, but he was a big follower of anything related to space. He loves Elon Musk, for example, considers him the wisest man on earth."

"Nothing you are telling me," Jorge shook his head. "Makes me think that this kid was even violent, let alone would shoot Athas."

"That's the thing," Marco shook his head. "Nothing is indicating that he even knew how to use a gun. He doesn't *legally* own a gun. No one in his household owns a gun. And the only reason he was even at the particular event downtown was that he was meeting some lady that he met online for a date. Not even at the event, but at a nearby coffee shop."

Jorge made a face.

"So," Marco continued. "I don't think he even did it. I think he's getting the blame because he's young, and pathetic."

"And the girl," Jorge asked.

"A bot, sir," Marco shook his head. "A fake account."

"Shouldn't the RCMP be investigating this?" Jorge asked. "Isn't this their job?"

"Well, they aren't," Marco replied. "I've hacked them too. They already decided this kid did it, claiming it was for attention. They are preparing a carefully worded statement. It is currently going back and forth between people to perfect it. And I don't mean necessarily other constables or even higher-ups. I mean PR people and professional writers."

Jorge's head fell back as he burst out in laughter.

"I know, sir," Marco started to giggle. "This must sound ridiculous to you."

"Marco, it is ridiculous," Jorge replied. "They are more concerned with having the correct speech than investigating this fucking case. "And people, they wonder why criminals get away with so much. Isn't it obvious?"

"And this is someone shooting the prime minister," Marco pointed out. "Can you imagine if this was just a regular person, someone with no status?"

"They would care even less," Jorge confirmed. "Sweep it under the rug and hope people forget about it."

"Sir, I always thought Canada was better than this," Marco commented. "Before I moved here from the Philippines, I thought Canada was the greatest country in the world, and they cared about its people. But now, sir, I am not so sure. Especially when I see things like this and knowing that the police are doing as little as possible."

"They only care about their reputation," Jorge reminded him. "And giving the public a satisfactory answer. That is all."

Marco let out a loud sigh and nodded.

"At any rate," Jorge pointed toward the computer. "Do not worry about what they say about me on social media. I will have Andrew and Sonny address it on their show. I will also have Makerson investigate. Maybe pass on what you know to him, give him some direction."

"I will, sir," Marco nodded. "I am still trying to find out who *actually* shot at Athas and from where. I can tell the general direction, but no one seems to have seen a thing."

"Their attention was all on the stage," Jorge suggested. "But still, yes, it is odd no one seen a thing."

"I am checking cameras, but it is so crowded," Marco sighed. "It is hard to tell even where the bullet came from."

"Maybe the bigger question is who did it," Jorge said. "We need to know who put the wheels in motion."

"I am curious about that as well," Marco replied. "The election is coming soon, so this might backfire on them. I was doing some reading, and sometimes if a contender is shot or attacked, it works to their benefit in the polls."

Jorge's eyes widened.

"Do you think it was someone in his party?" Marco cautiously asked.

"His numbers were already good," Jorge reminded him. "He was the rock star unless they don't want him leading?"

"Do you think it was more personal?" Marco suggested.

"This is possible," Jorge shook his head. "But I doubt it."

"Do you think we're wrong?" Marco asked. "And it wasn't planned? That it was some random person?"

"But this guy," Jorge pointed toward the laptop. "He does not look to have it in him."

"This is not making sense, sir."

"To either of us," Jorge confirmed. "The more we talk, the less I feel like I know."

"That has been my research all day," Marco shook his head. "Usually, by now, I find something."

"Just keep looking and…"

"Jorge," Chase stuck his head in the door, interrupting the two of them, holding his phone in hand. "You'll want to see this."

CHAPTER 41

"Andrew got this here?" Jorge squinted as Chase held the phone up to him. "And this is…."

"A friend of the guy accused of shooting Athas," Chase replied. "He's saying it's all bullshit, and buddy wouldn't even know *how* to use a gun."

Jorge exchanged looks with Marco, who raised his eyebrows.

"It is starting to seem more and more like this is a setup," Jorge said. "I must go see Andrew and talk to him. When was this posted?"

"Just now," Chase replied. "So Andrew is probably back at the production house."

"I will see him," Jorge started for the door, only turning back for a moment. "Thank you, and please keep me informed if anything new develops."

Jorge rushed out and headed to his SUV. Taking a deep breath, he got behind the wheel but hesitated before starting the vehicle. Why was this scenario playing out again? This wasn't the first time they arrested the wrong person, and if history had told him anything, the kid wouldn't see the light of day again, one way or another.

He drove to the production house, feeling a sense of heaviness as he did. Why would anyone go to such lengths to get Athas out of the way? Was this even about Athas at all? Were the bots on social media sending him a message? Was Athas being attacked for his policies or his advisor in the background?

Things were getting too complicated, and Jorge was getting too old. He was tired of games. Back in Mexico, he always knew who his enemy was and why; here in Canada, it was a whole other story. Things were much more insidious. People here liked to play games, especially when it came to politics.

Then again, maybe it wasn't so different. Maybe, Jorge was just tired.

Arriving at the production house, he parked in his usual spot and headed inside. Glancing around, he saw a rush of activity and decided to observe it rather than announce his arrival. It occurred to him that they'd be fine without him. Everyone knew their job. Everyone knew what he expected of them. A part of him wanted to turn around and leave. That's when Makerson walked out of the boardroom and spotted him.

"Oh, I'm glad you're here," he rushed toward Jorge. "We got something…"

"Yes, I saw the interview Andrew did with…"

"Nah, we got more than that," Makerson gestured toward the boardroom, and Jorge followed. "Everything is happening so fast. I didn't have time to let you know."

Jorge said nothing, following him into the room, closing the door behind them. Andrew and Tony were seated at the table. Both glanced up.

"Hey, shit *is happening*," Andrew remarked and pointed toward the laptop. "That interview started something. All these people are coming forward saying all sorts of shit. People are saying they think it was a sniper from on top of a building or from a window."

"Really?" Jorge sat down and glanced toward the screen. "It's all over social media."

"We're trying to get in touch with some of these people," Tony added as he tapped on the computer. "We put a call out all over social media, and we're getting tons of responses. Unfortunately, we have to try to decipher which ones are real and which ones are bullshit."

"Sonny is interviewing someone right now," Andrew added. "And we're trying to get this shit out as fast as possible before the censorship assholes at Big Tech shut us down."

"Why would they if it's true?" Jorge casually asked and got a look from Andrew.

"They gotta protect their criminal friends," Andrew muttered. "At least that's what I think."

"It's crazy," Tony said as he looked up from the screen. "Like, people are saying Athas had a ton of security, so how could they miss this stupid kid? It's not exactly like he's a professional shooter. And he was so far away, he would've had to be good to shoot with any accuracy at all. Besides, only a few people are said to be witnesses, and they've all but disappeared."

"Disappeared?" Jorge asked with interest. "Isn't that interesting?"

"If there were ever any witnesses at all," Makerson added as he jumped back on his laptop and started typing. "No one seems to know who they are or what they saw. Just a random kid was grabbed and said to be the shooter, and everyone went along with it. They wanted to feel safer, and that's all they cared about. Everything was resolved, and they could stop pearl-clutching and go on with their lives."

"As if those types ever stop clutching their pearls," Tony laughed. "It's these social elitists that have no value for anyone in a certain economic bracket that assume all poor people are fucking criminals. Especially if those people are kids. This guy has no record of anything. No warning, no red flags. Nothing. He never even got in trouble when he was in school. He was a loner. That's it, that's all they got."

"Yeah, his friend said he wouldn't know how to shoot a fucking gun to save his life," Andrew laughed. "He tried to go to mainstream media, but no one would talk to him. They don't care. They got the story they want."

"Yeah, the *story* they want," Makerson sniffed. "The story *someone* wants."

"Ok, so all this aside," Jorge jumped in. "Because it is clear this kid, he did not do it, I am wondering who put the wheels in motion."

"Another mystery," Andrew replied. "Maybe your friend Athas can help us with that."

"So far, he knows nothing."

"He's the fucking prime minister," Andrew laughed.

"He's the one that was shot," Tony jumped in.

"Yeah, well, the RCMP and CSIS, they hold their cards close to their chest," Jorge said. "They will not tell him anything."

"He should fucking *tell* them to give him information," Andrew threw in. "Or fire their pristine asses and hire someone who will."

"I think they have a union," Makerson suggested. "They're protected."

"Too bad Athas wasn't," Andrew muttered.

"It makes you wonder about all our safety," Tony added. "Or was I naive enough to think I ever was protected by our police?"

"You have someone better than our police looking after you," Jorge informed him. "You have me."

"Yeah, there's justice you won't find in the Canadian system," Andrew muttered. "Much harsher punishments."

Jorge grinned.

"The bottom line is the election is days away," Makerson reminded them. "And someone is getting nervous."

"Marco on it?" Andrew asked, and Jorge nodded.

"There's another debate tomorrow night," Tony jumped in as he typed.

"Athas, he must be a dragon in this one," Jorge replied. "I can have no pussycat answering the questions. He must show that he is strong in the face of what has just happened. They thought he would cower away, but he will not. The man I spoke to last night, he was ready to eat someone alive."

"That's what we need," Makerson insisted as their eyes met. "He's letting everyone else make the rules. Who the hell says he can't know more about the investigation? He's the fucking prime minister. He should have access to any information on whatever he wants. Especially when it's about his safety."

"This is the same old song and dance again and again," Jorge shook his head. "Nothing ever changes with Athas. Then again, maybe it will. If it does, I am anxious to see the results."

"Frederick Knapp is a pretentious old fuck," Andrew commented. "I would like to see Athas light him on fire in the middle of the debate."

"There will be no debate," Jorge shook his head. "This is the legacy media; all the questions are scripted in advance to suit whatever message they want to send out, and it's been clear from day one which candidate they prefer. They're having meetings right now on how to sell it."

"Do you think they'll ask any questions about this social media stuff that says Athas was shot because of you?" Makerson asked calmly. "I mean, I know it's not true, but…"

"I plan to coach Athas on all this later today," Jorge insisted. "When I am done with him, he will be ready to take on anyone and anything. I will prepare him for such questions."

"Do you need any help?" Makerson asked. "I've covered a fair share of debates over the years. I might be able to add some insight, let you know the kind of questions they'll throw at him."

"This here, it might be a good idea," Jorge nodded. "I want him to be as prepared as possible."

"We got any dirt on the other guy," Andrew looked up from his laptop and raised an eyebrow. "Dirt is always nice."

"He seems to be clean," Jorge replied. "But do not worry. If I feel we need dirt, I will look under every rock I can find. I have Marco on it. He's looking."

"Marco must be a busy boy," Andrew said.

"He usually is," Jorge commented as he started to stand. "Speaking of which, I must go now. Please keep me posted on anything new."

"Things might happen fast so…" Makerson began, but Jorge was already shaking his head.

"You know that I trust you," Jorge reminded him. "You do not need to check with me and meanwhile, I will keep an eye out for your alerts, and we will be in touch."

"Ok," Makerson stopped typing and nodded. "That sounds good."

Jorge smiled and headed toward the boardroom door. Turning on his phone, it sprang to life with messages. However, it was the first one that caught his eye.

CHAPTER 42

"Of course," Juan Perez ushered Jorge into his luxurious office at *Taza de Sol* the following afternoon. "Do come in and have a seat. Can I offer you some coffee?"

"No, it is late in the day for me," Jorge replied as he followed the older Mexican man across the room. "I try to avoid caffeine after lunch now. My heart it likes to jump around like crazy."

"How about something else to drink?" Juan grinned as he sat behind his desk and gestured for Jorge to have a seat.

"What you got?" Jorge was intrigued as he sat across from him.

Juan reached into his desk and pulled out a bottle of tequila. It wasn't the same kind he usually chose himself, but still, a good brand.

"You know," Jorge nodded as he stared at the bottle. "I may have to say yes to that one."

Juan laughed as he reached for two shot glasses behind him. Carefully pouring the liquor into each, he slid one across the desk for Jorge, who reached for it.

"To the health of you and your family," Juan said as he raised his glass, and Jorge did the same.

"*Gracias,*" Jorge said before downing the golden liquid, feeling it burn down his throat.

"You know," Jorge finally spoke. "I did not think I needed that until now."

To this, Juan laughed.

"We sometimes don't know," he shook his head. "We just go, go, go, and then, finally, we need to stop and enjoy the finer things in life."

"So, you called me over here," Jorge got right to business. "I assume you either have a proposition for me or something you might need help with?"

"Well, if I did need help," Juan said as he weaved his fingers together in front of his chest as he studied Jorge. "I know you are the man to call, but today, I have something *for* you."

"I see," Jorge was curious, although somewhat guarded. "And what would that be?"

"You are the man who works with Alec Athas. Am I correct about this?" Juan asked as he continued to study Jorge while appearing to relax. "Or is this just a rumor?"

"I advise him," Jorge gave a tense smile. "You might say that I am somewhat of an influencer. Why? Do you have something that you need me to influence on?"

To this, Juan raised his eyebrows and gave a wicked grin.

"Well, not at this time," he shook his head and opened a laptop in front of him. "But I may have something of interest to you."

"What is that?" Jorge was intrigued.

"Well, as you know, I have many locations of *Taza de Sol* throughout the country, but our highest demographic of customers is here in Toronto."

Jorge nodded as Juan signed into his laptop.

"One of these locations," Juan continued. "Just happens to be in the downtown area close to where Alec Athas was recently shot."

Jorge's face grew serious as his ears perked up. He sat up straighter, giving Juan his full attention.

"And according to your production house," Juan continued. "There was a lot of reason to believe that the RCMP got the wrong guy."

"It is looking that way," Jorge replied, "*si.*"

"When I hear this," Juan continued as he turned his laptop around. "I was curious. I thought it might not hurt to do a little investigating of my own. I wondered why the police never came asking to see if my cameras picked up anything since I was so close."

Jorge raised an eyebrow as the two men shared a look of understanding.

"As it turns out," Juan continued as he pointed at his greying hair. "I managed to find more in those few minutes with my old eyes than the police have found since the shooting."

"And what would that be?" Jorge was intrigued.

"The shooter," Juan bluntly replied.

"Is this so?" Jorge leaned forward in his chair.

"I will show you," Juan turned the laptop more in Jorge's direction before hitting play on the still image, causing it to come to life. "Watch the man wearing black to the left of the screen."

Jorge sat ahead and followed his instructions. The tall, slim man wore sunglasses, a dark baseball cap, and clothing. Alone, he seemed inconspicuous, sliding into a hidden corner between two buildings. Suddenly, with a gun in hand, he could be seen shooting toward Athas.

"This here," Jorge spoke up. "It is not a man who just bought his first gun yesterday."

"My guess," Juan nodded as Jorge rewatched the video. "Is, he's a cop."

"That would explain a lot," Jorge agreed. "This here is the opposite side of the street from where they said the bullet came from, which is interesting. And no one saw a thing?"

"There was so much chaos," Juan attempted to rationalize as he shook his head. "So many people, everything happened fast. My guess is this was well planned and by someone who had already prepared for all these factors."

"Not to mention," Jorge continued as he sat back in his seat, his eyes returning to Juan as the video returned as a still image on the screen. "That Athas didn't have good security."

"You would think a man with *so* much security would be safe."

"This here," Jorge nodded. "I have thought about it."

"Not to mention the range," Juan pointed toward the laptop. "If he wanted the prime minister dead, he would be now. There are too many concerning factors. That is why I decided to contact you, rather than the police. I do not have much faith that they are interested in knowing the truth."

"Mr. Perez," Jorge shook his head. "You may not have lived in Mexico in a long time, but you certainly know that there is often a fine line between the police and the criminals."

"Well, to be honest, Mr. Hernandez," Juan replied. "I have learned this here too in Canada."

The two men laughed.

"So, you would like me to have this," Jorge nodded toward the laptop. "I have an expert who can look at that and get all our answers."

"These are good experts to have," Juan nodded. "You are welcome to it. I figured you might want to use it for your production house or…maybe to investigate on your own."

"This here is exactly what I will do," Jorge nodded toward the laptop. "If you do not mind, I may have my IT guy come to look at it."

"I'm not techy," Juan leaned forward on his desk. "So, I'm not sure what to do, but if your specialist wants to come here, he can do whatever he wishes."

"I'll call him now," Jorge offered.

"Please do," Juan nodded. "I am curious myself. As I said, no police ever came to ask to see my security cameras. No one talked to my staff. No one even looked in our direction at all."

"Not to give you the wrong impression," Juan continued as Jorge reached for his phone. "I don't wish to have the police lurking around either. I just found it very…curious."

Jorge raised an eyebrow as his phone came to life.

"The police," Jorge finally replied. "My expectations are quite low for them."

"Well, even the situation with my daughter," Juan reminded him of how they met. "They've done nothing to this useless fuck of a principal. I thought an investigation would be in order. See what he did. Were there others? Maybe place some charges?"

"Nothing?" Jorge asked as he tapped into his phone.

"*Nada.*"

"That could change."

"That is my wish."

"Any thoughts on a reasonable punishment?" Jorge asked.

"You know," Juan grinned. "My father, he once fell down the stairs. He broke a lot of bones. He was in pain for a long time."

Jorge nodded in understanding.

"He had a lot of time to….reflect on life," Juan continued, "on some of his poor life choices."

"The only thing," Jorge reminded him. "Sometimes, a man falls down the stairs and suffers worse damage than you can imagine. Some are permanently injured or die. So, your father was a lucky man. Others may not be."

"It's a chance I'm willing to take," Juan's face grew cold.

"This here, I understand," Jorge nodded. "And I respect. I will…look into my crystal ball and see what I find."

"I know you, Jorge Hernandez," Juan returned with a smile. "You have a reputation in Mexico, and even though I have been gone many years, there are stories. If these stories are correct, you have a way of predicting the future. Especially when someone is going to have an accident."

Jorge grinned as a message on his phone pulled his attention away.

"My employee," he replied. "Is on his way. If you are sure that this is a good time?"

"I got all the time in the world to help you," Juan replied. "As I am sure you would do the same for me if needed."

"Consider it done," Jorge replied.

"These elections," Juan pointed toward the laptop again. "They are serious business."

Jorge was about to reply when his phone buzzed.

Glancing at the screen, he took the news in stride.

"Looks like," Jorge looked up at Juan. "They just got more serious."

CHAPTER 43

"Did you leave yet?" Jorge asked as he left the *Taza de Sol* office and headed for his SUV in the underground parking lot. Glancing around as he walked through, Jorge didn't freely speak until he was safely in his vehicle. "I got to talk to you before you do."

"I'm still at the bar," Marco confirmed. "I was packing up my stuff to head out. Why? Has there been a change of plans?"

"I wanted to make sure this guy, Juan Perez, he is ok?" Jorge asked as he started the SUV, putting the call on speaker. "You checked him out before?"

"He is clean, sir," Marco replied. "But also, if he were or is doing anything other than run a coffee business, he would have to be careful to hide this fact."

"This is true," Jorge replied as he pulled out of his spot and made his way out of the underground parking. "I have a few more ideas about that, but it will have to wait. He has something I need you to look at more closely at his office. I sent you the address?"

"Yes, I have it here, sir," Marco replied. "Is this technically speaking?"

"Yes," Jorge was careful not to give too many details. "Just something he needs you to look at, and I thought I would see if you could go over. I'm intrigued to see your thoughts."

"I am curious about this," Marco replied. "I will get back to you later today."

"Oh, there is something else, Marco," Jorge apprehensively continued. "I just received some….not so good news."

"Really?"

"The kid arrested for shooting Athas?" Jorge said before continuing. "He was found dead in his cell."

"Oh, sir, that is too bad."

"Especially considering," Jorge added as he made his way onto the road. "It was obvious that he was not the true suspect."

"I will…I will see what I can find out about this as well."

"I would appreciate it."

"We will talk later."

"*Gracias,* Marco."

After ending the call, Jorge took a deep breath and thought about the news he had just received. An innocent kid was dead while the truth was in plain sight. Of course, it was only plain sight if you bothered to look, something the police were not interested in doing. He wondered if Marco could figure out who the man was, but at the least, they could anonymously release it on social media to know the public saw it. They probably wouldn't otherwise.

His phone rang again, and Jorge took a deep breath before answering it. "Yeah?"

"Did you hear?" Athas' voice rang through the SUV.

"Yes," Jorge lowered his tone. "I did. This here is concerning."

"I don't think he did it."

"I *know* he didn't do it."

"You *know?*"

"I will have more for you later."

"I'm in Toronto," Athas continued. "I'm tied up every second until the election, but I think I'm…"

"This here," Jorge interrupted, "you will want to make the time. I will be in touch."

With that, he ended the call and called Makerson.

"Hey."

"How are things there?"

"Busy," Makerson kept his answer brief. "I got Athas coming over later to coach him...."

"Perfect," Jorge cut him off. "We might have something for you and him to see. Can you arrange a time for you, me, Athas, and Marco to meet? That way, I can kill two birds with one stone. I gotta be somewhere else now, but if you could arrange this, it would be perfect."

"What's it about?" Makerson asked. "Or is it....a surprise?"

"Nothing you are about to learn will surprise you," Jorge replied with laughter in his voice. "Trust me on that, but you will see later."

"Any specific time?"

"Whatever time works for everyone," Jorge replied.

"I was supposed to meet Athas at either 6 or 7."

"Just let me know."

"You hear about the kid in jail?"

"Yes, I did."

"He was suicided."

"You know this here for a fact?"

"I hear things," Makerson replied. "I have some sources. It would've been an educated guess regardless."

"I predicted this as soon as he got arrested," Jorge commented.

"I think a lot of us did."

"I will see you tonight," Jorge said as he drew closer to the *Princesa Maria*. "Just send me the time."

"Will do."

"*Gracias*."

Jorge ended the call and took a deep breath. Although he usually could take everything in stride, this situation made him uneasy. This kid was used as a fall guy and murdered when it looked like the truth might come out. Someone was going to great lengths to cover something up. Jorge had always assumed it was Big Pharma behind everything, but now, he wasn't so sure. But there was one thing he knew. Someone wanted Athas to run scared. They wanted him to run right out of the election.

Pulling into his usual parking spot at the bar, Jorge jumped out of the SUV and headed inside. Hoping to get Chase alone, he was irritated to hear Jolene's loud voice echoing through the room as soon as he walked in. He had hoped she would've been out of the picture by now, but no such luck.

Walking toward the empty bar, he could see her fat ass perched at the bar as she leaned forward and attempted to talk to Chase. With a clipboard in hand, his attention didn't appear to be on the conversation but work. Maybe there was hope for him yet.

"Jolene, don't you have something to do all day," Jorge sharply cut her off. "A life to ruin or something?"

"I do not have a job," She reminded him. "You said you would give me one, then you change your mind."

"Jolene, you're a pain in the ass to work with," Jorge reminded her. "You're lazy and argumentative. No one wants to work with you other than the dead people, and *you* changed your mind on that."

She made a face while Chase appeared to fight a grin.

"Anyway," Jorge continued. "Chase and I, we have to talk, so I suggest you go to the mall….or do whatever you do when you're not torturing people. Find something productive."

"I keep saying…"

"I don't want to hear it," Jorge put his hand in the air. "Jolene, go. Chase and I have work to do. It's important. So can you please leave?"

"Ok," She slowly got off the bar stool. "But I will prove my loyalty someday and make everything up to you. I promise."

To this, Jorge didn't reply. He knew that anything he said would prolong the conversation, and he didn't have time or interest. He waited until she was gone before he turned his attention to Chase.

"Let us go to the office," Jorge glanced around. "Clara, she has been in?"

"Yup," Chase nodded as he sat down the clipboard. "Did you need me for something?"

"I do," Jorge nodded as the two men headed into the office behind the bar, closing the door behind them. "It has to do with a conversation I had earlier today."

"Oh?" Chase appeared intrigued, if not a little withdrawn. "What do you need?"

"I need someone shaken up."

"Who?" Chase asked as he sat behind his desk and leaned back in the chair.

"Remember when I went to the school and walked in on the principal with the girl?"

"Yes," Chase thought for a moment. "I remember something about that. He was fired, right?"

"Yes, but that is all."

"No charges?" Chase shook his head. "Nothing like that?"

"No," Jorge replied as he sat across from Chase. "And this here is the problem."

Chase didn't reply but nodded.

"You recall I met the girl's father?" Jorge reminded him. "Juan Perez, he come here to see me?"

"Yes."

"Well, we had a conversation about something else earlier today," Jorge continued. "And he tell me that the principal lost his job, but that's where it ended, and this was a concern to him."

"It concerns me," Chase said in a low voice. "What do the police do all day?"

"Jerk each other off," Jorge shrugged. "Arrest the wrong people? Suicide them before they have a chance to defend themselves and expose the lies?"

"I heard about that," Chase replied, pausing for a moment. "It's disturbing."

"But not surprising," Jorge added. "Back to what we were talking about regarding the principal."

"So you want me to do something to him?"

"I want him to have an accident on the stairs," Jorge said with a raised eyebrow. "A very steep stairs and a painful accident."

"How bad?"

"Bad enough that he's in fucking misery for a long time."

"But alive?"

"Preferably," Jorge nodded. "But if a mistake happens, my heart won't break."

Jorge and Chase shared a smile.

CHAPTER 44

"In Mexico, we have an old proverb," Jorge began to lecture Alec Athas from his seat at the head of the conference room table. "They tried to bury us but forgot we were seeds."

"I've heard that one, sir," Marco spoke up as he glanced across the table at Makerson before looking back at Jorge. "That definitely applies to this situation."

"The problem is," Andrew loudly spoke up. "the motherfuckers *literally* wanted to bury him."

"If they really wanted to bury him," Jorge shook his head. "He would be dead now, not sitting at this table."

There was a collective silence as they each shared a look.

"So, what you're trying to say," Athas finally found his voice. "Is what doesn't kill you makes you stronger?"

Jorge turned his nose up at the expression.

"What I mean," Jorge replied. "This is your chance to rise, to be the most powerful you have been in your life. They do not expect this, and they certainly don't want it. That is why you're coming out like a lion at the debate tomorrow night. Not like a pussycat, like you usually do."

Athas seemed to take his words seriously, nodding as he listened.

"Make it obvious that you plan to find out who is *behind* the shooting," Makerson suggested. "Without actually saying it, imply you haven't let this go yet. They need to know you're taking them on, head to head."

"How do I bring it up?" Athas appeared confused.

"Don't worry," Jorge shook his head. "They will bring it up to you. They want to rattle you. The best way to do so is remind you that someone had a gun pointed at you just the other day."

"And shot me," Athas reminded him. "That's an important point."

"Yeah, but come on," Andrew turned to Jorge. "This ain't an everyday occurrence with most people."

"Do you think that I spend much time on that other side of a gun?" Jorge countered. "That's why I carry one with me at all times."

"Just do that, Athas," Andrew mockingly suggested. "Pull out a gun and slam it down on the podium and be like, 'any other questions, motherfucker' and people, they won't fuck with you no more."

Marco started to giggle and looked down.

"I'm not saying this is a bad idea," Jorge went along with the joke. "Sometimes, a man must let them all know who's fucking boss."

"From the Jorge Hernandez school of etiquette," Andrew continued with a grin. "Always sound advice to mark your territory in the world."

"Again, you are preaching to the choir," Jorge seemed to relax. "But we must get back to business."

"Well, as much as I would like to haul out a gun and swing it around," Athas grew agitated. "Here in the real world, I have to play the game."

"Yeah, but you don't have to play nice," Makerson reminded him. "This is the end of the line. You don't pull any punches at the final debate. You throw them."

"This here, it is sound advice," Jorge nodded. "And Frederick Knapp, he's an old fucking man, so it won't take much to knock him out."

"Yeah, you're younger and stronger than him," Andrew threw in.

"Better looking," Makerson added. "The polls say that women between the ages of…."

"Is this even relevant?" Athas appeared slightly embarrassed. "I mean, the whole rock star thing was a bit weird. Do we need to get into these stats too?"

"People, they sometimes think with their hormones," Jorge shrugged. "We take them any way we can get them."

"Yeah, promise to fuck anyone who votes for you," Andrew snickered. "That always works."

"Ok, can we be serious?" Athas grew more agitated.

"Hey, he already did that," Jorge ignored the prime minister. "Remember the lovesick reporter?"

"Is that the boring one with the big tits?" Andrew jumped in.

Athas continued to look annoyed, which gave Jorge pleasure.

"I bet she couldn't get enough of you," Andrew continued to mock Athas. "Or at least your…."

"I have another meeting," Athas sharply cut him off.

"Hey, that attitude," Jorge pointed at Athas. "That is what you'll use at the debate tomorrow night."

"Can we get back to that, please?" Athas shot Andrew a look, which only caused him to laugh. Marco did the same.

"Ok, so, this here is your chance to make a lot of noise," Jorge continued. "To stand out."

"Yeah, we want them talking about *you* the next morning," Makerson insisted. "Not the other guy."

"Technically, we aren't the only two parties," Athas reminded them. "There's four on the debate stage."

"*Technically*," Jorge shook his head. "No one gives a fuck about the other two parties. They are like the uncool friends of the hot girl at the party. You only talk to them because you're trying to fuck the hot one. Same with this debate."

Andrew laughed, and Marco quickly joined in.

"I…can honestly say, I've never thought of it that way before," Athas grinned this time.

"He's kinda right," Makerson agreed. "I mean, no one thinks those other two parties will win, so they're there, but they're kind of *not* too."

"Hey, at least Jorge is saying you're the fuckable one," Andrew added. "You may never hear that again."

"This is true," Jorge agreed.

"So, you're doing commentary on the debate tomorrow night," Makerson shifted his attention to Andrew. "You and Sonny? I'm thinking about adding my voice to the discussion."

"Yeah, man, join us," Andrew nodded. "We're going to do a live show. Stuff like check out Twitter comments, talk about the winners and losers, that kind of thing."

"That's the *Raging against the Machine* show?" Athas asked.

Andrew nodded.

"And you are too?" Athas turned his attention to Makerson.

"I was going to do my own show, but I think it would work better if I join them."

"That would be interesting," Jorge nodded in approval.

"So, the main things you must do," Makerson turned to Athas again. "Is push the issues you talked about the whole election. The indigenous rights, the child abuser law you want to bring in, and of course, Big Pharma. Which, by the way, I want you to refer to as the Pharma Cartel throughout the debate. My hope is that catches on, especially on social media."

"We can make it catch on social media," Andrew reminded him. "That's the plan anyway."

"Pharma cartel...." Athas nodded.

"That's what it is," Andrew shrugged. "Fucking legal drug dealers."

"No joke," Jorge commented. "And what was it you mentioned to me earlier, Makerson?"

"Oh yes," he nodded and turned his attention to Athas. "Make sure you also say, 'with all due respect' as much as possible."

Marco looked puzzled.

"Why is that?" Athas asked. "That sounds very...courteous."

"It's not," Makerson corrected him. "With all due respect in political talk means to fuck off."

"Or you could just say fuck off...." Andrew suggested.

"Nah, trust me," Makerson replied. "This is much better. It *does* seem respectful in the real world, but in the political world, it means fuck off. *Trust me.* People will know."

"I didn't know that," Athas replied. "So, all the times that...."

"They were telling you to fuck off," Jorge cut him off. "So, now you know."

"Now you know, son," Andrew shook his head. "Now you know."

Athas looked annoyed.

"I cannot believe you didn't know that," Jorge spoke up. "What the fuck does your campaign manager tell you?"

"He tells me what to talk about," Athas replied. "He said to be respectful and polite because that's what people want from me. They said to be charming, speak slowly, gently…"

"Your campaign manager is a fucking pussy," Jorge shook his head. "I should've been doing this all along!"

"Look, I have to go shortly," Athas glanced at the clock. "Can we talk about the kid who they say shot me…"

"He didn't shoot you," Jorge cut him off. "That's why he was suicided."

"He was….wait," Athas took in the information. "You don't think…"

"Not even for a fucking second," Jorge answered his question. "And we got the recording of the person who did."

"Sir," Marco finally spoke up. "The tape, it was real. I checked it today. The man I could not identify, but he was someone who had some experience targeting someone because the crowd was thick, so it was not an easy task."

"Do you have it?" Jorge asked.

"Yes, sir,' Marco nodded. "Any thoughts on what to do with it?"

"The police?" Athas suggested.

"Why?" Jorge shrugged. "So they take a piss on it and say it no longer works? No, we're going to release it on social media on the sly and have it publicly directed at HPC accounts, so many eyes will see it. This ensures that the police, they do not deny it. They will have to admit it wasn't the man they blamed."

"It wasn't even from the same angle," Andrew added. "Like, how fucked up is that."

"Can I see it?" Athas cut in. "This is all news to me."

"Things happen fast around here," Jorge replied.

"Where'd you get it?" Athas asked as Marco fired up his laptop.

"I cannot say," Jorge replied. "I know people."

"It's easy to miss," Marco confirmed. "But, when you zoom in…"

Athas looked ill at ease as Marco turned the laptop in his direction.
The screen lit up, and Athas moved closer to look.

"Can I watch it again?" He asked when it finished.

"Of course," Marco replied and replayed it.

Athas leaned back in his seat and thought for a moment.

"I know who that is."

CHAPTER 45

"I'm happy like Christmas," Jorge commented as he leaned back in his office chair, exchanging looks with both Makerson and Marco on the other side of the desk. "That debate last night, it could not have been better."

"Wow, sir, it's all over the media today," Marco commented with wide eyes. "People have a lot to say."

"They had a lot to say last night, as it was going on," Makerson added.

"That argument between Mr. Athas and Mr. Knapp," Marco started and hesitated as if looking for the right words. "I thought they were going to get into a physical fight, sir."

"It kind of looked that way for a while," Makerson added. "Talk about taking off the gloves. Both made a lot of low blows, and neither was listening to the moderator."

"They had to cut their mics at one point," Marco gleefully giggled. "It got crazy!"

"I must admit," Jorge finally jumped in. "When I tell Athas to go into it like a lion, I did not think he would take my advice so much to heart. But he did prove me wrong. He was no pussycat last night."

"If there was a winner," Makerson commented. "It had to be Athas. People are talking, and they sure have lots to say about him today."

"He argued a lot about the welfare of children," Marco nodded. "Both at reserves and in general, which is hard to argue with, but Mr. Knapp, he tried."

"Not a good political move," Makerson let out a laugh. "I think the words flew out of his mouth before he realized what he said."

"Which works to our advantage," Jorge reminded them. "This here, it is good."

"Athas provoked him a lot," Marco pointed out. "He knew how to get under his skin."

"That was a little something we threw in at the last minute," Jorge said. "Just to spice things up."

"We haven't even talked about social media yet," Makerson continued. "Today #Pharmacartel and #withallduerespect are trending, which was what I hoped."

"Oh yes!" Marco nodded vigorously. "We got some fake accounts, but most were real. People have a lot to say, and some famous people have also jumped on board."

"Freelancers, influencers, politically junkies have commented too," Makerson nodded. "That helps to keep the fires burning because they have so many followers."

"The show you did last night," Jorge directed his attention on Makerson. "That was good. Andrew's reaction to various moments in the debate has been trending?"

"It was a good dynamic," Marco jumped in. "Andrew is so reactive, whereas Sonny is more on the other extreme, and Makerson is in the middle."

"Viewership was huge!" Makerson nodded. "We got numbers."

"I was surprised the shooting was barely discussed," Jorge admitted. "I thought more would be brought up about that topic. At least, to rattle Athas."

"I think it's because Athas didn't come across as a victim," Makerson admitted. "I think if he had, they would've played that card more, but since it wasn't working to their benefit, they didn't seem to bother."

"This here makes sense," Jorge nodded. "But it will be coming out very soon."

"We will release it later tonight," Makerson nodded. "A fake account will bring it out and share it. Then another fake account will tag us as if it wanted to bring it to our attention."

"And the police, they cannot trace this here?" Jorge asked with interest.

"Sir, they couldn't trace cookie crumbs to the jar," Marco laughed. "I am hardly worried."

The three men laughed.

"But do not worry," Marco shook his head. "I have it all covered. It will seem authentic yet untraceable. They won't even know what country it comes from, let alone who's IP address."

"This here is perfect."

"They might put some extra effort," Makerson pointed out. "Because this leaves egg on their faces. It makes them look incompetent and stupid."

"It is what it is," Jorge shrugged. "Let them burn."

"Do you think Mr. Athas was right?" Marco grew serious. "About who the shooter is, or do you think he's mistaken? It is a grainy image to know for sure."

"He seems certain," Jorge replied. "But I guess that will come out later tonight."

"Nothing surprises me at this point," Makerson added. "I just wouldn't think that…"

His words were cut off when Jorge's secure line rang.

"Speak of the devil," Jorge leaned forward. "That would be him now."

Marco giggled while Makerson sat upright.

"Athas," Jorge answered the phone. "You were a man on fire last night."

"I don't know what came over me," Athas admitted on the other end of the line. "I just looked at Knapp, and I was furious."

"That is the perfect way to be in this situation," Jorge commented. "You are all over the news and social media today, which is what we wanted a few days before the election. Your name is on the top of everyone's mind, and hopefully, it stays there when they reach the voting booths."

"I'm having a lot of reaction to the debate," Athas admitted. "People are seeing me with new eyes."

"Good," Jorge nodded in approval. "Very good. Now you keep up this momentum for the next few days, and you should make an easy slide back in on election day."

"So, what about that video?" Athas asked with some apprehension. "Are we still going to…."

"It will be out tonight," Jorge reminded him. "And you're going to be shocked."

"I will…I mean, I was when I saw it."

"Remember, Athas, this is not the time to put your weapons down," Jorge reminded him. "I know, last night, it went good, but we have to stay on the ball until election day. You still have a couple days left, and you must not let Knapp get ahead. He still has his die-hard fans who think he can do no wrong. Your job is to keep people in your corner. Keep showing strength. That is what this country needs now."

"I know," Athas assured him. "I will. I'm just worried about when that video comes out tonight…."

"It will not hurt you," Jorge reminded him. "If anything, it will only help you."

"I suppose," Athas didn't sound convinced, but Jorge just glanced toward the others to observe their reaction.

"Look, this here," Jorge continued. "Makes other people look bad. It will create compassion for you while starting another shitstorm. And for that shitstorm, you will come out strong, taking the reins and assuring everyone that you have it covered and that you will take immediate action *as soon as* you are back in. People need to feel that you are a consistently powerful force, especially now. I promise you this will only work in your favor."

"I hope you're right."

"I'm always right," Jorge reminded him. "Now, I have another meeting to attend."

"That's fine," Athas replied. "I gotta get going here too."

"We will talk later."

"Yes."

Jorge ended the call and started to stand up.

"I, unfortunately, have to go," Jorge said as he exchanged looks with both men. "But I cannot say enough that things went very well last night, and this here is mostly because of the two of you."

"Thank you, sir," Marco replied.

"We do our best," Makerson added. "Let's hope things keep going strong."

"Remember, tonight...."

"I will be on top of it," Makerson assured him. "It's going to be a long day, but worth it."

"I am interested in seeing the numbers for last night," Jorge continued as the three headed for the door.

"I will have more details later," Makerson replied. "I'll send them to you."

"*Perfecto.*"

Ten minutes later, Jorge was in his SUV and heading toward the *Tazo de Sol* head office to meet with Juan Perez. The sun was shining, and things were going well, but Jorge couldn't shake the feeling that something was off. He just wasn't sure what yet.

He arrived at the same office he had visited earlier that week, parked his car in the same area, and headed for the elevator. Perhaps he could get this over with and take a nap afterward. It had been a late night, followed by early morning.

Arriving on the floor of Juan's office, Jorge went inside. He was greeted by the secretary.

"Mr. Perez is waiting for you."

"*Gracias.*"

Jorge entered the room to find Juan behind the desk. He looked up, automatically standing when he saw his guest.

"Mr. Hernandez," he smiled as Jorge closed the door behind him. "I do appreciate this early visit. I know you have a lot to contend with, with the election coming up, the debate last night."

"It went well," Jorge admitted as he crossed the floor and sat down. "Even better than I expected."

"Well, you are a man who gets things done," Juan commented as they sat down. "I know I appreciated what you did for me."

"I hope the results are satisfactory," Jorge commented. "A few broken bones, minor concussion, and our Mr. Anthony didn't see his attacker."

"That's the best way to have it."

"It's the only way," Jorge corrected him. "I hope this brings you some... satisfaction."

"Yes, but not as much as I had hoped," Juan admitted. "My daughter, she is still a little off, you know. I still worry."

"I know," Jorge nodded in understanding. "Believe me, I know."

"We worry so much," Juan took a deep breath. "And the recording I gave you?"

"It's about to come out," Jorge replied. "And it's going to shake things up."

CHAPTER 46

"I think Sonny and Diego are back together," Maria informed Jorge as the two sat in his office later that evening. "I saw Sonny going there tonight with a bottle of wine in his hand."

"Is that so?" Jorge was intrigued. It was always interesting to see what his daughter noticed. "This here, I didn't know."

"I was surprised," Maria crossed her legs and leaned back in her chair. "I thought Diego dumped him when he went all crazy and stuff."

"Well, Maria, I'm not sure he went *all crazy* as you suggest," Jorge grinned at his daughter. "But he was having issues with the *cocaina,* and you know life issues."

"It's never simply one thing, is it?"

"Not usually, Maria," Jorge shook his head. "These things are complicated."

"So, did he tell you that he and Sonny might get back together?"

"No, he did not," Jorge admitted. "Shamefully, I have been so busy with the election that I have not had much time to check in with Diego lately. That's why I thought you and I should have a conversation tonight. I have hardly had much time to catch up with you either."

"I was busy with school too," Maria shrugged. "You know, and stuff."

"And your boyfriend?" Jorge raised his eyebrows, noting that Maria looked slightly embarrassed.

"I guess," She blushed. "He's nice."

"*Nice,*" Jorge observed. "You do not sound very enthused."

"I don't know," Maria shrugged again. "I like him, but maybe not as much as he likes me."

"Just be careful, Maria," Jorge warned. "Teenage boys can be snakes. Their hormones say more than their heart."

"*Papá!*"

"Well, Maria, this is true," Jorge insisted. "I am sorry if this is not what you want to hear, but I know teenage boys. I *was* one."

"Well, maybe you were different," Maria attempted to justify. "He seems sincere."

"Maria, he may be sincere," Jorge assured her. "But, believe me when I tell you that teenage boys are little perverts. I do not care how nice he is or that he has good intentions because under all of that is raging hormones, and they often do not realize it."

"*Papá,* do we have to have this conversation?" Maria continued to blush. "Would you say this about Miguel? One day, when he is older?"

"Of course, I will!" Jorge laughed. "He is my son with that Latino blood running through him. If anything, he will be worse than any boy you know now."

"But will you sit *him* down and give him this lecture?" Maria challenged.

"Yes, Maria, I will," Jorge assured her and began to laugh. "But I can only handle one teenager at a time. So thankfully, we have a few years yet."

"Can we change the subject?"

"Yes, Maria, we can."

"So, I heard you and Paige talking, did Chase...."

"Chase pushed your former principal downstairs, *Si,*" Jorge spoke candidly. "But like with everything in this office, it does not leave this room."

Maria nodded.

"And that's because of what he tried to do with that girl?"

"Yes, her father approached me," Jorge told her. "He is the man who owns *Taza de Sol.*"

"I heard her father was super rich," Maria spoke dismally. "Everyone's parents at my school are loaded."

"Yes, well, he is a man who earned it," Jorge reminded her.

"*Papá,* sometimes I wonder if I would rather go to public school."

"Is that because your boyfriend is in public school?"

"*Papá!*"

"Well, Maria, this here is a legitimate question."

"No, it's because I would rather go to school with normal kids," Maria spoke honestly. "The kids I go to school with are pampered."

"*Pampered?*" Jorge wrinkled his nose. "I am not sure if I am familiar with this word, Maria."

"It means spoiled."

"In fairness," Jorge countered. "There are a lot in public school that are spoiled too."

"So, like, Chase threw Mr. Anthony downstairs," Maria returned to their original topic. "Was he hurt bad?"

"Yes," Jorge nodded. "He is currently in the hospital."

"Is he going to be ok?"

"Maria, I do not care," Jorge shook his head while his daughter lowered her eyes and nodded. "I worry that he has done terrible things to other children, and Mr. Perez said that his daughter, she is still not ok. So, if the man is in pain or suffering, I do not care."

"Is Chase still with Jolene?"

"Maria, I do not ask," Jorge replied. "But I assume she will be there until she either finds another man or he kicks her out."

"So, probably forever," Maria replied.

"You know, Maria," Jorge observed his daughter. "You and Chase were always close, so it is unfortunate that you no longer speak. Do you think you will ever be friends again?"

"Not as long as Jolene is around," Maria replied. "I can't even look at them together, and I remember that day…"

"Maria, I am sorry you had to see that," Jorge leaned forward in his chair. "That was not appropriate of either of them. And Chase, he knew you worked at the bar that night. It is not like you were barging into their bedroom."

"Apparently, any room will do," Maria rolled her eyes, causing Jorge to laugh.

"Oh, Maria, I am sorry you had to deal with this," Jorge said. "But you had to learn the truth."

Jorge's phone beeped. He glanced at it, and his eyes returned to his daughter.

"Was that them?"

"It was Makerson."

"So, everything is happening now?"

"*Si.*"

"Can I turn my phone back on now?" Maria gestured toward her iPhone on the chair beside her.

"Yes," Jorge nodded. "You are more techy than me, so I will have you look through Twitter until you find something. But do not share, like, comment, anything. Let me know what you see."

"Ok," She nodded and went to work.

Jorge sat back in his chair and glanced toward the bulletproof window. Things were about to happen quickly, and he was looking forward to it.

"I think I found something," Maria spoke up a few minutes later. "Is this the video?"

Turning her phone around, Jorge leaned ahead and nodded.

"That is it."

"This guy posting the video shows it far away," Maria commented. "Then zooms in on the face. I'm not sure who it is."

"Athas, he thinks he knows."

"Really?" Maria looked up, wide-eyed. "I thought it was some random guy."

Jorge shook his head, amused by her reaction. Everything amazed her, and he envied her intrigue with the world around her. He never wanted that to go away, as it had with him.

"This is getting shared like crazy," Maria continued. "Like, non-stop."

"This is good."

"A lot of people are tagging Athas and the news," Maria continued to tap on her phone. "I see where HPC news just shared it, asking if it is real. Wow….it's just blowing up, *Papá.*"

"This is good, Maria."

"People are tagging the police," Maria observed. "Like everyone is going crazy, it's trending now. Wow, that was fast!"

"Can you read the comments and tell me if anything is relevant?"

"Sure," Maria agreed as she pulled both feet up onto the chair and found a more relaxed pose. "This is good stuff."

Jorge merely nodded. He watched his phone to see who would call him first. Of course, no one would because they were too busy working behind the scenes.

Ten minutes later, his phone rang.

"Makerson, I see things are...busy tonight."

"It blew up," Makerson confirmed. "Faster than I expected."

"Maria is here," Jorge proudly smiled at his daughter, who briefly looked up, but quickly returned to work. "She is keeping me posted."

"The shooter has been identified on social media."

"Is that so?"

"Athas is quiet so far."

"I think this here is better," Jorge replied. "It is more appropriate he waits, as if to learn the news, then to confirm before speaking."

"It's going to throw a wrench in the election," Makerson insisted. "But to his favor."

"It would never get out otherwise," Jorge replied.

"*Papá,*" Maria turned her phone around to show a professional image beside a screenshot from the video. "They say it's this guy."

Jorge leaned forward and nodded.

"You saw that?" Makerson asked from the other end.

"Yes, I am looking at it right now."

"I wonder what the public will think when it's confirmed?"

"They will have no choice but to accept the truth."

CHAPTER 47

"Did you know that Sonny and Diego are maybe back together?" Jorge asked Paige as he climbed into bed later that night. "This is what I learn from Maria tonight."

"He has been considering inviting him back into his life," Paige replied on the other side of the bed as she sat her book down. "But I think he was overwhelmed when he came back to town. Trying to live his life clean was enough for him to contend with, let alone when starting back to work. But now that things are calmer, he thought he might see how it went. They decided to spend some time together and take it from there."

"Probably just wanted to get laid," Jorge spoke skeptically.

"Jorge!" Paige shook her head. "Why are you so cynical? I think there was a little more to their relationship than that, and by the way, you shouldn't tell Maria that her boyfriend is just a little pervert. That will make her distrust all men as she gets older."

"She *should* distrust men," Jorge insisted as he stretched. "Come on, Paige, teenage boys are only out for one thing, and she should know this fact."

"I don't think that's always the case," Paige shook her head. "I think you've been hanging around the soulless political world too much lately, and you forget that not all people are assholes. Even the social media aspect of politics is a dumpster fire."

"Are you saying Athas is an asshole?" Jorge challenged, winking at his wife.

"I'm saying most people connected to that world *is* an asshole," Paige corrected him. "And that it brings out the insanity in people. Look at everything that came out tonight."

"In fairness," Jorge teased her. "It only came out to the public tonight. We already knew."

"You know what I mean," Paige pretended to hit him with her book. "I don't like this side of you when you get into the political world."

"What side of me?" Jorge was surprised by her remark. "I am the same as always."

"You are not the same as always," Paige corrected him. "You're more cynical, and you see everyone as an enemy. Alec is *not* your enemy. And it colors your whole world, like what you said to Maria tonight. I've met Nico. He's a nice boy. He's harmless."

"Wait, you met him," Jorge cut her off before she could continue. "How come I did not meet him yet?"

"Gee, I wonder," Paige rolled her eyes. "Probably because Maria doesn't want you asking him if he's a little pervert trying to take advantage of his daughter."

"I think that's a fair question," Jorge countered with a grin. "Oh, Paige, you know I wouldn't say that to him, don't you?"

Paige looked into his eyes for a moment before answering.

"No, I don't know that."

"Oh, come on, this here wouldn't happen," Jorge laughed. "I would, however, read between the lines."

"Maybe he's just a nice kid who has a crush on your daughter," Paige reminded him. "And maybe Maria is hesitant because she's been through so much already. How could she ever believe in people with everything she's seen in the last few years?"

"Yeah, well, walking in on Chase banging Jolene probably didn't help," Jorge reminded Paige. "This here, I am still angry about."

"Well, that was highly inappropriate," Paige agreed. "I could see if she barged in the office, but…"

"Yes, she barged into her workplace," Jorge reminded his wife. "With the key I gave her because the bar will someday be hers. I thought this is good. It teaches her responsibility. It shows her I have trust in her. Instead, she catches one of the people in my *familia* fucking the town *puta* against the bar."

"She told you it was against the bar?"

"Chase, he forgets we have cameras everywhere," Jorge reminded Paige. "Marco and I looked it up. You should have seen my little girl's face when she walked into the *Princesa Maria*. My heart, it broke for her, Paige."

His wife shared a concerned look with him, but she didn't reply.

"But it showed Maria who Chase really is," Jorge continued. "And now, she will always be careful about men. And this isn't my cynicism because I've been so involved in politics, but because the world can be a cold place sometimes, and my daughter she needs to know that now."

Paige didn't say anything.

"Also, tonight, Paige," Jorge said as he moved closer to his wife. "She asked about the way we met."

"Why would she ask that?"

"She is reading *House of Hernandez*. I have already told her most of the truth," Jorge grinned. "She did not believe that you just happened to come to my door by mistake."

Paige started to laugh.

"So, I tell her."

"I hope you didn't tell her everything," Paige turned more in his direction, her voice lowering. "You know…"

"Yes, Paige, I tell her that I removed your thong with my teeth that night," Jorge said and started to laugh. "No, Paige, I did not tell her *everything.*"

"So, what did you say?" She pushed. "I need to know that we have the same story."

"The truth," Jorge shrugged. "That you come to my hotel room by mistake, and I invited you in for a drink."

"And?"

"And that it was business related," Jorge admitted. "But she would have to ask you for the rest of the story."

"So, she doesn't know I was an assassin who almost killed you by accident?"

"Paige, this here it is up to you whether or not to tell her," Jorge shrugged as he snuggled a little closer. "This is not my secret to tell. If you choose to and *when* you choose to it is up to you, not me."

"I often wonder if I should tell her," Paige admitted as she sunk further down in the bed and sat her book aside. "But, maybe it's too much."

"Paige, she knows we all have killed," Jorge reminded her. "This includes even her when she shot that man that broke in. I think she can handle this information. It is not exactly like she thinks her father is a saint either."

"True."

"You worry too much," Jorge commented. "Maria, she can take all this information. I think it should be a little at a time. That is why I slowly introduced her to lessons about running the family this summer. I continue some in the fall. Today, I had her on Twitter when information came out about Athas' shooter. She was involved and helping. I tell her about Chase pushing the principal downstairs. I keep her in the loop without overwhelming her. A few bites at a time, you know?"

"So, about the Twitter thing," Paige whispered. "What happens now? Alec didn't make a statement tonight? I assume he's going to give it time to sit overnight."

"We think this here is better," Jorge confirmed as he reached out to run his hand down her arm. "You know, give it time to swirl around social media. Eventually, mainstream media will pick up the story."

"What about HPC news?"

"Tomorrow," Jorge replied. "Tonight, Makerson had a brief story stating what was on the internet and simply saying it's 'still under investigation' to show that we aren't jumping on the bandwagon too fast. That is what they want. We must show the people that we take our time to get the facts."

"And the facts are?"

"The facts are that some people," Jorge moved closer to his wife. "That some people will burn tomorrow, and Athas will come out the hero."

"And then when this election is over….." Paige continued to whisper, causing Jorge's thoughts to drift elsewhere. "Am I finally going to get more of your time and attention?"

"You make it sound like I do not fulfill all your needs," Jorge leaned in, his face close to hers. "I thought I always addressed this, have I not?"

"I think I need a little more of you than Alec needs," She replied as her hand ran over his chest and toward his stomach. "After Monday, it's time you let him fly on his own."

"Paige, I couldn't agree more," Jorge said as he swooped in to kiss her.

The following morning, he was awake before his wife and was hesitant to get out of bed. He briefly considered waking her to see if he could get a repeat of the previous night but decided it was best to let her sleep. He felt getting out of bed was like being removed from a magical world of passion and pleasure, to the dark and dismal reality of the political world. It occurred to him that, at the very least, he could appreciate that this was Athas' life and not his own. At least he could advise then walk away.

Slowly making his way to the shower, he was under the warm water when it occurred to him that he forgot to check his phone yet. Maybe this was something he had to make a point of doing more often. He wondered if Paige was right and if it was time for Athas to fly solo. Perhaps he relied too heavily on Jorge, and it was time he stood on his own two feet. Was that even possible?

Getting out of the shower and dressing in a suit, Jorge made his way downstairs and turned on the coffee maker. He loved it when the house was silent. The kids were still sleeping. He could have some time alone to collect his thoughts.

With some hesitation, he finally looked at his phone to see what awaited him.

It was unexpected.

CHAPTER 48

"Last night, some evidence was leaked on social media regarding the recent attempted assassination of our prime minister...."

Jorge grinned to himself and glanced toward his bulletproof window. They were suddenly so dramatic about Athas being shot. Only days earlier the whole event was brushed under the rug as fast as possible. The suspect had been caught, Athas was fine, and they tied it up with a bow. Now they were suddenly backtracking, speaking of it as if it were a tragedy, like they gave a fuck.

"...shows that mistakes were made, and as a result, I have reached out to the parents of..."

Jorge shook his head. The parents of the man falsely accused, then most likely killed and made look like a suicide, would be paid off to let it go. It was easier for everyone involved that it didn't get too much media attention, and a potential trial would drag out the whole story and malfunction of the RCMP into the public. Not to suggest that it wouldn't happen anyway, but it was clear they were rushing to clean things up to make less of a scar. The parents of the innocent kid were in a vulnerable place and would most likely comply.

"...we continue to investigate the information found. We want to be sure it is legitimate and wasn't doctored...."

Jorge laughed. It wasn't, and they knew it. This was them attempting to give the impression that they were thorough and careful when examining evidence. It was too little too late. Of course, the argument was compelling, and people wanted to believe that law enforcement was trustworthy, so they would take anything they had to say as the truth.

"…we won't be answering any questions at this time. As I'm sure you can understand, this information is still pretty new, and we want to look into it more before we make any further comments…."

Jorge rolled his eyes. He didn't want to answer the questions because they hadn't decided yet what they could say, so they didn't seem like incompetent morons. Chances were they had to run their official comments through someone in PR to spin it, plus go through several officials to be sure it was worded the right way and gave the right impression. It was all bullshit.

Noticing a familiar voice, Jorge looked back at the laptop to see Athas standing at the podium.

"In light of the new information we learned last night, I would like to apologize to the…."

Jorge looked away and fought the urge to shut his laptop and stop listening. It was just more politically correct bullshit, sifted through a layer of people who told Athas what to say.

Athas took full advantage of a chance to get his face out to potential voters before Monday's election, this time showing his compassionate, caring side. He talked about his years in social work and how it gave him the gift of being able to see both sides of almost any situation, although he also admitted this one was a little hard to swallow. Jorge laughed and rolled his eyes.

After rattling on for about ten minutes, he finally ended his speech and stepped back. He was the last person to speak at the press conference, which caused the reporters to panic, throwing questions at the prime minister in hopes he would give them more information. However, with no answers given, the questions were as revealing.

"Is it true the shooter is an RCMP officer?"

"Has anyone been arrested?"

"Wasn't the video shot on the opposite side of the street? Does that mean the RCMP neglected to look at all the evidence?"

"Do we know why this man was shooting at the prime minister?"

"Was anyone else involved?"

It didn't matter the question because everyone on the stage rushed away, acting as though there wasn't an anxious audience at home. Did they not deserve answers?

Jorge sat back in his chair and closed his laptop.

There was more to come.

His secure line rang.

"Athas," Jorge answered. "I saw your little speech."

"The reporters were like vultures."

"They always are, Athas or is this something new?" Jorge mocked him. "Of course, in this case, wouldn't this here be helpful to your cause?"

"It would if I could answer the questions."

"And you know, that will not be allowed."

"I had a pretty good idea what to say to each of them," Athas admitted. "I'm just not allowed. I barely could address the family of the man who died in jail even though he did nothing wrong."

"Of course, it showed you might be accountable."

"They're afraid it will give them a reason to sue the RCMP."

"That is all they care about."

"And covering their ass," Athas added.

"They certainly have a lot to cover," Jorge replied. "So, it was one of the men that was once protecting you?"

"It was one of the men *still* protecting me," Athas replied. "In fact, after shooting me, he came back to work the next day. It's just a bit unnerving. His name is Constable Isaac McQuaid."

"If I were you, Athas," Jorge relaxed in his chair. "Heads would roll."

"They're fucking rolling all right," Athas grumbled. "But he's not talking. He's all lawyered up."

"Good lawyer?"

"*Pricey* lawyer," Athas corrected him. "But we have to find out who hired him and why."

"I am meeting with Marco this morning," Jorge said. "To see where he is with all of this."

"My first assumption was Big Pharma," Athas admitted. "But now, I'm not so sure."

"Why do you say this?" Jorge was intrigued. "Have you pissed off anyone else lately, Athas?"

"I think that's my main job some days," Athas sighed. "But it was clearly to rattle me, not kill me. At least, not originally, but now, I'm not so sure."

"Let me look into this more," Jorge replied. "Do I need to hide you in my safe house until the election?"

"I can't," Athas replied. "I have to be around this weekend. The opposition would love it if I went into hiding."

"This is true," Jorge thought for a moment. "I can send you over someone…."

"No, look, I got security up my asshole right now," Athas said. "People aren't even allowed close to me at this point. It's getting fucking crazy."

"Once we sort this out," Jorge reminded him. "It will calm down, especially after the election."

"I hope you're right."

"I'm always right," Jorge insisted. "Now, I got to go see Marco. Maybe he's got something for me."

"Thank you," Athas replied. "I know I don't say that enough, but I know you got my back."

"Just try not to get shot this weekend," Jorge suggested. "I will personally take care of whoever is behind all this."

They ended the call, and Jorge stood up and reached for his phone. He checked his pocket for his gun.

On the way out, he gave his family each a quick kiss before heading to the door. Once in his SUV, his mind began to race in several directions. Although he didn't want to alarm Athas, he still had some concerns that someone was hoping to get him out of the picture before the election on Monday. It was his job to make sure that didn't happen. Someone was going to die that weekend, but it wasn't going to be Athas.

He found Chase at the bar as soon as he walked in. He looked up from his paperwork.

"Marco here?"

"In the VIP room," Chase pointed in the general direction. "I think he's got something for you."

"Thank you, by the way," Jorge said as he walked toward the VIP room. "Our Mr. Anthony won't be bothering anyone now that he's taken a tumble."

"That's my hope," Chase grinned. "He knows why he took the tumble too."

Jorge smiled, nodded, then walked into the VIP room.

"Marco," Jorge said as he found his seat. "I got your message. I came over as soon as I talked to Athas. So, what you got for me?"

"It's complicated," Marco admitted. "At first, I *did* think it was Big Pharma behind this because of a series of emails stating they wanted Athas out. But then, it sounded like they wanted to manipulate him to go along with them instead. They thought he would be easier to work with than Knapp if he got elected."

"Wait, isn't Frederick Knapp backed by Big Pharma," Jorge was curious. "Did I not understand that?"

"That's how it looked," Marco shook his head. "But now, he's back paddling."

"Now that they've already thrown some money his way?"

"Yes, sir, that's the weird part," Marco shook his head. "It almost seems like they wanted to shoot *him* from these emails and texts I've read."

"You don't suppose this is to get you off track?" Jorge wondered. "Maybe they know you were looking…"

"No," Marco shook his head. "Something seemed to go down between Knapp and some top guy in Big Pharma. So, getting back to what I was saying earlier, it doesn't make sense that they want Athas shot."

Jorge thought for a moment.

"Not even to create compassion for him," Jorge realized he was grasping at straws. "Maybe get the vote that way."

"No," Marco shook his head. "They were making jokes about him getting shot, so they didn't know about that either. No, I think someone else is behind all of this."

"So, no clues?"

"Just one," Marco appeared worried. "But I'm not sure of what it means."

"What is it?"

"On the day of the shooting," Marco began as he tapped on his laptop and turned it around. "This man, McQuaid, is on the phone talking to someone just before he does it. If I can hack his phone, maybe I can see who he was speaking to."

Jorge moved in to look at the image.

"That might be our answer."

CHAPTER 49

"McQuaid, he was talking to someone on the phone just before he shot you," Jorge informed Athas through the secure line an hour later. "Do you know who this could be? Marco and I haven't been able to find a thing."

"It *literally* could be anyone," Athas replied, causing Jorge and Marco to share a look.

"Well, what about someone who might want you out of the picture or to shut you up?" Jorge pushed harder.

"Again," Athas sounded exhausted. "It *literally* could be anyone."

This time, Marco rolled his eyes, and Jorge grinned.

"Oh, come on, Athas," Jorge said. "If someone try to shoot me today, even though I could fit all the people who hate me in a ballpark, I still would be able to narrow it down to a few people. Even on instincts alone. How could you not have any idea? Any hunches? Anything?"

"Well," Athas thought for a moment. "Big Pharma hates me. The opposition hates me. The legacy media hates me. Should I go on?"

"This is true, sir," Marco agreed as he moved closer to the phone. "But when I look at all these guys at Big Pharma, although they seem happy someone shot you, none of them indicate who did it. Many are asking between themselves who shot you. The opposition? I don't think he would go this route. The legacy media wouldn't either."

"Maybe it's more personal?" Athas wondered.

"No," Jorge automatically answered. "Personal wouldn't get you no RCMP."

"He's not talking either," Athas replied.

"Well, maybe we will make him talk," Jorge insisted. "The motherfucker will talk to me."

"They aren't going to let you in," Athas insisted.

"Want to fucking bet?" Jorge countered. "If you want answers, I suggest you find a way to get me in."

Athas was quiet for a few minutes. Jorge looked at Marco, who nodded vigorously.

"I'm going to look into that and get back to you."

"You do that."

Jorge ended the call and exchanged looks with Marco.

"Sir, this will work," Marco insisted. "If you can get in, that man will talk. I can even make sure the cameras are off."

"This will have to be the case," Jorge said. "We are running out of options, Marco. If you can't find anything, then we aren't looking in the right places. But where do we look?"

"That is the problem, sir."

The phone rang shortly afterward, and Jorge answered.

"We can get in."

"Perfect," Jorge replied. "When?"

"Later today," Athas said. "I arranged for the guards not be there, no cameras, nothing."

"And who knows?"

"People who want to keep their fucking jobs," Athas said.

"Athas, this new attitude," Jorge grinned. "I think I finally hear your Jorge Hernandez side coming out. This here is good. This will make you win the election."

"Polls are good since the debate," Athas confirmed. "But I gotta make it to the election. I feel like an ax is hanging over my head."

"Well, that's because there is one," Jorge suggested. "But it's coming down on someone else's head, and it's coming fast."

Jorge arranged to meet Athas at the time and place when the right people would be gone for lunch, and the other people would look the other way. Isaac McQuaid was in an undisclosed location due to the public outrage over the vigilante RCMP officer, especially because a kid was falsely accused and was now dead. This wasn't sitting well with an already wary public after being told these establishments were trustworthy and encouraged to believe in them.

Arriving at the building, Jorge briefly considered burning it to the ground to send a message, but he would try Plan A first and take it from there. If that were the case, the staff would have strict instructions to let the fucker burn. Sometimes, it was the only way to send a message.

Once inside, as previously agreed, Jorge didn't leave his gun or phone at the door. He didn't have to sign in or leave evidence that he was ever there. This was his stipulation, and Athas made it happen.

The building was dark, dank, like something in a horror movie, but that didn't bother Jorge. Nothing did. He walked down a long hallway, where he met Athas just outside the room that held McQuaid.

"You ready for this?" Athas asked Jorge, which caused him to laugh.

"I could ask you the same," Jorge shook his head. "Son, this is not my first rodeo."

Athas looked down and nodded before opening the door and entering the room. Jorge followed, quickly getting a whiff of stale air, his eyes landing on Isaac McQuaid, who sat in handcuffs at the table. He showed no reaction to Athas walking in but was surprised when Jorge followed him. Athas sat down, but Jorge didn't.

"What the fuck is this?" McQuaid asked as his eyes jumped from one man to the other.

"This here," Jorge pointed at Athas. "Is the man you shot, the same man you were supposed to protect? And me? Just consider me an interested party."

"I want my lawyer."

"*I* want fucking answers," Athas shot back.

"I'm not talking to either of you."

"Do you want to fucking bet?" Jorge countered as he crossed his arms over his chest. "We ain't going nowhere till you talk."

"I don't talk to fucking criminals." McQuaid glanced at Jorge but looked away.

"Don't look like me sitting in handcuffs."

"It should be."

To this, Jorge laughed.

"Enough of this bullshit," Athas snapped at McQuaid. "Why did you shoot me? Who paid you?"

"Why do you assume anyone paid me?" McQuaid shook his head. "Like I told my lawyer, the stress of the job just got to me."

"Who the fuck were you talking on the phone with before you shot Athas?" Jorge asked.

"No one," McQuaid tensed up.

"Does 'no one' go by another name?" Jorge countered.

"I don't remember."

"You don't remember?" Jorge laughed, then suddenly lurched forward to backhand McQuaid on the side of the head, briefly throwing the constable off track. "Think a little harder, motherfucker!"

"You forget what I do," McQuaid snapped back as he glared at Jorge. "You can't shake me up like you do other people. I *know* this game."

"No, I assure you," Jorge shook his head, getting closer to the man. "You do not know *my* game. It is not like *your* game. You see, in my world, there are no lawyers. I won't spend hours trying to wear you down. I don't offer deals. No, you do *not* know my game."

He said nothing.

"Do you think those cameras are on?" Jorge glanced up at the device in the corner. "Do you think the sound is on? Do you think there is a guard outside waiting to help you? Do you think they care if you make it back to your fucking cell tonight? You are, after all, someone who makes all of them look bad. A dirty cop. Do you think your life means anything?"

"I would tell him what he wants," Athas suggested. "Because this will get a lot harder before it gets easier."

"That man," Jorge pointed toward Athas. "He trusted you to protect him. No matter what you think of me, or my people, we protect one another. We show loyalty. You're a traitor to your people. So try, one last time, to be a real man and tell us the truth. Who hired you? Because I am going to kill someone today. And if it's not the person giving the instructions, it will be the person who pulled the trigger. You know it is not uncommon for someone to be hung in their cell. Kind of like that kid who took the blame for your crime. Did he deserve that? You weren't even enough of a man to speak up. You had some fucking kid take the rap. Did you manipulate the investigation?"

McQuaid finally showed some emotion as he turned away.

"It was a distraction," he replied. "I didn't think…"

"Yeah, well, his parents would feel much better knowing how little you thought," Jorge yelled at him. "Again, do you think anyone in this building cares if you're dead before the day is over? You've put a dark mark on their reputation, and they do not take too kindly to that."

"He's right," Athas replied. "How did we get in so easily? How come Jorge has his gun on him? They didn't check at the door."

Jorge unbuttoned his blazer to show a gun.

McQuaid shrank in his seat.

"What happens if I tell you?"

"You get to fucking live," Jorge replied.

"Will I get a lighter sentence, at least?"

Athas thought for a moment. "Something might be arranged."

Jorge stood back and waited.

The silence was almost too much. Jorge was starting to think he wouldn't answer when he suddenly replied.

"It was someone at CSIS," McQuaid said, looking at Athas. "A woman, her name is Susanne Nestor."

"What?" Athas was confused. "Why?"

"Because she's part of a secret group, who more or less runs the country from behind the scenes," McQuaid explained. "They decide how things should be and then find people to push for those changes. You're pushing back, and they don't like that. Especially now, where they think you'll win."

"What's this here group called?" Jorge asked.

"That, I'm not sure," McQuaid shook his head. "She refers to them as *we* when she talks. So she will say something like, *we* discussed it and decided that Athas needs to go."

Jorge and Athas shared a look.

"Can you keep your fucking mouth shut about this conversation?" Jorge asked.

"Trust me," McQuaid replied. "The last thing I want is for them to know that I told you any of this because they *will* kill me. They've done it to others before."

"Does that include the kid blamed for your crime?" Athas asked.

"I'm assuming," McQuaid replied. "They don't let anyone get in their way."

Jorge exchanged looks with Athas.

CHAPTER 50

Honor. It's not a word we hear as much anymore, probably because it doesn't mean much anymore. It's cheapened. It's weak. Those in power think it's automatic simply because of their position or title, but it doesn't work that way.

Honor is a slow process that builds over time. But it's time that people aren't willing to give.

"Sir, I think I found something," Marco said without looking up from his laptop. "This lady, Susanne Nestor, it looks like she comes from a long line of powerful people. And this group, which they don't seem to name in any of her emails or texts. It looks like she might have fallen into the position due to her family's legacy."

Across the desk from Marco, Jorge listened but didn't say anything.

"I found text messages that seem to have transpired between this group, and they all report back to her," Marco added. "There are some well-known and powerful people in this group, sir. Celebrities, politicians, CEOS, some I have never heard of, but most I have."

"That's interesting," Jorge finally commented as he continued to consider this new information. "I have heard of such a group before, Marco, but never here in Canada."

"They are well hidden," Marco admitted. "For all the research I've done over the years, I've never even stumbled on them before. Then again, I've never researched anyone in it."

"Do you see anything on Athas?"

"I see where they originally thought he could be steamrolled," Marco replied. "But as the election got closer, they started to have doubts. They even talked about changing the polls to manipulate people but feared this wouldn't be enough. They call him *Snow White* on here, by the way."

Jorge grinned.

"They say his policies are a little too 'Snow White' and think he's spending money on useless causes that should only get him limited votes, so were surprised when he exceeded their expectations."

"Who knew that having honor would be so popular?" Jorge quipped.

"These people, sir, do not have honor," Marco shook his head. "They talk about the Canada they want, and it's scary. They have some unrealistic ideas that cannot happen unless people suffer. They talk about lowering the population to use less government funding, changing the education system so children are more compliant, and having people eat more foods grown in a lab. They even talk about how it will make people sick, but that's ok because the pharmaceutical industry can step in. This also helps them lower life expectancy and therefore cut the population."

Jorge remained expressionless as he thought about the words.

"It just goes on and on, sir," Marco shook his head. "So, this is why they want Athas out of the picture. They even say he isn't willing to play the game. They thought he would drop out as soon as he got shot. Now, they are in a tailspin trying to figure out what is next."

"Athas, he is protected tonight," Jorge insisted. "Paige and Chase took him and the kids to the safe house. His security thinks he is still in his own home, with a bug, sick, so he is safe for tonight, but we may not be able to keep this going for long. We must get to the bottom of this before they get to him."

"It looks like," Marco frowned. "That is their plan. They figure nothing else will work at this point other than getting rid of him."

"We will see about that," Jorge said. "So, I must figure out a way to get to this woman who leads the group. It will send a message to the others."

"Will that be enough, sir?"

"Marco," Jorge thought for a moment. "I honestly don't know."

"I will continue to look, sir."

"Make sure they are not suspicious of anything," Jorge reminded him. "Also, have you seen anything about me?"

"Not yet, sir," Marco shook his head. "I will keep looking."

"Also, see where to find this Susanne Nector," Jorge continued.

Grabbing his phone, he turned it on. As soon as it came to life, he sent a message to Andrew.

Jorge noted a text from his wife. It was a simple thumbs up. That meant they had arrived at the safe house; all was fine. Anything else would've set off alarm bells since this was agreed on before they left.

He had to take care of things before these psychopaths attempted to kill Athas. This time, for real.

"Sir, I think I found something," Marco spoke up. "And it's big."

"What is that?"

"They're currently having a conversation through their message group," Marco said and stopped to read. "I can see their messages to one another."

"Is it about Athas?"

"They mention him canceling his events tonight," Marco stopped to read again. "They think he's at his house. They comment on how he probably got food poisoning, and one jokes how this could've been their way to get him out of the picture."

Jorge raised an eyebrow.

"So, they have no suspicions," Marco continued. "They are talking about how the election is Monday, and it's now or never. Although, someone pointed out that if they kill him before, it will send a message that if you oppose their ideas, you'll never make it to the finish line."

Jorge nodded as he listened. Thoughts flowed through his head.

"They want to do it tonight."

Jorge felt himself grow tense.

"Sir…it looks like they want to go to his house," Marco frowned. "When his security changes, they plan to slip one of their people in at the last minute. They think they can make it look like he had a heart attack."

Jorge remained silent.

"This is scary," Marco shook his head. "How many times do you think this has happened?"

"Probably more than we want to know," Jorge admitted. "They cover their tracks well."

"But…..oh, sir," Marco sat up straight, his eyes widened.

"What is it, Marco?" Jorge asked.

"It looks like Isaac McQuaid is dead. They said he was too much of a liability."

"This here is not a surprise."

"They say now that he has been taken care of," Marco continued. "That Athas is the next problem they plan to remove."

"There is some disagreement," Marco continued as he squinted to read the screen. "This is going so fast, sir, but it seems this Susanne lady wants to kill Athas. The rest, they feel they can coerce him in some way. She is getting mad because they are backtracking on her. They are telling her to wait, to see. They think they can change his mind. And if not, later, they can make it look like an accident."

"He travels a lot," Marco continued to read. "They say it can be an accident. It looks too suspicious if it's now."

"So, she is the main person calling the shots?" Jorge asked and watched Marco nod as he continued to read. "If you want to disorientate the group, you must first take care of their leader. And you must do so in a way that shakes their foundation."

"Yes, sir, do you want me to find out where she will be tonight?"

"Yes, Marco," Jorge replied. "I will kill her myself."

"But sir," Marco shook his head. "Do not go alone."

"I can get Diego," Jorge insisted.

"He is away for the weekend with Sonny."

"Then I will go alone."

"Sir, I think…"

"I can take on this woman, Marco," Jorge laughed. "Please, I will be fine. Where the fuck is she?"

"Tonight," Marco appeared hesitant. "She is alone in her penthouse."

"No family?"

"Her kids, they are grown and away," Marco confirmed. "Her husband, he died last year."

"Did he have one of those sudden heart attacks?" Jorge quipped.

"I do not know," Marco shook his head. "Sir, if you want…"

"No, Marco, this here will be fine," Jorge insisted. "I will take care of her on my own."

Reaching in his desk drawer, he pulled out a gun.

"You stay here. Text me if anything else comes up."

"I will, sir," Marco replied. "Please, be careful."

Jorge nodded as he headed for the door. A few minutes later, he was in his SUV and on his way to Susanne Nestor's penthouse. This would end tonight.

To his surprise, Jorge didn't find security at her building, nor did he have issues getting inside. Marco had already assured him cameras were off in the building and surrounding areas. No one would see a thing, and wearing gloves on the crisp fall night didn't make him stand out. He knew all the moves to slip into her place before she realized he was there. But when she did, it was on her way to the kitchen when Susanne found him in the hallway. The middle-aged lady barely reacted to her intruder.

She tried to grab a nearby glass vase but Jorge pulled out his gun.

"Don't move, lady," Jorge snapped. "Because I got no problem blowing your fucking brains out right here."

"I was wondering when the *real* Jorge Hernandez would come out to play," She spoke fearlessly. "Not the fictitious character in the fairytale that Makerson wrote about in *House of Hernandez,* but the murderous psychopath you are. The one that controls Athas."

"If you thought I was a murderous psychopath, then why you fuck with us, lady?" Jorge countered.

"Because I have my own security."

Jorge felt a gun touch the back of his head.

"You forget that I play in your world, with your rules," Susanne Nector smirked. "I knew you were coming. I wasn't sure when, but I knew. And I was ready for you when you did. And…"

A shot rang out, and a heavy weight overpowered his body. Blood was everywhere. Overtaken by regret, he recalled Marco's warning that he shouldn't go alone. Why hadn't he listened? Why hadn't he taken this more seriously? He was going to die. He would never see his family again. After all the years of putting himself in danger, this was how it ended. His heart throbbed, and the next few seconds felt like an eternity as he grew weak.

That's when he realized it wasn't his blood on the floor. The heavy weight behind him was a body falling against his back. Jumping ahead, a large black man fell dead at his feet. Jorge looked behind him to see his wife standing, pointing a gun at Susanne Nector.

"Jorge, could you move a little to the left," Paige calmly asked. "I want to make sure I have a clear shot. This bitch is going down fast."

"Paige, I…."

"You're sure lucky I was on my way back when Marco called," Paige cut him off. "That's all I'm gonna say."

"Please!" Susanne spoke up. "I…"

"This is for Alec," Paige shot the woman in the arm in the same area where the prime minister had been grazed. When she cried out, begging her to stop, the former assassin coldly replied, "And this one is for my husband."

The second bullet shot into her chest, instantly killing her.

Honor may be a rare thing. But it still exists in the *House of Hernandez.*

If you enjoyed this book, please give it a review! Learn more about the Hernandez series at <u>mimaonfire.com</u> Thank you for joining me on this adventure!

Printed in the United States
by Baker & Taylor Publisher Services